PRAISE FOR ESHKOL NEVO

"Eshkol Nevo writes beautifully, funnily, and wisely about men and women ... Friendship, envy, love, misery, endurance—he captures the lot."
—Roddy Doyle, author of *Paddy Clarke Ha Ha Ha*

"Eshkol Nevo is a fascinating storyteller who gives the reader a broad and diverse picture of Israeli society."
—Amos Oz, author of *Judas*

"Eshkol Nevo is a brilliant literary chemist who succeeds in extracting from daily life's most mundane events the deepest crystallized essence of the contemporary Israeli psyche."
—Etgar Keret, author of *The Seven Good Years*

Praise for
THREE FLOORS UP

NATIONAL JEWISH BOOK AWARD FINALIST

"Mesmerizing ... this book and its conflicted apartment dwellers stayed with me long after I finished reading."
—*New York Times Book Review*

"Smart and absorbing ... Nevo shows us life's complexities in a thoroughly satisfying read." —*Library Journal* (starred review)

Praise for

THE LAST INTERVIEW

"A compelling page-turner...Nevo pushes the boundaries of fiction both formally and thematically, challenging the reader at every turn to reconsider their conceptions of the relationship between truth and fiction. A daring, triumphant work of searing beauty." —*Kirkus Reviews* (starred review)

"Engrossing...Nevo's latest is a clever, delightfully unreliable, occasionally head-shaking, sometimes eye-rolling portrait of an artist as a not-at-all-young man."
—*Booklist* (starred review)

"Eshkol Nevo's *The Last Interview* is a generous, graceful book— at once wry and raw, mournful and hopeful, ironic and tender. This book is a moving story of loss, love, and friendship, a thoughtful meditation on the porous borders between reality and fiction, and a true joy to read."
—Moriel Rothman-Zecher, author of *Sadness Is a White Bird*

"In Eshkol Nevo's extraordinary *The Last Interview*, a writer reflects on that which sustains and troubles the human heart, including the fragility of love, the friability of truth, the constancy of friendship, and the certainty of loss. Through engaging prose, poignant storytelling, and the sorrowful yet irresistible voice of Nevo's unforgettable narrator, we are asked to consider the question: How should we be in the world? Always heartfelt and often heartbreaking, *The Last Interview* is ultimately a balm for those of us living in these troubled times."
—Judith Claire Mitchell, author of *A Reunion of Ghosts*

ALSO BY ESHKOL NEVO

Homesick

World Cup Wishes

Neuland

Three Floors Up

The Last Interview

INSIDE
INFORMATION

Eshkol Nevo

*Translated from the Hebrew
by Sondra Silverston*

OTHER PRESS
NEW YORK

Song lyrics on pages 37, 69, 83, and 137–38 from "Let Love In" by Knesiyat
HaSechel. Lyrics on page 176 from "The Last Summer" by Shviut Zmanit. Lyrics
on pages 314 and 356 from "Homecoming" by David Broza. All translated from
the Hebrew by Sondra Silverston.
Song lyrics on page 170 from "Don't Stop Me Now" by Queen,
from the album *Jazz*, 1978.

Production editor: Yvonne E. Cárdenas
Text designer: Jennifer Daddio / Bookmark Design & Media Inc.
This book was set in Vendetta and Impact by
Alpha Design & Composition of Pittsfield, NH

1 3 5 7 9 10 8 6 4 2

Library of Congress Cataloging-in-Publication Data
Names: Nevo, Eshkol, author. | Silverston, Sondra, translator.
Title: Inside information : a novel / Eshkol Nevo ; translated from the Hebrew
by Sondra Silverston.
Other titles: Gever nikhnas be-pardes. English
Description: New York : Other Press, [2023]
Identifiers: LCCN 2022049822 (print) | LCCN 2022049823 (ebook) |
ISBN 9781635423235 (paperback) | ISBN 9781635423242 (ebook)
Subjects: LCGFT: Thrillers (Fiction). | Novels.
Classification: LCC PJ5055.35.E92 G4813 2023 (print) |
LCC PJ5055.35.E92 (ebook) | DDC 892.43/7—dc23/eng/20221221
LC record available at https://lccn.loc.gov/2022049822
LC ebook record available at https://lccn.loc.gov/2022049823

Publisher's Note
This is a work of fiction. Names, characters, places, and incidents
either are the product of the author's imagination or are used
fictitiously, and any resemblance to actual persons, living or dead,
events, or locales is entirely coincidental.

DEATH ROAD

My lawyer said that even if we decide to lie in court, we should be sure about the truth. And the best thing would be for me to write down the events exactly the way they happened. So here goes.

Until that moment, I had never seen a picture in the paper of someone I knew—dead. I know that's pretty incredible in this country. With all the wars and so-called military operations that are actually wars, at some point you're likely to open the newspaper and come across a picture of someone who was a schoolmate or army buddy.

But no. Somehow, I managed to get halfway through my life without having that experience. And maybe that's why the chills running down my spine were so intense. We usually say chills because we can't find a more precise word, but I really did feel cold between my shoulders, all the way down to my tailbone. I totally froze when I saw the small picture, which wasn't on the front page but on one of the last ones, facing the obituary page. I didn't have to look twice. It was him. We'd only spent a few hours together in La Paz, but his face was etched in my memory. The chiseled nose. The eyes you could tell were blue, even in the black-and-white newspaper photo. The goatee that looked like a monk's beard.

The short piece under the picture told the story of Ronen Amirov, a twenty-eight-year-old Israeli trekker who was killed in an accident on Death Road in Bolivia while on his honeymoon. The bicycle he was riding, it said, veered off the road and plunged into the chasm. His wife, Mor Amirov, who was with him when it happened, called for help, but by the time the rescue crew arrived, he was already dead. His body was being transported to Israel and the funeral would be held sometime in the next few days.

I had no reason to cry about the story. During that period, I had more personal pain in my life than the death of a guy I hardly knew. And in general, I hardly ever cry. I cried when Liori was born—or to be exact, when I held her for the first time. I cried the first night without Liori, in my new apartment, after she asked me on the phone to visit her in her dreams. And that's it, more or less.

Who knows, maybe every time you cry over something, you're crying about other things as well, things that have remained hidden until that moment. Like previously unreported income on your annual tax return. In any case, after a few days of pretend indecision, when you actually know from the start what you'll decide in the end, I went to the shiva. But it wasn't until I finally escaped from the Tel Aviv traffic jams to the highway that I realized how excited I was at the prospect of seeing Mor from La Paz again.

Excited—what a shitty word. There isn't a workshop I teach where my students don't say, "I'm so excited to be here." And from so much use, it isn't exciting at all. Maybe ... eager. Yes, that's the word I'm looking for. The closer I got to my destination, the more eager I became. My stomach clenched as if I were making a muscle. My thoughts flew out the window. The music coming from the radio went in one ear and right out the other. And my mind filled with more and more images of Mor's surprise nocturnal visit to my room two weeks earlier.

She spoke to me in the middle of the street. Asked in her Israeli-accented English if I knew how to get to Juan's Ice Cream Parlor. For a moment, I couldn't decide whether to play the game and answer her in English, but there was something about her look that must have turned me on from the first second. So I answered in

Hebrew that I was on the way there and they were invited to come along.

Her eyes lit up and the fleeting touch of her fingers on my arm was electric. Israeli? she asked. No kidding! With your height? I never would have guessed.

Yes, I said, I know. A lot of people say that. And I'm not exactly . . . the right age. For a post-army trek, I mean.

Why, how old are you?

Thirty-nine, I admitted.

You don't look it, she said. Not in a flirty way. Just stating a fact.

The guy she was with, who hadn't said anything until then, reached out to shake my hand. Ronen, he said with a formality trekkers never use.

Omri, I said, and shook his hand. Nice to meet you.

And I'm Mor, hi! she said. And kept her hand close to her side.

We're on our honeymoon, Ronen said, and put his arm around her. Not only did he put his arm around her but he pulled her and her curly head close, as if to say: She's mine.

Congratulations, I said and smiled, trying, like a couples therapist, to shift my gaze between both of them without lingering too long on either one.

And you? Mor asked as we began walking. What are *you* doing here "not at the right age"?

A post-divorce trek, I said.

No kidding, she said, staring at me. That's original!

Ronen didn't say anything. He had a pointed, well-trimmed beard, and he stroked it with displeasure. As if we had violated some unwritten commandment like, "Thou shalt not converse during a walk."

Later, at the ice-cream parlor, he ordered one flavor. Vanilla. And she asked to taste a few flavors before she decided on caramel. Then I ordered and paid, all in Spanish. I'd already taken a week of classes and enjoyed rolling the words around on my tongue.

Your Spanish is great! Mor said, turning to me with a spoonful of ice cream in her hand.

It's no special talent, I said, I'm taking a course.

Even so, she said and smiled at me.

There was nothing flirtatious in her smile. More than anything, it reminded me of a religious girl's smile. Kind of modest. Shy. If anyone had asked me at the time, I would have bet she was religious. Or had been once. The large earrings. The exaggerated vivacity. The curls pulled back with a kerchief. The sweatshirt and sharwal she was wearing. I once held a workshop in a religious girls' school in Carmiel, and that's what they looked like there. But on the other hand, there was something in the way she looked at me when Ronen wasn't watching. With a boldness that stopped short at becoming desperation.

Something hungry. That was the word I was searching for. Her glance was hungry. For what, exactly? I still had no idea.

We sat down to eat our ice-cream cones. How long does it take to eat an ice-cream cone? Five minutes? Ten? She even licked her ice cream like a religious girl. Small, delicate licks with the tip of her tongue, not missing a single spot on the cone. We had an idle, backpacker's conversation. That is, she and I spoke and Ronen focused all his attention on his ice cream as if he were a scientist trying to calculate the algorithm of its melting speed.

Mor said, We started in Bolivia and now we're trying to decide where to go from here.

A lot of people recommend Peru, I said.

Yes, she said, but her tone was skeptical, as if she wasn't sure other peoples' recommendations were relevant for them.

How much time do you have? I asked.

A month and a half.

I'm jealous.

Why? How much do you have?

Two weeks tops, I said, I can't stay longer than that. Because of my daughter. I miss her to death as it is. And there are visitation rights to settle. And work. In short, even two weeks is problematic.

8

I hear you, she said, giving me another hungry look as she rested her head on Ronen's shoulder, snuggling into him in a way she seemed to have done a thousand times before.

And he was still observing his dripping ice cream in silence.

They walked me to my hostel. That is, they wanted to go to the Witches' Market and my hostel happened to be on the way.

We stopped on the sidewalk in front of the open entrance gate.

Mor said, It's really nice here, and stood on her tiptoes to see past me, as if she were peering over the walls of a forbidden city.

I looked too—at the bit of skin that was exposed when she stretched and her sweatshirt rode up a little—and said, The inner courtyard is nice, the rooms are pretty basic.

Speaking to me for the first time, Ronen said, Okay, so . . . we'll probably see you in the city again.

Yes, I said.

And that was it. No hug. No kiss on the cheek. No lingering glance. No curls suddenly bouncing as they walked away. No sign of what would happen later.

———

I turned right at the Cabri intersection. A sign said that the distance to Kfar Vradim was fifteen kilometers, and it occurred to me that there's never a cardboard sign saying "To the Shiva." Only "To the Wedding."

I slowed down and drove seventy kilometers per hour on the highway as if I were trying to delay the inevitable. Or gain more time to remember.

The knock on the door of my room in the hostel came shortly after midnight. I had just ended a video call with Liori, who told me that she'd been alone at recess again the day before, and then asked once more whether I was doing dangerous things on my trek. I reassured her, definitely not, and suggested we do a little beatboxing on the phone. As usual, I moved closer, placed a hollow fist to my mouth in order to exhale a basic rhythm, and she joined in, as usual, drumming on her body. We began to improvise rhymes with her name, Lior-Lior every apple has a core, happy days are in store, love opens every door—but before we managed to get into the rhythm, Orna came on the line and said they were late for school and Liori still had to comb her hair, so we moved our lips close to the screen and made a loud kissing sound. And that was it. I went to bed, exhausted from the effort of trying to be happy for her, and I thought, What did you expect, you idiot, that at the age of thirty-nine you could go on a worry-free, post-army trek? I picked up the Salinger book I'd insisted on keeping when we divided up our belongings, *Raise High the Roof Beam, Carpenters*, and began reading where I'd left off the night before.

I love the rhythm of Salinger's sentences, and at first the knocking at the door fit right in with the beat of the story. But after a few seconds of silence, it started again, and this time it was harder. And syncopated. I opened the door, and she was standing there. The girl from the ice-cream parlor. Wearing tights and a checked shirt that was totally and secularly skintight.

Can I come in? she asked, and walked past me without waiting for a reply. I caught a whiff of her freshly shampooed hair. The scent of a woman. I asked her whether she wanted something to drink, and immediately apologized that actually, I didn't have anything in the room. It's a kind of habit, offering guests something to drink, I said, and then said, wait a second, I just remembered that I have some mineral water.

Sure, she said, and I handed her the bottle. She took a swallow that seemed to go on forever, as if she were drinking from a beer bottle to imbibe some courage.

Then she sat down on the edge of my bed and said, Can I ask you something?

I said, Of course, and sat down on the bed too, but not close to her. Something about her seemed to say it wouldn't be appropriate. I leaned back against the wall and stretched my legs forward, but not too far forward, careful to keep my feet from touching her knees.

She pushed her hair behind her ears so that her earrings showed, and only then did she turn to me and say, Did you know in advance?

I thought I understood what she meant. But still, to gain time, I played dumb: Know what in advance?

That it wouldn't work, you and…your wife. I mean…before you got married, or let's say…your first year, were there signs that…?

Lo-o-k, I drew out the word…I had no idea what to say.

Then she got up and began pacing around the room. It was a small room, so she didn't have a lot of space. An open suitcase, a desk, a wastepaper basket, a wall, two pairs of shoes, one pair covered in dry mud. With flushed cheeks and swaying earrings, she maneuvered hypnotically between all those things—it was like watching a dance performance. A dance of discomfort. She gathered up her hair, then let it fall loose, she picked up a pen that was on the desk and clicked it, she spun around on her heels and almost banged into the suitcase, but no, at the last second, she slipped past it, she pulled her shirt down and tapped her fingers on her tights in a regular rhythm as if they were a metronome, all the while speaking, half to me, half to herself: I'm so sorry, I shouldn't have come here, how could I drop in on you this way, in the middle of the night, you don't even know me, forget it, I'll just go now, oh, how dumb is this—

Don't go, I said.

She stopped walking. Then sat down. And wrung her hands. Without looking at me. She had beautiful fingers with nails painted purple to match her shirt.

You asked a big question, I said.

Yes, she said, and her lips curved into an unhappy smile. She stared at my Converse All Stars.

And ... I don't want to just toss off an answer. That's why I didn't respond right away.

Okay. I thought I scared you—

And also ... everything's so fresh. I still don't have a perspective on it.

When did you split up? Is it okay for me to ask?

Three months ago.

That really is fresh, she said and took a sip of water from the bottle. A smaller sip.

I took the bottle from her and drank too.

I think that . . . no, you know what, no, I didn't know in advance, I said.

Mor nodded slowly, and I thought I could see disappointment in her nod.

But that doesn't mean . . . it's not that I don't understand things in retrospect.

What, for example? She turned her whole body toward me.

For ex-am-ple—I spoke slowly so I could have time to think—maybe because I'm on a trek now, I remember something that happened on our post-army trek.

Where did you go?

That's just it, we couldn't decide between Australia and India, and in the end, because of the money, we settled on India. And then one morning, I wake up late in the guesthouse in Dharamshala and see she isn't in bed, so I go to the restaurant and find her sitting there alone looking like the world had ended. Before I could order coffee at the counter, she blurts out: We should have gone to Australia. It turned out that she'd sat down for breakfast with some Crocodile Dundee who told her stories about the Australian deserts that had turned her on. But honey, I say, the Himalayas are above you and the most beautiful valley in the world is spread out below you—

It really is beautiful there. I've seen pictures.

Exactly! So I said to her, What's with Australia now? And she insisted: We have to go to Australia, Omri.

And that was a sign?

At the time, I didn't think it was a sign. But in retrospect, she was never satisfied. Not with her job, no matter what it was. Not with the house we lived in, no matter which house it was. Not with Liori's day care teacher, no matter who she was. She always thought that the real thing was somewhere else. We had a kind of standing joke that I was the only thing she wouldn't change.

And in the end, that's what happened.

Not exactly.

At that point in the conversation, I remember, Mor was already stretched across the width of the double bed in my room. The position she was lying in emphasized her beautiful curves. But I didn't think she was aware of it. I didn't think she would have done it deliberately.

What do you mean, not exactly? she asked, cupped her chin in her hand, and looked at me with eyes that seemed to say that the words about to come out of my mouth would have enormous significance for her.

Relationships are pretty much...a jungle, I said. The tangled undergrowth trips you up and it's hard to know...what's the cause and what's the effect. The easiest thing is to blame each other. But that's a lie. I am...I was just as responsible for it as she was. You have to learn how to live with someone who's dissatisfied most of the time. And I moved away from her as if it were contagious. There were other things too, things you can't know in advance. Our daughter . . . let's say she's . . . very sensitive. In the ninety-ninth percentile of sensitivity. And . . . we each developed in different directions, and . . . I don't know, maybe being together for fifteen years without killing each other is actually an achievement and not a failure? Sorry, I think you're looking for clear answers and . . . I still don't have any.

It's okay, you're helping me, she said and looked me straight in the eye.

Really? I stretched my legs a bit, and now my wool socks were almost touching her thin waist.

Yes, really.

We didn't speak for a while. Each of us stared at a different spot on the wall. And I thought it was weird and beautiful that although we barely knew each other, our conversation already had a beat. Including that silence, which came at exactly the right time. I thought: I've met so many people since we split—students, friends, colleagues, I even went to a psychologist twice—and I've never experienced this rare thing with them, the feeling that the person with me and I are the only people in the world at that moment. And I thought: Mor has plump cheeks, and I might be the only man in the world who thinks plump cheeks are sexy.

I don't know what else to tell you, I said after waiting four bars. The truth was that I'd barely spoken to people since the breakup. Not like that.

Mor looked at me again. Her gaze was warm but not entirely readable. She didn't move even a millimeter in my direction and was still scratching her tights with her nails in such a way that made it seem more like a tic than a real itch. And something else: Even though she was lying across my bed, she hadn't taken off her shoes. Her shod feet grazed the bed frame as they dangled ten centimeters beyond it.

I thought to myself that if she takes them off, it would be a sign. But I wasn't even sure I wanted her to take them off. Like those phantom pains that soldiers feel where their amputated limb had been—it seemed to me that since the split from Orna, I'd been suffering from phantom monogamy: I knew I should celebrate my new freedom, but in reality, I didn't. After fifteen years with the same woman, I couldn't picture myself being intimate with someone else. The idea even stressed me a little. I wasn't sure I'd be able to function.

In the end—I think she'd been in my room for an hour, tops—Mor stood up and said, I have to go back, Ronen might wake up by mistake.

But wait. I stood up too. Aren't you going to tell me why... all those questions?

I can't, she said.

That's not fair. I pouted like a kid who'd been denied something he wanted, and she said, Sorry, and smiled, but her tone was serious: It feels like a betrayal.

Okay. I put my hands together and gave her a Japanese bow. So... I'm glad I could be of service. Her hand was already on the doorknob, but I took the chance anyway: Can I tell you something else?

Yes, she said.

I'm shooting in the dark here, and the worst-case scenario is that you'll think I'm talking crap, but a trek is... an extreme situation. It brings out the best in some people, and in others...

I know, she said. And her eyes filled. All at once. Usually, eyes fill slowly, but with her, it happened very quickly. She turned to the door to hide them from me, and then turned around abruptly, took two quick steps toward me, stood on her tiptoes, and kissed me.

At first, I didn't see her at the shiva.

The house was full of people who had come to offer their condolences, standing in two clusters: one in the living room, six or seven gray heads surrounding an erect woman who was apparently Ronen's mother, and the second near the dining room, four or five young guys and one young girl, without curls, who was leaning on one of the guys, looking as if she were about to cry.

A grand piano stood between the living room and the dining room, its lid open as if someone was about to sit down and play, or had already played before I arrived. Beside it was a fireplace, the flames inside it crackling. The entire space was filled with the kind of humming you hear only at shivas. Sad, restrained voices, with a louder voice occasionally rising above it like a musician playing a solo.

Just when I began to think that the visitors should be handed little cards like the ones they give out at weddings that direct you to the tables where you can sit with people you know, and if you don't know anyone, they direct you to the table where people who don't know each other are sitting—

Ronen Amirov suddenly appeared, walking toward me.

I mean, the guy coming toward me looked so much like Ronen Amirov—the height, the slightly stooped back, even the monkish goatee—that for two bars, my heart stopped beating.

Then he reached out his hand and said, Gal, Ronen's brother. We look amazingly alike, people always tell...told us that.

I'm sorry for your loss, I said.

We haven't really taken it in yet, Gal said. We're all in shock. Where . . . do you know my brother from?

Bolivia. I met him and Mor there.

In La Paz?

The truth is, yes.

You don't say, he said, and I noticed that his tone suddenly dropped half an octave. It's nice of you to come.

I nodded.

He opened his mouth as if he wanted to ask something else, but then changed his mind and said, Mor's over there, as if there was something offensive about it, and pointed to one of the side rooms.

It was the long, narrow study of an older person. A desk. A large lamp. Shelves packed with books. And the space between the books and the shelf above them was also crammed with books. A few black plastic chairs stood close to the bookshelves, and under the window, at the far end of the room, was an office chair. On which Mor was sitting.

In lotus position. Thick wool socks on her feet.

Plumper than I remembered. More beautiful than I remembered. Wearing dark jeans and a light-colored sweatshirt with a picture of Frida Kahlo on it.

Her curls were gathered with a functional clip and her ears were earring-less, but a delicate gold chain lay on the honey-colored skin of her neck.

There was no place for me to sit, so I remained standing. She was busy talking to one of her girlfriends and didn't even notice that I had come into the room. She said, From the luggage conveyor belt. With my backpack.

Oh, that must have been so awful, her friend said.

All his clothes are in it, his books, I haven't unpacked anything yet, Mor said. I can't bring myself to do it.

Everything in its own time, her friend said. And they were silent for a few seconds, the silence that follows a cliché, and then Mor looked up and saw me, bewilderment in her eyes.

I walked over, bent down, and hugged her. Lightly, without pulling her body to mine.

Omri, I said when we broke apart. From La Paz.

I know, she said in a weak voice.

And that was it. She didn't say anything else to me. Or look at me. When a seat in a corner of the room became empty, I sat down. I tried to catch her eye, but it was impossible. She was otherwise occupied. I tried to listen to what she was telling her friends, but she spoke so quietly that I couldn't combine the occasional words I caught into sentences. I noticed that although almost every girlfriend tried to get her to talk, she had them talking about themselves in no time at all. But she did even that in a low voice I couldn't hear. So I picked up one of the photo albums that was being passed around and pretended to browse through it, while intermittently raising my eyes to get a better look at her. I noticed that the small scar between her eyebrows had deepened into a furrow that added several years to her age. But it actually made her more attractive to me. Her features had softened a bit. Her expressions had become subdued. Instead of an overly optimistic religious girl pretending innocence, a clearly sad woman was sitting before me. Even the Frida Kahlo on her sweatshirt looked unhappy. But she wasn't totally drained. Though her face showed profound sorrow, her body revealed a kind of jumpiness. Disquiet. She kept switching back and forth from lotus position to crossed legs, and after every few sentences her girlfriends spoke, she put her gold necklace into her mouth, all the while scratching her jeans, a tic I remembered from my hostel room.

Gradually, the small room emptied out almost entirely. Only Mor, one of her friends, and I remained. And still, she showed no sign of wanting to speak to me. Just the opposite. She spoke quietly to her friend, clearly excluding me from the conversation.

I felt like an idiot for driving all the way to Galilee to console a woman who looked right through me. So I said to myself, One more album and I'm gone.

There was a series of wedding photos in the one-more-album-and-I'm-gone, each one with different relatives who all looked like they were from his family. There wasn't a single curly haired person among them. She looks good in a dress, I thought. It emphasizes her waist. Even though you could tell from the way she was standing that dresses didn't come naturally to her. Definitely not the kind she was wearing. Ronen stood beside her, glowing. It turned out that the uptight guy I met in La Paz also had a generous smile that made his eyes slant and softened the angle of his nose, turning him into a pleasant-looking guy. It was the kind of smile that makes you like the person it belongs to. And feel a bit sad that he died.

Then there was a picture of the two of them sitting side by side, looking at something happening on a stage—it might have been the congratulatory speeches—and although they weren't touching, their faces were illuminated by the light of intimacy. Then there was a picture of them kissing. And another one of them kissing. And another, from a different angle—

Enough.

I stood up to leave.

She ignored that too, but when I reached the front door of the house, I felt a touch on my shoulder. The very lightest of touches.

I turned around.

Thank you for coming, she said, and extended her hand.

Her handshake lasted longer than is usual. Which gave her time to leave a note in my palm.

I nodded. And made a fist around the note.

Only when I was in my car did I dare to read the note.

Drive to the end of the street, then turn left at the traffic circle and go straight until you reach the monument. Wait for me in the parking area. It'll take me a while, but I'll find an excuse and come.

The first thing I did was call Orna. I asked her to pick up Liori from day care for me.

She said, This is so you, to fight with me about custody, then disappear to Bolivia for two weeks and now back out of picking her up.

I told her not to exaggerate, it was the first time. And she knew how important Liori was to me.

She said I couldn't leave them in the lurch like that, at the last minute. Liori doesn't react well to these sudden changes, she said, and she's going through a bad period as it is.

I told her I had no choice, I was in the north and couldn't get there in time. She asked what I was doing in the north. I lied to her.

You've become a really hard worker since we split, she said.

I always was, I said. And now I have alimony to pay.

Okay, she said, I'll pick her up, even though you don't deserve it.

Bitch, I hissed, moving the phone away from my mouth, then said to her, Thanks, Orna.

I got out of the car, went up to the monument, and read the names of the fallen soldiers from Kfar Vradim, first from right to left, then from left to right. Then from war to war. It occurred to me that since the separation, Liori had been asking questions about death. When will you die, Daddy? When will Mommy die? Where do we go when we die? Can we come back from there? Are you sure we can't?

I looked at my watch and decided that if Mor didn't come in the next five minutes, I would take off. So I could get back in time to hug my little girl today.

But ten minutes later I was still standing at the monument.

———

In the end, Mor arrived. On a bicycle. I saw her appear at the curve of the street, and my heart went out to her. Maybe because women who ride bikes usually look happy. Full of energy. And there was something hurt and forlorn about the way she was riding. Maybe because the street was totally deserted. And wide. Which made her look like a lone cowboy. Or a little girl running from a group of kids who are chasing her.

She was pumping the pedals hard. The wind and the speed whipped her curls around, and she pushed them behind her ears. But they blew free again in the next gust of wind, and that make me think of how she must have pedaled behind her husband on Death Road. Of the panic. And once again I felt the same urge: to make sure that no one hurt her.

She stopped at the monument, raised a surprisingly long leg over the bar, leaned the bike on the memorial wall, and came over to me. She was breathing hard, and her breasts rose and fell quickly. I didn't know whether it was because of the riding or because of me. The situation was so unclear that I didn't even know if I should hug her. Fuck it, she's a widow.

She stood on her tiptoes and kissed me—a quick kiss on the cheek—and said, I forgot how tall you are. I'm sorry I was so awful before. I'm living under a magnifying glass. I think they sense something. I don't know, maybe it's all in my mind. His mother is actually okay with me. But his brothers...they...I mean...it's possible that...I'm so happy you came. She stopped and gave me a weary smile. You have no idea what I'm talking about, eh?

I nodded.

She looked around quickly, as if she were afraid that someone was watching us, and then said, Come on.

Behind the monument was a footpath I hadn't seen earlier, and she began walking toward it, assuming I would follow.

It was mid-February. February 17, to be precise. I remember the date because Liori's birthday had been two days earlier.

Spring hadn't yet fully burst forth, but it was no longer winter. The cyclamens had already withered among the rocks. The anemones, on the other hand, had only just begun to open. The sun shone between the nearest clouds, but the ones in the distance were heavy and black. Only a few of the almond trees we passed were blooming, but the others had not yet begun to blossom. The path was a bit muddy from the rain that had fallen on Saturday and driven Liori's birthday guests from the garden to the living room, which had once been my living room as well. (Liori noticed that I had stopped at the threshold, hesitant about whether to enter, and without a word, took my hand the way an adult takes a child's hand before crossing the street.)

Mor walked more heavily than I remembered from La Paz. There, when we left the ice-cream parlor, she and her curls had skipped lightly down the street. Now there was something stooped about her gait.

I followed her silently until we reached an enormous flat rock that was at least the size of a double bed. It was surrounded by spiny broom plants that left only one side open to the view: green hills sloping westward down to the sea.

She sat down.

Water still dripped from the crevices in the rock. I found a dry spot not far from her, but not too close either.

She hugged her knees, turned her head to me, and gave me that two-stage look that begins directly and ends with averted eyes, and asked, How are you?

How *am I*?

Yes, how are you, Omri?

So many people have been asking how I am recently, I thought, but no one asks it *like that*. With a genuine curiosity that invites a sincere response. It's incredible how, in three words, she once again created a bubble around us.

I think that...you're going through...slightly more dramatic things, I said.

Have you kissed anyone else since we kissed in La Paz?

No.

Are you a monk or something?

I'm selective.

What do you actually do? I don't know anything about you.

I'm a nuclear scientist.

No kidding!

I'm a musician.

I don't believe it. You're a violinist too?

Why, who else is a violinist?

Ronen...was.

I play drums and percussion instruments. So...do you want to tell me what...happened?

Yes, but let me do it...at my own pace.

Are you cold?

What?

You're shaking. You want my coat?

It won't help. I've been like this since...Death Road. Always cold. It doesn't matter how many layers I wear. The coldness comes from inside.

I took off my coat and spread it around her shoulders. I'm sorry, I said, but I can't stand seeing you like this.

Thank you, she said, and let the sleeves dangle without putting her arms in them. So . . . you manage to make a living as a musician?

Are we still talking about that?

She nodded. Twice. And the scar between her eyebrows deepened.

I said, I started a workshop called HeartBeat and I hold it in schools.

And what happens in your workshop?

Are you really interested?

Really, she said, and cupped her chin in her hand, just the way she had in La Paz.

I teach them to listen through music. Their whole generation is one big attention deficit disorder. Most of them can't even carry on a dialogue. The fact is, they have a total communication disorder, not just an attention deficit disorder. So through playing percussion instruments together—

It wasn't an accident.

What?

Ronen's fall—it wasn't really an accident.

———

She slipped her arms into my coat. Left arm. Then right. She released the curls that had caught in the collar, zipped it all the way up and then unzipped it. All the way down. She moved a finger on her cheek as if to wipe away a tear. Even though there was no tear there. She lowered her arm back to the side of her body.

I wanted to caress that hand, but restrained myself.

She said, We used to take walks here a lot, Ronen and I, in the wadis.

Are you from ... here?

I'm from Ma'alot. I used to hitchhike here to see him and we used to take walks. He was a mess after his dad died—

Yes, I saw in the albums that his dad stopped appearing at some point.

A heart attack. Ronen was home when it happened. He tried to save him.

Shit.

I used to take him for walks so he wouldn't lose it completely. His head was so buried in violin scores that he didn't know any of the paths in the area until he met me. Even the path along the Kziv stream was new to him. Sometimes we would walk for an hour, sometimes for a whole day.

No kidding.

The rule was that we walk until he smiles. One real smile was enough. It didn't matter how long it took.

Now her tears were real, and one, only one, ran down her cheek. When Liori was little, I used to catch her tears with my tongue and that would make her laugh and stop crying. Since the split, I think she cries inside.

Mor wiped away her single tear herself with a quick movement of her finger and snuggled into my coat.

They asked me to identify him, she said in a choked voice. A cop took me to the hospital. Or the morgue. In La Paz. Or Coroico. I don't remember. The first few days are all jumbled together. The cop spoke Spanish to me the whole time and I just kept nodding. I didn't understand what he said.

There wasn't anyone from the embassy with you?

They closed the embassy after Israel's last military operation.

Fuck.

There's an Israeli couple that lives in the city and helps trekkers, but they were on vacation in Israel.

So you're saying that, even later on . . . through all the investigations . . . and the procedures . . .

Totally alone. They kept me there four days.

I put my hand on hers. An instinctive movement. Like drumming on the bongos. I didn't think too much.

She didn't move her hand away, but neither did she return my touch with her own.

We sat like that for a few minutes, without speaking. Each with our own mental images.

The black clouds that had been only on the horizon earlier now moved closer. The water dripping from the rock crevices began to ripple in the wind. I was starting to feel cold, but it didn't enter my mind to ask for my coat back.

I thought about her bicycle, which wasn't chained near the monument, and about the fact that if it were in Ramat Gan, it would be stolen in a minute.

I thought about my bike rides to day care with Liori when she was little, and about the time we fell when I lost my balance and she toppled headfirst onto the sidewalk, and about the too-long seconds that passed before she started to cry.

I thought about Liori's torn look when I told her—I spoke first to show Orna that I was coping, that I was on my feet—that "Mom and Dad aren't...getting along, and that's why Dad is moving to another house." At first, she didn't understand. She didn't understand at all what we meant. She even had a kind of odd smile on her face, as if we were telling her a joke.

I thought it was still a bit strange that Mor had skipped out on her husband's shiva like that. And that they had banished her to a side room. And that no one from her family had been there with her. No mom. No dad. No sister. My mom wouldn't have moved an inch from my side if such a disaster had struck me.

I asked, You want to tell me what happened?

She hesitated a little before replying, I do, but I'm afraid to.

It'll stay between us, I said, putting a hand on my chest as if I were taking an oath.

That's not it.

So what is it?

If you don't tell anyone, it's like it didn't happen. And you can tell yourself that it's all in your imagination.

Whatever you want, I'm here in any case, at your service—

You're terrific.

I'm not terrific at all.

Really? So tell something not-terrific about you.

Now?

Yes. It'll help me. Because what I'm about to tell you isn't the least bit terrific.

I hesitated. On the one hand, I didn't want to lose the look she'd been giving me up to then, a kind of clean look, not yet muddied by insults and scores to settle and knowledge of the other person's dark side—so maybe it wasn't appropriate to tell her why I was suspended by the conservatory, for example—

On the other hand, it was clear to me that, if I wanted to understand exactly how her husband had fallen into the abyss on Death Road and what she was doing here with me instead of sitting shiva for him, I had to reciprocate.

Okay, I started, so when... I came back from... Bolivia?

Yes.

Orna, my ex-wife... suddenly refused to do what we had agreed upon in mediation and demanded to cut down the number of days Liori would be with me. She said Liori wouldn't have a stable environment at my place because... I lost my job at the conservatory and didn't have another permanent job, and then I disappeared abroad for two weeks. And that, in general, I wasn't stable, just like my dad. So I called her and said I wanted to meet face-to-face. She said she preferred our lawyers to be present, and I said that, for her own good, the lawyers shouldn't be there. Not at that meeting. She met with me that evening at a café in a neighborhood that was once our neighborhood. I told her there was no way I would give up one minute with Liori, the girl needs her father, and if she doesn't go back to the original custody agreement immediately, I'll report her to internal revenue for her office's double bookkeeping. Then she said she didn't believe I would sink so low, and I said that if she didn't want her new man to go to jail, she should rethink her moves. Omri, this is me, why are you doing this? And then I just got up and walked out of the café. Without paying.

But why did she say all those things about you? Mor asked, and I felt her hand move slightly in discomfort under mine.

Because actually...I kind of fell apart a little after the divorce. And my dad really was a nothing. One of those men who can forget his kid in the car with the windows closed in the summer. And I'm not too good at nine-to-five...I can't seem to stick to it. But Liori? She never felt it. With her, I'm a rock.

I believe you.

You're only hearing my side. It's easy for you to believe.

No. That's one of the first things I picked up about you in the ice-cream parlor, Omri, that you're one hell of a dad.

But how...

I asked you how long you were going to stay, and you said, "Two weeks tops, I can't do more than that. Because of my daughter." You said you missed her to death.

Right.

It was because of that remark that I went to see you in the hostel. Because of the way you talked about your daughter.

Really?

I knew you wouldn't take advantage of the situation.

No kidding.

But Omri, she said, then was silent. And scratched her jeans with her available hand. Dug into them.

What? I asked.

My story . . . is a lot worse.

And as she said that, she returned my touch for the first time. Her delicate fingers wound around my thick ones, as if she wanted to guarantee I wouldn't run away after I heard what happened. Her wedding band wasn't on any of those fingers.

But what exactly happened? I asked.

She didn't reply, just breathed heavily and bent her head like an animal surrendering to a stronger animal.

Sometimes, during people's silences, I hear a song. Like a movie soundtrack. Sometimes I understand right then and there why that song in particular. Sometimes only in retrospect.

You're most beautiful when you're drunk
And you can't tell right from wrong
Not even beauty . . .

Those lines, from a forgotten Knesiyat HaSechel song, began to play in my mind.

You know what? I said, I have an idea. It's something Orna and I used to do in couples therapy—

Which re-a-l-ly worked, of course, Mor said and raised her head.

I laughed out loud and thought, I never had a girl-friend with a sense of humor. That was always my job, to be funny. And I said, Whenever one of us had a hard time saying something, the therapist suggested we switch to third person.

Third person?

He, she, them.

Like in a story?

I nodded.

À la "Once upon a time there was a girl with curls who loved a boy and went on her honeymoon with him under the illusion that everything was fine"?

Exactly.

Okay, give me a minute.

Take your time.

She untied the laces of her red Ultrastars. Then retied them, tighter. The right shoe, the left shoe. As if she were about to set out on a journey. And then she began to speak.

Okay . . . so that . . . that girl, with the . . . curls . . . if there was anything she was sure of before the honeymoon, it was that she knew her husband. After all, they'd been together since high school, together they missed each other terribly in the army, together they lived in a one-and-a-half-room apartment for all their undergraduate years. He studied math at the Technion and she switched majors four times until she finally settled into a fast-track master's degree program in clinical sociology. When they graduated, they felt it was time to do the post-army trek they hadn't done, except that there was one small problem—she was doing shifts on the ERAN suicide hotline and he was giving private violin lessons—and they didn't have a pot to piss in. Then I had an idea—I mean, the girl with the curls had an idea: Let's get married at your family's place, on the grass. Your friends will handle the music, we'll do the catering ourselves, and with the money we get as gifts, we'll go to South America. And that's how it was. Even without any dramatic proposal scenes, it was clear to both of them that it was for life, and even if she was sometimes curious about other guys—after all, she was a girl who could take hours to decide which flavor to get at an ice-cream stand—she never let her curiosity raise its head until La Paz. And the truth is that, even there, nothing would have happened if he hadn't started acting weird.

Can you manage to understand anything with this third-person thing?

Yes.

When I talk about it this way, it's as if it happened to another girl.

That's the idea.

If only it had happened to another girl. It's going to rain. Omri. You want your coat back?

Don't be silly. Go on.

Okay. So...it had already started on the flight. He complained the whole time. About the food. About the service. About the quality of the movie earphones. And she was actually enjoying that empty time. When the plane shook over the ocean, he stressed out while she mellowed out. Sitting on her other side was a guy in a suit who was playing with a kind of upgraded Rubik's Cube, and when she asked him what it was, they got into a pleasant conversation. Ronen didn't say anything, but when they were waiting at the luggage carousel, he said, You know, not everyone has to be your friend. She'd had no experience with poison arrows shot at her from his direction, so she simply didn't answer. But when they reached the hostel, it turned out that he wasn't satisfied with the room either, and he insisted that they move to a different one. And at night, he talked in his sleep, words that didn't connect into sentences, something he hadn't done since his father died.

A few days later, it was obvious that something bad was happening to him. He didn't smile at her at all, and he was always busy trying to save money or calculating how much they'd already spent and how much they had left. At night, he talked to himself and it was impossible to touch him at all. Every time she tried, he drew back as if she were contagious, and the only time they... had sex, he went at her furiously, as if she meant to harm him. She told him she didn't like it that way, and he complained, so you're saying we can't change it up sometimes? And from that moment on, he completely lost interest in... being intimate with her and moved to the far side of the bed. On the other hand, when they were with other people, on buses or in cafés, he stuck to her like glue and didn't even let her go to the bathroom without watching her like a hawk.

Sounds stressful, I said.

You're looking at me as if you want to ask me something, Mor said. So *yalla*, ask.

Our fingers were still laced. The clouds above us threatened to burst.

If things were so bad for you both, I asked, why didn't you get on a plane and go back home?

You mean, why didn't *they* get on a plane.

That third-person thing is really working for you, isn't it?

Seems like it.

I'm listening.

So after a week, when . . . her husband was still keeping her at arm's length, she really did ask him if he wanted to go back to Israel, and he said no. So she said, You don't seem to be enjoying yourself, and he looked into her eyes and said, Sorry, I don't know what's going on with me, I keep having thoughts about my dad, flashbacks of him collapsing in the living room, and in general, my mind is full of bad thoughts that I can't stop. She told him they'd work on it together, and stroked his back. That time, he didn't pull away at her touch, and she thought that was a good sign.

And really, the next few days were days of honey for them, of small kindnesses from him, like: Come on, I'll carry your backpack. Shall I get you coffee from the restaurant? That sharwal is really beautiful, and that shirt, why look at the landscape when I can look at you? But all that ended in an instant when she stopped to talk with the guide in Salar. She just wanted to ask how the Red Lagoon had become red, and she may have touched his elbow during the conversation, because that's how she is, she touches, but that definitely did not justify the scene Ronen made later, when they reached their room. She can't even describe it now, that's how humiliating it was, but he called her, among other things, a slut and . . . an idiot. In any case, that was her breaking point. In a single moment, all her efforts to understand him and accept his shifting moods turned into icy fury. She told him he would never talk to her like that again because next time it happened, she would just leave him, honeymoon or not, she refused to be treated like that. She was sure he'd argue with her, but instead, he kneeled down on the filthy floor of their room, kissed her hand, and begged her to forgive him. He promised it would never happen again and suggested that they go back to La Paz the next day and he would go to a pharmacy to buy tranquilizers, anything to keep her from leaving him, because he wouldn't be able to survive that, it would break him for good—

So in fact . . . I met you in the ice-cream parlor in La Paz right after that?

Yes, two days later.

What timing.

Tell me, Omri, what . . . did you think of me then, in the ice-cream parlor?

That you weren't really as thrilled as you wanted people to think, I wanted to say. But instead, I repeated her question: What did I think of you?

Yes.

Now she gave me her first flirtatious smile, which was also a bit sad. As if she knew only too well how all flirtations end.

I liked you, I said, smiling back. That's for sure. But it never occurred to me that—

I'd knock on your door in the middle of the night.

Wearing tights and a red checked shirt. With the top button open.

You remember.

Could I forget?

The truth is that it never occurred to me either.

So what happened that...

Maybe... we should continue the story?

The next day, they took a bus to La Paz. He fell asleep on her shoulder during the ride. She, on the other hand, couldn't fall asleep. It was as if she'd caught his negative-thoughts virus. She thought about how she would ever survive another month with him like this. Maybe she should pretend to have a terrible illness, and then ask him to arrange for an earlier flight to Israel, let him feel strong. But how do you fake an illness, who pretends to be sick on their honeymoon, it's not supposed to be this way. They weren't supposed to have sex only once in two weeks on their honeymoon, he isn't supposed to call her a slut and an idiot on their honeymoon, and she isn't supposed to feel like a slut and an idiot just because he called her that. Maybe he isn't attracted to her anymore? Maybe they'd played at being in love before they got married, and now they're like an off-season tourist town? His head was heavy on her shoulder. She moved it, but every time the bus swayed, it fell back on her again, pressing hard on her bones—

More than anything, she felt the need to be alone for a little while, a few hours for herself. To organize her thoughts. So on the morning of the day they met the . . . tall divorced guy, she asked, Is it okay if I take the morning to wander around the city alone? She asked in the nicest way, but he just said, No, I'm sorry, and added, I think the pills are helping, but I still don't feel ready to be alone with my thoughts, definitely not in this depressing room. She wanted to remind him that they had a recommendation for a gorgeous hostel downtown and that he was the one who turned it down because of the price, and that's why they're in "this depressing room," but instead, she said, Okay, so let's go have some ice cream, I heard there's an ice-cream parlor not far from Lobo that has special flavors. And on the way, they met the tall divorced guy, who was actually the first person apart from Ronen to speak Hebrew with her since the beginning of the trip. At first, she thought he looked like a Viking, with that height and the long hair pulled back into a ponytail, so she spoke English to him, but he answered in Hebrew, and something in the way the conversation flowed and the warmth that radiated from him only made it clear to her how complicated and frustrating and hopeless things were with her husband, who sat with them in thunderous silence during the entire conversation. Then they walked with the Israeli Viking—who, it turns out, also had a lovely name, Omri—to his hostel, which was the same recommended hostel she had wanted to move to. Over his shoulder, she saw that there was a burbling fountain in the inner courtyard, and of all the things in the world, it was that fountain that ignited her anger and made her realize all at once that, from the beginning of the trip, she had in fact been living in a dictatorship.

True, the dictator was miserable, but his misery was exactly what enabled him to control her, and also to remark a second after they walked away from Omri, It's pathetic, the way you have to get attention from every man who enters our radius. She didn't reply to that nasty comment, and got into bed that night in her tracksuit as if nothing had happened, let him hug her as if nothing had happened, and waited for the tranquilizers he'd bought himself in the pharmacy to knock him out. After he fell asleep, she pulled his beard very gently to make sure it didn't wake him up, and only then did she change into tights and a shirt, put on her earrings again, and leave. At first, she really didn't know where she was going and just breathed in the free air. But then her legs took her to Omri's hostel. She still had no idea that the visit to his room would develop the way it did.

The way Mor had kissed me in the hostel, I recalled, was no less surprising than the actual fact of the kiss: She totally abandoned herself to it. Which made me totally abandon myself to it as well. Her mouth was wide open and hot. Very hot. I breathed heavily, I heard myself panting. Since the unsuccessful operation to correct my deviated septum when I was in the army, I mostly breathe through my mouth. And since my mouth was very busy, I had no air. But somehow, I didn't care about panting near her. Maybe because she too was trembling, a slight movement that was transmitted to me through her tongue, which was curling around mine. It had been the kind of kiss during which your hands automatically begin to wander around the other person's body. But as soon as I started to caress her waist under her checked shirt, she broke away from me. Sharply. She pushed me away with her hand and gave me one last, indecipherable look. Then she stroked my cheek with the same hand that had pushed me away, whispered good night, and went out.

Did you ever cheat on Orna? Mor asked, pressing my hand gently, returning me all at once to Galilee. To now.

No.

Did you want to?

A little, with the psychologist who treated Liori, there was something so...supportive about her that I found myself fantasizing about her between sessions—I wanted to say. But instead, I said, Toward the end, yes, to get back at her. But something...stopped me. I don't know. Maybe I'm just not the type.

"She" isn't either. The girl with the curls.

She isn't what?

From the first day she was with Ronen, she hadn't touched even the little finger of another man.

No kidding.

But after that happened, when she left the...Viking's room in the hostel and walked along the empty streets, she didn't feel guilty. To her great surprise. Just the opposite, she felt that, with a single kiss, she had solved a serious problem that had been burdening her, and when she got back into bed beside her husband, she thought that now that she had regained her liberty, she could love him again. And in the morning, when she opened the shutters to let the sun in and said to him, Get up, we're going on a hike, and he said, How, what, when. Now, honey. Remember the walks we used to take after your dad . . . we walked and walked until you smiled? Remember how that helped you? So that's what you need now: to be in the fresh, open air. He began to say, Yes, but—but she interrupted him and fired the doomsday weapon: And hikes are a lot cheaper, Ronch. Every hike saves us fifty dollars!

The hike known as El Diablo starts high up on the Andes and descends for two or three days, depending on how fast you walk, until you reach Coroico, a small town on the edge of the jungle. Most of the path is not marked, so they navigated according to the hiking journal written by a German named Dieter Lemke that she had printed from a hikers site: *From the spot where you get out of the truck, walk five hundred meters to the house. A path begins at the house. If you're lucky*—and they were lucky—*you can see alpacas on your left. After the alpacas, climb on the right bank until you reach an empty cabin.* And so on and so forth.

On the first day, Ronen walked behind her without speaking. Only on the morning of the second day, when they finished taking apart the tent, did he say, It was a good idea to go on a hike. And she said, You have no idea how happy I am you said that, Ronch. And he said, We haven't met a single person since we set out. She asked, You don't think that's weird? And he said, I like it.

The landscape changed as they moved forward on the trail. The snow melted into small waterfalls they tried to walk under without getting wet, and into raging rivers they crossed on rope bridges. Every time they had to jump over a missing slat or leap from rock to rock, he gave her a hand, and she took it every time he offered it. They both knew that with every touch, they were re-creating and reconfirming the moment their love came into being, at the Bridge on Mount Halutz, right after she showed him the spot that overlooked both the Mediterranean Sea and the Sea of Galilee, and they turned around and started back. They'd been dating for almost two weeks then, but neither one of them had dared to be the first to move from talking to touching. Truthfully, she was beginning to be afraid that he wasn't into girls. And then she stumbled. On one of their rock-to-rock jumps. A slight stumble. He gave her a hand and she took it and didn't let go of it even when they reached safe ground. And so they walked hand in hand all the way back to his house. For almost an hour. And there, behind the door to his room that had a dartboard hanging on it, they kissed and he undressed her, stopping occasionally to make sure by looking at her that he could continue, and when he saw the large birthmark shaped like Africa to the right of her navel—she thought it was ugly and was so ashamed of it that for years, she had avoided showering in the locker room—he got onto his knees and kissed it, whispering, It's so beautiful, you're so beautiful.

On the second day of their hike, it started to pour.

According to Dieter's hikers journal, they were supposed to reach a small village soon, so they ran there, their backpacks bouncing, to find shelter before it got dark and knocked on the door of the first cabin they came to. The man who opened the door had no teeth and he spoke in an ancient language that had lots of consonants. Not Spanish. They tried to explain with their hands about the rain and their wet clothes, and he nodded and gestured for them to follow him. Ronen whispered to her in Hebrew that it looked dangerous, and she said loudly, No way, he has good eyes. And in fact, the man led them to a small building in the middle of the tiny village, jangled a huge bunch of janitor's keys, and opened the door of a school classroom with chairs, desks, and a blackboard in it. The downpour continued outside, but now they were completely protected in their Noah's ark. They spread their sleeping bags on the podium meant for the teacher and slept so well that they didn't hear the children come in and gather around them. Only when the teacher shook them by the shoulders did they wake up, and something in their shocked expression must have been funny because all the kids—seven in number—along with the teacher laughed uproariously, and their laughter was so unrestrained that they joined in, that is, she laughed and Ronen smiled, actually smiled under his small beard. After giving the children candy from the supply in their backpacks—the hikers journal explicitly recommended buying candy to give to kids, that's how thorough Dieter was—they folded up their sleeping bags, left the classroom, and continued walking in the countryside that glittered with raindrops and sunbeams. They sang a duet as they walked: She was the soloist and he was the violinist, crooning the high-pitched sounds and moving his hand as if he were bowing the notes. When they finished, he said, Maybe when we go back home, I'll start performing again. That would be wonderful, she said, thinking, Finally! My Ronen—who spread love over all my childhood wounds, who made me finally understand what it means to feel at home—has come back to me.

But when they finished their hike and returned to La Paz, her Ronen went back to being as tight as a wire. She fantasized about a few days of recuperating—taking hot showers and lying in a hammock—but he complained that La Paz was ugly and all the blind people and cripples in the streets stressed him, and that people were always trying to sell you something, and this room, in the hostel, who rents out a room without a window? The empty aquarium in the lobby, what the hell is that supposed to be? Where's the water? Where are the fish? And he was afraid that the bad thoughts would start again, and there's another hike that Dieter, that same Dieter Lemke recommends—actually a bike trip, on Death Road, I mean, it was once Death Road, but today, because of the many disasters that happened there, it's closed off to all vehicles except bicycles, and Deiter wrote in his blog that the views are amazing—

She wanted to tell him that she'd planned to rest a little, but she was also afraid that the bad thoughts and weird behavior would start again and didn't want to endanger the renewed closeness developing between them. So in the end, having no choice, she agreed that they would set out for Death Road the next day.

'm talking so much, Mor said, and put a finger on her lips as if to stop herself from speaking, and then gave me the look that I haven't been able to describe until now. Maybe the thing about it is that lowering her eyes modestly after staring brazenly at you isn't really modest because her eyes stop at the opening of your shirt as if they were undressing you—

It's okay, I said, go on.

In general, I'd really rather listen, she said, not lowering her glance from the open top button of my shirt.

I remember, I said, from La Paz.

It's so weird how things happen to you when you... She stopped for a moment, then began again, When I was eight, I had a callus on my vocal cords. They operated on me, and I wasn't allowed to talk for a month. For a whole month, I just listened.

A preparatory course for the ERAN suicide hotline. Exactly.

But continue now, okay? I'm listening.

I have a kind of burning in my throat, Omri. As if, if I continue, I'll end up... crying.

And that's bad?

If I start to cry—I won't stop. And that's not good. I have to be strong now.

Why in fact, does she have to be strong? I wondered. And asked, Don't you... I mean, I have no problem staying here until tomorrow, but don't you... have to go back to the shiva at some point?

I do—she gave a small sigh that sounded like a moan of pain and looked up at me again—but I also have to get this story out of me.

Okay.

Good. She took a breath, a long breath, and only then did she continue: When she...woke up, she wanted to go out for breakfast, but discovered that the door to their room was locked from the outside and that her husband had taken the spare key, so then— Wait, Omri, maybe...before we go on, we need to say something about that "she." She has four sisters, all of them "good girls" except for her, and their dad, who was afraid she'd be a bad influence on them, used to punish her all the time. If she came home too late after being out on the town. Or she was fresh to him, disrespectful. One of the punishments he liked best was locking her door from the outside and not letting her out until morning, not even to the bathroom. So when she saw that her husband had locked her in the hostel room, the memory of all those humiliating nights she was forced to pee from the window into the yard of their apartment building enraged her and she tried to smash and kick the door open, which did nothing but cause intense pain in her shoulder, so when he came back with the bikes, she had already lost it completely. Maybe if he had lied that it was a mistake, that he hadn't planned to take the spare key, she might have calmed down. But he did the opposite—he explained in an unapologetic tone that he took the key because he went to rent the bikes and didn't want her to go for breakfast and flirt with all kinds of people.

She asked, So you made yourself my jailer? And he said, You didn't leave me a choice.

Now, as she's telling me all this, and in the third person, no less, it's clear to her that that was the moment she should have understood how totally unhinged he was and acted accordingly, that is, start protecting herself, maybe get someone else involved, maybe fly him back to Israel straight to a hospital, and definitely not keep arguing with him. But at that moment, she was deeply entrenched in her rage and completely incapable of seeing things objectively, and more than anything, she wanted to get back at him, hurt him, give him a verbal slap that would restore her Ronen, and that's why she told him about the middle-of-the-night meeting with the divorced Viking in La Paz. She said, I went to see him. She said, After you fell asleep. She said, A kiss. She also said things that didn't happen. And then—she had never hurt a fly and didn't know she had it in her, but when she saw that the verbal slap had no effect on him at all—she started to punch him in the chest. You see? Punch. This is what happens when you lock me in! Punch. It's all because of you! Punch. You pushed me to this!

———

Don't look at me like that, Omri.

Mor jerked her fingers out from under mine.

Like what?

As if I made a terrible mistake by telling him about us. Clearly I made a terrible mistake.

Eagles began to circle above us. Or above some invisible carcass. Mor looked at them. And I looked at her and noticed, for the first time, that several strands of silver she was too young to have were entwined in her curls.

Isn't it true that in movies, she said to me, when a woman punches a man in the chest, he always hugs her tight until she calms down?

Yes, it's true.

So in real life, it's different.

What happened in real life?

Ronen only pushed me... her away, smiled bitterly, and said, I knew it, and she said, Idiot, and he said, My mom always said you were an alley cat who would go with anyone who gave you a bowl of milk. I could answer you, she said, but I won't stoop to that level. He sat down on the bed and stuck his hands under his thighs as if he were trying to control them before he couldn't control them, and said angrily, not pleadingly, Don't you understand that I can't live without you? She sat down close to him and said, You don't have to live without me. I'm sorry, Ronch, I'm sorry I went to him. He smiled the bitterest smile, didn't touch her, and looked at the two bikes he'd brought that were now standing in the middle of the room, and said, I paid a fortune for them. Is that what he's interested in now? she thought, but said, So *yalla*, let's go for a ride, and he said, unenthusiastically, Okay. But on one condition. I'm listening, she said. Your phone, he said, I hold on to it. So you don't text with that Omri behind my back. And she said, I don't even have his number. Through clenched lips he said, That's my condition. She was so anxious to atone that she took her phone out of her pocket, handed it to him, and said, Take it. Hoping that would pacify him.

But from the minute they left for Death Road, he withdrew into himself again and barely spoke to her, and he also kept a distance from her as they pedaled, always two or three pumps in front of her. She waited for him to stop feeling offended, hoping that his willingness to go riding was a good sign, and didn't say anything about how narrow the road was at a scary spot, or why wasn't there a guardrail, or how she was trying to look only straight ahead and to the left so as not to look to the right at the deep wadi. She didn't even glance or nod at the other riders they passed. On the one hand, she was filled with self-contempt for surrendering to the dictator, and on the other hand, she was a prisoner of the hope that it was possible to save their honeymoon from falling into the abyss. She had no idea that another decision was taking shape in his mind. He had become a total stranger to her. Even when they passed the small crosses planted in the ground in the memory of the people who had died on that road—each cross froze her blood and made her pedal more slowly—he didn't say anything. He remained as closed as his sleeping bag was when zipped all the way to the top.

At night, in the tent, her calf muscles sometimes cramped from the strain and the cold. He pedaled quickly, and during the few breaks they took, he was silent with her and looked at everything but her, and a minute or two later, he'd say, *Yalla*, I'm done, and jump on his bike. She had to make an effort to catch up so he wouldn't vanish in the fog—there was fog almost the entire time—but she didn't want to ask him to slow down so as not to arouse some demon, and also because she hoped that with all the furious pedaling and sweating the anger would seep out through his pores and then maybe he could forgive her for the stupid things she'd done and for the ones she hadn't done that existed only in his mind. Yes, at that point, she still believed there was a chance it would all work out, reminding herself constantly what the Viking had told her in his room, that a trek is an extreme situation that brings out the best in some people and in others—remember telling me that?

Of course.

And suddenly, she remembered the only vacation they'd taken over the last few years, after college graduation, and how, from the beginning, Ronen had complained about the outrageous price they were paying for the next to nothing they were getting, and it was too hot, and then too cold, and all that sand everywhere. At dinner with all the other guests, while she chatted with people, he took out a book about Hitler's last days in the bunker and read it without turning a page even once. At some point, he leaned over and said to her, *Yalla*, I'm done, but you can stay here and flirt with anyone you want. On the way to the cabin, he walked half a meter in front of her, and when she asked why he was walking so fast, he didn't answer. When they reached the cabin, he kicked the door open and threw himself onto the mattress, exhausted, even though he hadn't done anything all day, turned his back to her, and fell asleep really quickly. He talked in his sleep that night, fragments of sentences, the way he'd done at his father's shiva—

Sounds horrible—

Not all couples have to be compatible trip-wise, she told herself. We just have to survive Death Road, then go home and never go on a trip together again.

I worried about you after you left my room in the middle of the night, you know?

Really?

I woke up in the morning and looked for the two of you in every hostel in La Paz. I had a . . . bad feeling.

What a sweetie, she said.

Her intonation annoyed me. "What a swee-tie." Swee-tie? What am I, a little kid? So I didn't tell her that, in the end, I followed them. Instead, I encouraged her, with a slight nod, to keep talking.

She continued. Totally immersed in the events.

The agonizing pain of cramping muscles woke her at night in the tent, but she didn't cry out, so as not to wake her husband, and she didn't go out of the tent to pee, even if she had to, so that God forbid he might wake up and think she was going to see someone else again. And now that she's talking about it, she realizes how much, at that point, everything was already twisted beyond repair. She wasn't even enjoying the views—they were there, occasionally emerging from the fog. After all, the Andes, with their white peaks, the silvery, winding thread of a river, the wild vegetation, the low clouds, the waterfalls that splash onto the road itself—they were there, but they left no impression on her, like a painting in a museum that you see is beautiful but have no emotional reaction to. And yet, because of the love she still felt for him, and because of the what-did-I-do-why-did-I-kiss-another-man-on-my-honeymoon feeling she had that made her think she might really be a slut, as he claimed, or a floozy, as her father had always said, she dragged herself out of the sleeping bag every morning, packed everything into the backpack every morning, got on her bike every morning, and pedaled two or three meters behind him every day, and sometimes, when they had to slow down because of a rockslide that blocked the road, she also tried to toss him bits of verbal bait, maybe he would take one of them:

It looks a little like Sha'ar HaGai, no?

Did you see that monument of stones with the names in Hebrew? I think I read about their accident. Eight people. A jeep.

She even tried songs. She sang softly. Maybe he would join her with that pretend-violin thing of his. Or just sing along with her. A minute passed, another minute, another minute, and yet another, until she gave up. How long can you talk and sing without getting a response? And without feeling stupid?

Her father used to punish her with silences. Sometimes they lasted a whole day. Sometimes, if he found cigarettes in her backpack, two days. And once, when he found out about her affair with the drama teacher, it went on for an entire month. She would talk to him and he would just ignore her, not answer her. And if he had to ask her for something, let's say to pass the pepper at a meal, he would ask her sister Elisheva to ask her. There's nothing more humiliating than that, right?

Right.

Thanks for answering.

You're welcome.

Always answer me, Omri. Promise?

Promise.

I liked that she said "always." "Always" meant we had a future. And suddenly I had a flash-forward. I saw us in another few months, standing together, relaxed and comfortable, like a couple, in the Barby Club. At a performance of Knesiyat HaSechel. With the beat of the bass guitar shaking the floor under us.

Mor continued: They rode along the last section of Death Road in total, heavy silence. The chirping of birds, for example, could be the most wonderful sound, but also the most depressing if all it does is underscore the silence. She still remembers the sound of his bicycle chain, which squeaked a little, and the sound of her brakes on the downhill sections, and the scrunch of earth being crushed under the wheels, his, hers, and the buzzing of mosquitoes near her ears, above her eyebrows.

They had started riding in the mountains near La Paz, five thousand meters above sea level, and descended, kilometer after kilometer, to a jungle teeming with stinging insects. The weather changed too, almost abruptly, from cold and dry to tropical and sweaty, and it started to rain, like now, small drops of fog, the kind that wouldn't cause you to stop biking but did make the sides of the road wet. You have to understand, there is nothing on Death Road that separates riders from the abyss, only narrow shoulders, and when they're damp, they can crumble and disappear under your wheels.

They pedaled quickly in the fog. According to Dieter, the closest shelter should be eight kilometers away, and they hoped to reach it before darkness made their ride even more dangerous.

They rode in the center of the dirt road. He kept five or six meters in front of her. And then he veered slightly to the right.

She said, Watch out, Ronch, don't go to close to the edge.

He didn't reply. And instead of moving away from the edge—he moved closer to it.

Then she shouted, You're crazy. What are you doing?

That is, she thought she shouted, it all happened so fast that she isn't sure about the exact words, they were swallowed up in the fog—

Yes, I'm crazy! he yelled. And started pedaling faster.

Stop, Ronch! She started pedaling faster too, and now she caught up to him. She could hear his rapid breathing and see the sweat glistening on his temples.

The rain intensified, whipped their faces and wet the words coming out of their mouths.

Ronch, please, don't ride on the shoulder—

Why do you even care—

What do you mean? I love you—

You don't—

I do. Stop, Ronch, please. It's dangerous. Dieter specifically wrote that before a curve you have to stay close to the cliffs—

So what—

You'll skid!

So I'll skid!

I'm begging you, get away from the edge!

The sharp descent into a curve began. I pressed the handbrakes to stop—but Ronen continued to fly forward. I turned my handlebars to the left to stay close to the cliffs, but Ronen stayed in the middle of the path. I wanted to yell, but I had no voice. In those last few seconds I froze, do you understand? I didn't do anything.

I stopped and watched it happen. The way you watch a movie. He kept riding straight ahead and fast, as if there were no curve and no fog, and when he reached the curve, he turned his handlebars sharply and intentionally to the right, and just...just rode into the abyss.

Later, when suspicions arose and question marks took shape, I thought about Mor's description and began to have doubts about it: If it was so foggy, and if Ronen sped ahead while she stopped, how did she even manage to see so clearly what happened? And why did Ronen have to turn his handlebars to the abyss? After all, if there was a sharp curve there, steering straight ahead would have been enough. And how, damnit—with all due respect to the exercise I stole from couples therapy—was she able to tell me such a thing in the third person, as if it was just a story, and switch to talking about herself only at the end?

She rested her head on me. First her curls touched my shoulder, then her cheek. That surprised me no less than the kiss in La Paz. You have to feel very close to someone to allow yourself to rest your head on them, to admit to them and yourself that life is too much for you and you no longer have the strength to deal with it.

We didn't speak for a long while.

I got a strong whiff of her scent. In La Paz, I'd barely had time to notice it, and all I remembered was that it was pleasant. Now I had time to inhale it deeply: a faint scent of lemongrass from her hair, a strong aroma of freshly baked butter cookies from her neck, and a new smell she hadn't had in La Paz, maybe of fear.

The drizzle had almost stopped, and the wind carried only a few drops in our direction, as if they were falling from leaves after a delay.

I should have been deeply horrified by her story. Or, alternatively, I should have been deeply suspicious of the details that didn't hang together.

And it's not that I wasn't horrified, and it's not that I wasn't suspicious, but at the time, I began to feel a different, more intense emotion.

A halfhearted sun appeared between the clouds, already close to the sea, almost touching it—but not quite yet.

I'm always beating up on myself, Omri, she said. In first person. Sounding crushed. Her head still rested on my shoulder. Her thigh pressed against mine.

But what could you have—? I started to say.

You know, she interrupted me, when Ronen got weekend leave from the army, I'd pick him up at the bus station, and just before we hugged, he'd take the sunglasses off his shirt where he always hung them so they wouldn't get in the way of our squeeze. That's what we called it, that tight hug where nothing was hidden, the hug that lasted until we both managed to silence the underlying fear of abandonment that started to surface whenever we were apart. You get it? Maybe if I had held on to him like that, as hard as I could, on the first few days of our honeymoon, and forced a squeeze on him, he would have calmed down. And maybe if I hadn't spoken to the guide at Salar, and maybe if we hadn't gone to Bolivia at all, and maybe if I hadn't gone to see you in the middle of the night, and maybe if I hadn't agreed to go on that bike trip on Death Road—

There's no way of knowing, Mor. All those "maybes"—

I had a plan, Omri. I knew where I was going in life. And I knew that I wasn't traveling alone. Now I'm totally lost. I have no idea what to do.

It seems to me—I cautiously put my hand around her shoulders—that that's the whole idea of a shiva, no? To postpone all those questions until later.

She pressed up against me, signaling that she wanted the embrace.

But I still wasn't sure it was okay, what was happening here. And I thought: Why did you mention the shiva, idiot, in another minute she'll remember, give you the brush-off, and go back there, and you'll never see her again.

Our bodies, however, fit together without effort or hesitation. The eagles flew off to another place.

Another Knesiyat HaSechel song played in my mind again. I tried to push it away, but pushing a song out of your mind is as impossible as stopping yourself from falling in love.

You're most lost when you know
What you want
I'm like that too.

I don't feel like going back to the shiva, she said after a long silence.

Why not?

His family . . . I didn't tell them the truth. I said it was an accident, that he rode close to the edge and just skidded, and now I think they suspect, and—

But what is there to—

They keep checking to see if I'm grieving enough. If I'm acting the way a widow should. But my tears must have dried up on the flight. I boarded the plane a total mess after four days of not sleeping—and I still couldn't fall asleep. So I drank cognac in plastic cups and cried. At some point I must have really lost it because people called the flight attendant.

No kidding.

She came over and asked what happened, did I need anything, and said that maybe I should take it easy on the drinking. So I told her what had happened. Her eyes opened wide and she sat down in the empty seat next to me, put her hand on mine, and asked me to tell her a little bit about Ronen. So I told her. About the notes he used to leave me on the fridge. And how, when I was sick once, he played Brahms for me, a private concert for an audience of one woman who applauded with her feet at the end of every piece because it was hard for her to move the rest of her body. And how, at our wedding, when he saw me standing off to the side and my family didn't even come over to me, he came and put his arms around me and said, You're not alone, Mor. I talked and cried and cried and cried, and in the end, the flight attendant started to cry too, moved me to business class and brought me more cognac.

Nice of her.

His brothers had something to say about that too, you know? On the way from the airport, his brother asked me, Tell me sister-in-law, are you drunk?

But . . . why didn't you tell them the truth?

They wouldn't have believed me. The stinginess, the need to control, the madness—that's not Ronen. For the entire two weeks, it was as if he were a bad actor in a local community center play where every line he says reminds you that it's a play. They just wouldn't have believed me if I'd told them that he deliberately threw himself into the abyss. They would have imagined worse things.

I wanted to ask, What are worse things?, but I couldn't get a word in.

You believe me, don't you? she asked, raising her head from my shoulder and giving me the look of a little girl in an orphanage when parents-buyers are there, shopping for a child to take home.

Yes, I said. I tried to sound doubt-free.

You're only hearing my side, so it's easy for you to believe, she said and smiled.

I smiled back at her.

She reached out and stroked my cheek. I reached out and trapped a curl between my fingers. It was softer than I had imagined, and I wound it around and around slowly—

And then I leaned toward her, not because I decided to but because a hidden rope pulled me to her. Really hard.

———

That was a softer kiss than the one in La Paz. And slower.

My hands caressed the back of her neck and her hands caressed the back of my neck, and then my arms, and then my chest, and slowly moved under my shirt.

Everything was very gentle at first. I felt that something in her was still being cautious. Still hesitant about whether it was possible here, on the rocks. Of whether she even wanted it. I hadn't completely decided whether I wanted it either. Or could do it. Then I returned her caution with my own gentleness, but slowly, as her touches grew more pleasant and moved farther south, my body began to awaken from its long hibernation, and when she moved her leg onto mine and sat on me, it came fully to life. And the warning voices in my head—what are you doing, you lunatic, she's a widow, her husband killed himself in the middle of their honeymoon, and you're outside, someone might see you—all those voices were temporarily silenced.

Orna and I had had almost no sex over the last few years. And when we did, she banned more and more ways I could touch her as time went on. That didn't feel good. This hurt her. She didn't feel like doing that anymore. Not on her stomach. And not with my fingers. And not with my tongue. Sex with her was like walking through a minefield. The main thing was not to misstep.

With Mor, on the flat rock, the moment the let's-go-for-it switch was flipped, it was like a good duet, a duet of bodies in which everything fit and flowed with a naturalness that should not have existed between a man and woman who hardly knew each other, a duet in which every touch was desired and truly needed by both sides. But that didn't make them selfish, just the opposite, it made them generous. The rhythm was unpredictable. Changing. It was the sort of rhythm where you could wind a curl around your finger for long, lingering seconds, then abruptly grasp a handful of curls. You could suddenly laugh, because a bit of protruding stone ended up where it shouldn't be. And laugh again because a rear end slipped into a small puddle. It was the sort of rhythm where you could feel the joy of discovering new continents, look, a birthmark shaped like Africa, and this is how it feels to press your lips to her nipple, and though her fingers might look delicate, they scratched hard, really hard, blood-drawing hard—

It was the sort of rhythm where, in the eye of the storm, you could still stop for a moment and look around, filled with what-the-hell-are-we-doing panic. She was supposed to be sitting shiva. Someone might wonder where she'd disappeared to. Come here to look for her. Maybe, to be on the safe side, we should—

And then they pressed up against each other again. Bare stomach to bare stomach. Neck to neck. Cheek to cheek. Drawing courage from each other for a long moment before they went at each other again, kissing and biting. And removed the last bits of cloth that still separated them—

It was the sort of rhythm where the woman is so wet when the man enters her that you can't call it penetration. Maybe: blending.

The sort of rhythm where, at a certain point, there are no more words, only syllables.

Even so, I remember that she said a few words right before the climax—

Don't be alarmed.

What? By what?

When I come ... it sounds ... like ... I'm ... choking.

And although she warned me, when it came, when she came, those grunts and gasps didn't sound good at all, and her eyes rolled back in their sockets. Then there was a bone-chilling silence. She stopped breathing completely, air didn't go in or out of her. I was afraid, that's it, I've lost her, and I was horrified—images raced through my mind—how do I dress her and drag her body to Ronen's house? Who the hell brings a body to a shiva? How will the guests react? And what exactly will I say to the police when they ask me what she died of? An orgasm?

Then she opened her eyes, slowly—

And said, Hi. Thank you.

You're alive? I asked.

Yes, she said, thank you.

For what? I protested. Anytime, I said with a leer.

I'm sorry, she said, then sighed and spread her arms to the side like Jesus on the cross. I've been trying to avoid touch.

What does that mean?

Exactly what it says.

Did you used to be religious?

Something like that, she said, suddenly looking terribly sad.

Is everything all right? I checked again.

You know, she said, my husband's dead.

Sorry, I said, I didn't mean—

It's okay, I . . . needed that, she said.

Glad to be of service, I said, and kissed her ivory shoulder.

What about you? she said. You don't want to come today? It's a little cold. And I have to get back to the shiva soon.

We walked back to the monument. The path, which had been a little muddy when we first walked along it, was now completely muddy, and Mor suddenly looked around, as if she were afraid someone was watching us. I didn't understand why she started being afraid only now, but I didn't want to say anything. I felt the scratches she had dug on my back, and it occurred to me that it was a good thing I had proof that this whole thing had really happened. Because what were the chances. And then I felt her hand searching for mine, and spread my fingers to receive hers, and we continued walking. Close to each other. Hand in hand. And I thought that we walked at exactly the same pace. That we walked well together.

You know, I said, I followed you. To Death Road.

What?

I tried to catch up to you.

But . . . how?

When you left my room at night, you were so . . . I was afraid something would happen to you. And the truth is . . . I wanted to see you again. So I walked through the whole city. From hostel to hostel. You can't believe how many hostels there are in that city. It took ages to find the one you were registered in. The clerk at the reception desk said you'd gone out on a trip, then came back and went out again first thing in the morning, and she complained that you left a *quilombo* behind.

Quilombo?

A mess. She said she heard shouting from your room, but she didn't stick her nose in her guests' lives. And later, when she went into the room, everything was upside down and the bathroom mirror was on the floor. Broken into pieces. Only you Israelis act like that, she said to me.

Disgraceful. I apologized in the name of the Israeli people and asked her where she thought you'd gone. She said that, because of the bicycles, she thought the Yungas Road. I told her I'd never heard of it. And she said that Yungas Road is what the gringos call Death Road. That really stressed me out. I flew out of there to the center of town, rented a mountain bike, and set off.

Wait a minute—she stopped me suddenly—where exactly did you ride to?

There was a kind of police barricade, I lied to her. After the large waterfall? They didn't let riders through. So I had to retreat back to La Paz. And that's it. Two days later I took off for Israel.

Is that so, she said, and exhaled a lot of air. Then she was silent. A digesting-new-information silence. And finally, she added in a different tone, It's the intention that counts.

When we reached the car, she took off my coat and gave it to me.

Thank you, she said.

My pleasure, I said.

You solved a tough problem for me, she said, giving me a warm, open look, the kind that's not trying to seduce or impress.

I'd be happy to be your permanent problem solver, I said.

You would, eh? she said in a bitter tone I hadn't heard her use before.

Do you want me to come see you again this week? I have a workshop in the north on Thursday.

Better not, she said. It'll raise questions.

Okay. So . . . what? We'll talk after the shiva?

Yes.

What number should I call?

I still don't have . . . my phone fell . . . with Ronen.

No kidding. So where . . . ?

I'll find you.

Okay. Can I hug you?

Not here.

So imagine that I'm hugging you.

Okay, she said, smiling weakly. You imagine it too. Then she got onto her bike.

I waited. I'd already started the car but still hadn't moved. I waited to see whether she would look back. I wanted to enjoy that warm, open look one more time. She didn't turn her head. But even after she disappeared around the bend in the road, I didn't move. I don't know why. Maybe something inside me knew what was going to happen. Or maybe I was just hoping.

In any case, two minutes later, three tops, her bike reappeared. She was riding back to me, quickly, as if she were going downhill, even though it was uphill, and when she reached the car, she threw the bike onto the sidewalk and sat down on the passenger seat beside me.

Drive, she said. Panting. Red-faced.

What happened?

I can't go back there.

What? Why? What happened?

Will you please drive?

I released the handbrake and drove according to her directions, turn after turn, out of the town.

I glanced at her. Her face had changed. It was tense now. Tough. She bit her lip. Even her soft, plump cheeks seemed to have sunken. Making the bones more prominent. Creating a sharp, unattractive angularity that hadn't been there before.

Where are we going? I asked when we finally reached the main road.

If I knew, I would tell you, she said, her tone unpleasant. Gruff.

I pulled off the road and stopped. I put a hand on her thigh. To calm her.

She pushed it away and said, You're keeping me from thinking.

I put my hand on the wheel and thought: Why is she talking to me like that. And I also thought: I can get back in time to see Liori if I cut this short now.

Okay—Mor had come to a decision—drive straight ahead, take a left at the intersection. Two or three minutes after that, you'll see a dirt road on the right.

Only now, in retrospect, do I see how many suspicious signals there had been all along. But that's just the problem with such signals: You see them only in retrospect.

For example, the way she was greeted by her friend from her teens—the one who, during the drive, she described as "my lifesaver in high school," "the only girl in my grade who understood my humor," and "the only one in the whole city, except for me, who listened to Radiohead."

When we reached her friend's mud-brick house, it was already dark. The house was dark too, except for a few lit candles in the windows. Afterward, I understood that the entire village wasn't hooked up to the electrical grid, and there wasn't any phone service or Wi-Fi either. It was an ideological thing.

We knocked on the wooden door. A young woman about Mor's age opened it—and gaped. As if Mor had come back from the dead.

Mor was thrilled to see her, but the woman did not reciprocate. They hugged in the doorway, but it was clear that the woman wanted to cut the hug short.

"Oh, Ophelia," Mor cried, her arms still around her friend's waist, "How fares her highness after so many days?" An amiable-looking guy wearing a white sharwal came out of the kitchen with a baby in his arms. Why don't you ask them to come in, love? We're about to have dinner.

Shouldn't you be sitting shiva now? I mean, I'm... sorry for your loss...I was planning to come tomorrow, Ophelia said and took a step back.

I had to get some air, Mor said, stepping inside. You remember Ronen's family, how they drag you down.

This is Omri, she finally introduced me. He was in Bolivia with us. This is Gili, my friend since...We were Ophelia and Hamlet in the youth community theater. And this is...her husband. Remind me what your name is?

Osher, the guy said, gesturing to the low table surrounded by cushions.

We ate dinner. All kinds of healthy stuff. Green salad. Hummus that had chunks of chickpeas in it. Beets. Rice crackers. Food that Orna liked and I couldn't stand.

Mor didn't stop oohing and aahing over the food and asking in-depth questions. And she listened intently to the answers.

Osher replied enthusiastically. They built the house themselves. The birth was natural. They lived without buying things. Corporations trample the common man.

Mor nodded in understanding and told us about a conversation she once had with a man in distress when she was working for the suicide hotline: He'd been fired from the Pri Hagalil juice factory where he worked and was ashamed to tell his wife. He used to leave the house "for work" every morning, with his briefcase and everything, and hide in Biriya Forest until evening.

I watched her as she spoke. She knew how to tell a story. The pauses. The hand movements. But there was also a kind of melancholy chord underlying everything she said. I thought: What do you expect? Her husband died right in front of her a few days ago. And I also thought: That movement, the way she tosses her curls from side to side, it's so beautiful. And: She'd get along great with Liori. Liori would be wild about her. And: Don't get ahead of yourself, cool it.

I barely spoke during the meal.

Gili didn't speak much either and watched Mor with a look that might have been hatred or love, I couldn't decide.

Later, at night, I got my answer.

Osher brought mattresses and bedding to the living room. Mor fell asleep in seconds. Actually, I'd never seen her features relaxed. They were always showing one expression or another—attentiveness, seductiveness, contemplation. I could totally imagine her performing dramas in a youth community center theater.

But now she was asleep. A rebellious curl lay on her cheek. I moved it back to its place behind her ear. Lines from a Knesiyat HaSechel song—*You're most beautiful when you're drunk, and you can't tell right from wrong*—played in my head. I pressed my body against hers. We usually say: I felt the heat of her body. But the truth is that I felt the cold of her body. And I remembered that earlier, on the rock, she'd said she was cold inside. And I thought: Her husband died. What is she doing here with me instead of sitting shiva. And I thought: Who said you only have to sit shiva. You can also walk shiva. Or drive shiva. I wound my arms through hers and pulled her close to me. But I couldn't fall asleep that way, so I got my phone and did what I always do to relax myself: I read old messages Liori sent me on Orna's phone. A lot of heart emojis. Very few words.

Then I heard Gili's voice.

At first, I could only hear the tone. And something in it made me move closer to the wall. And listen hard.

It turned out that mud walls aren't very soundproof.

Don't you think it's weird? Gili said. Yes, it's her . . . the one I told you about, remember? . . . Isn't it just like her to show up with a guy when she should be . . . That's her style, all right . . . Alley cat . . . First the drama teacher . . . And then I . . . And then she saw that Ronen playing the violin on the grass at the Acre Festival . . . Her husband, remember? The one who was killed in Bolivia . . . And from that moment on, I . . . I didn't exist for her . . . And now, all of a sudden, I'm her "best friend" . . . I'm telling you that something here . . . It doesn't seem weird to you that her husband's dead and she isn't even...Don't tell me that she worked her magic on you too...Stop with the flattery...It's possible...So what?...Even so, there's something bizarre...So what are you saying?...Compassion? What does compassion...No way...Tomorrow morning she's gone.

don't usually remember dreams. And there must have been other parts to the dream I had in the mud-brick house. In the part I do remember, I lost Liori in a forest that looked like the one that was on the far side of the moshav where I grew up. She cried out to me: Daddy! Daddy! And I was riding a unicycle as if I'd been riding one for years, following the sound of her voice and trying to find where the hell she was in the heavy fog that had settled on the forest, while my mother, I mean her voice, was in the background, warning me in Italian, over and over again, *"Si raccogliere quale che si semina."* You reap what you sow. In the dream, I was worried about Liori. Very worried. But at some point, my mother's voice faded away and the fog itself began to envelop me. Dampen me. Caress me gently. And it was hard not to abandon myself to its caress. I mean to Mor's caress. I mean, I woke up to Mor's actual caresses. Her hand was under my shirt, on my back, stroking me with endless gentleness, as if she knew that my bad memories were kept there and wanted to heal them with her touch. Only after long, patient minutes did she pull off my shirt. Slowly. Then turn me onto my back. And kiss my chest, and below it, and below that too.

Orna would only go down on me on birthdays and anniversaries. And only if I asked her explicitly. And always, a few seconds before I was about to come, I had to remember to move her head to the side. In case, God forbid.

I tried to move Mor's head too.

I lifted the blanket slightly and whispered, I'm coming. But she didn't move her head.

And so, at the age of thirty-nine, in a village that doesn't appear on Google Maps, as the first rays of sun shone through the shutters, I experienced for the first time that extreme pleasure that borders on pain.

When I opened my eyes, I said, Thank you.

Then I lifted the blanket and asked, What about you? Do you want me to . . .

She slid upward under the blanket until her curls surfaced and her body lay beside mine and said, Not here.

After a brief silence, she turned her head to me, looked into my eyes, and said, My love. She touched the edges of my smile with her finger, and asked, Why are you so good to me?

I answered with the truth, Because I really like you, Mor.

She sighed sorrowfully, and put her head on my chest, and we breathed together for a few minutes, without speaking. I was so grateful and relaxed that I told her about the conversation I'd heard through the wall as if it were an entertaining anecdote.

She found it a bit less entertaining.

Come on, she said, standing up abruptly. We're leaving.

But—

She might even call Ronen's brothers.

Can you explain to me why you're so—

Questions later, Omri.

My car wouldn't start.

I began to tell Mor that since the divorce, I hadn't had time to go to the garage to get it serviced—

But in the middle of my explanation, she got out of the car, opened the hood, and bent over. Then she signaled for me to try again, came back to her seat, buckled her seat belt, and said, Drive.

My mom used to be a secretary in a garage, she said, answering unasked questions. She took me to work with her during every vacation.

———

Now explain to me what happened, I demanded when we were back on the paved road. A warning light lit up on the dashboard. Gas was running out.

First coffee, she said.

What coffee?

I didn't even have time to brush my teeth after . . . after you, she said giving me a partners-in-crime look. Besides, I have to think about where to go.

I remembered when Orna asked me—in a guiltless tone that drove me crazy—exactly what did you think would happen, Omri? And after I responded by smashing her laptop, I drove to my mom's place, and even though I arrived in the middle of the night, she didn't ask questions and opened the sofa for me and spread a sheet on it—

So I asked Mor, What about your family? Are they from around here?

Yes, she replied, her voice bitter, but they're not an option.

Can I ask why—

In a nutshell, they more or less cut me out of their lives.

Why?

It's a long story, she said. And after a brief pause, she added, You know how when an employee exposes corruption in an organization, he's the one who gets fired? So it's something like that.

You mean that—

Forget it, I don't have the strength to get into that now.

I half turned my body to her.

She put a fist to her mouth and bit one of her fingers. Suddenly, I could picture her as a little girl. I actually saw the picture. A curly haired kid. With a defiant expression. Holding a lollipop.

If you ever have the strength to get into it, I said, I'm all ears.

Thanks, she said, and gave me that warm, open look.

So what do you think about coming to my place, I offered, without giving it much thought.

I'm not sure that's a good idea, she said. Isn't your daughter there?

She's coming for the weekend. She's at her mom's now.

I see.

The truth is—I warned her—that I only straighten up and clean before she comes, so it'll be pleasant for her, but now . . . my apartment is pretty much of a *quilombo*. I haven't even had time to assemble the furniture I bought at IKEA. I mean, I couldn't get myself to do it. And there are dirty dishes in the sink... You know, a guy who lives alone. But if that doesn't bother you—

Definitely not, she said. But her tone hinted that she still had doubts.

It's better if I stay in the car, she said when we stopped at a gas station.

Instead of asking, Why?, I asked, How many sugars?, and only after the coffee was ready, as I was handing the money to the cashier, did it flash through my mind: I left the key in the ignition.

I looked over at the car—and saw her step out of it, one foot, then the other, and walk over to the driver's side.

I grabbed the cups from the counter and started to run.

The coffee sprayed onto my shirt as I ran. And I cursed. I ran and cursed, and managed to get the door open and sit down on the passenger seat before she could start the car.

What's up? I asked. In my calmest voice. And I thought: Alley cat.

She didn't say anything for a while, and lowered her glance to her Ultrastars.

I was still holding on to her coffee. On purpose.

I restrained a powerful urge to slap her. And then tell her to get the hell out of my car.

She finally raised her eyes, gave me a vulnerable look, and said, I'm sorry, Omri. I'm really sorry. I shouldn't have done that.

I was so amazed that I couldn't get a word out.

Through all my years with Orna, she never once apologized. I'm not good at it, she'd told me when we'd just started dating. And from then on, the whole business of apologies in our relationship was solely my responsibility. And now it seemed that there was another way.

I nodded. And tried as much as possible to make my nod look adamant, I didn't want to give away the fact that her "sorry" had taken the wind out of my anger.

You helped me so much, Mor went on, but I really think I should go on alone from here.

Is that so? I put the coffee on the seat and folded my arms on my chest.

You have no idea the mess you're getting into, Omri.

Maybe I want to get into it.

Why would you want—

I've been completely out of sync since my divorce, Mor. I'm a robot during the day. At night, I go the local kiosk to watch soccer with all the Romanian workers. I can't stay home. The sound of the TV in a living room that doesn't have a woman and a little girl in it . . . echoes too loudly.

I can understand.

The truth is that you can't. You can't understand what it is when they call you from your daughter's school to say that she's been crying since the morning, and you ask the secretary, Why? And then there's a kind of silence on the line because it's clear to both of you why. And you have no idea, Mor what it's like to hear your little girl ask you twice a day, "You'll definitely die before me, Daddy?" And realize that because of you, she'll be afraid her whole life that people will leave her. And you have no idea what it's like to get up in the morning and go to her room to wake her up by kissing her and tickling her back and discover she isn't there because according to the fucking agreement, it's not her day to be with you.

It really does sound—

And you don't have the energy for anything. The conservatory suspended me because I lost it with a student who answered his phone in the middle of a group rehearsal and threw a drumstick at him. And I don't give a crap about the workshops I developed, but I force myself to go to them and to the recording studios only because I have to pay the rent. The only two times in the last six months that I felt a desire for something, Mor, when I felt my heart beating, were when you came to my room in Bolivia and when I saw you pedaling to the monument.

Okay.

So don't suddenly tell me that you want to go on alone and . . . and don't do stuff like this to me anymore. It's out of line.

Okay.

We didn't speak for a few moments. She continued to look down at her Ultrastars. I took her coffee cup out of the holder and took a sip—and burned my tongue. Fuck, I hissed, and saw that she wasn't sure whether the word was directed at her or the coffee. I wanted to tell her, You and the coffee both. And when a car, with a couple in the front seat and two kids and a dog in the back, slipped into the spot on our right, I said, Okay, *yalla*, let's fill the tank. We'll drive to my place. And on the way, you'll explain to me exactly what kind of mess I'm getting into, because I think I have right to know, don't I?

Even now, as I reconstruct the events, I'm not sure whether the whole scene at the gas station wasn't staged just to give me the illusion that I was in control, that I was deciding (after all, she could have moved to the driver's seat while I was waiting for the coffee and just driven off, she had enough time), or whether she had really tried, for the last time, to keep me from slipping into the abyss with her.

I usually drive a hundred and thirty, a hundred and forty kilometers an hour on the highway. After the divorce, there were nights when I would get into the car, drive to the highway, and burn rubber at a hundred and sixty. Just let anyone try and stop me.

Now I drove at eighty, tops, because the fog was as heavy as in my dream.

I suddenly remembered how once, on the way back from a family vacation in the north, Liori asked us what fog was. Orna was driving so I could rest, and the Pixies singing "Where Is My Mind" was on the radio, and I put a hand on her thigh so she would know that it also made me think of Friday mornings in our apartment on Tchernichovsky Street, and with my other hand, I did what parents in the twentieth century do when they don't know how to answer a question their kid asks and don't want to make fools of themselves: I checked Google. After I read Liori a simultaneous translation for kids of the entry "fog" in Wikipedia, she bit her lip, the way she always did when she was thinking, and asked, So fog is really just a cloud that falls out of the sky?

———

A few minutes after we turned onto the highway, Mor began to speak.

In first person.

I thought to myself: First person, that means I passed a test.

I couldn't go back to the shiva, she said, because his brothers were standing outside the house. With their arms folded on their chest like two . . . mafiosos. Waiting for me.

But why—

Yesterday, right before you came, they showed me emails Ronen sent from Bolivia.

He sent them emails from Bolivia?

At first, I didn't believe it either. When did he have time? They said, Sit down, in a commanding, threatening tone, then opened the computer and stood on either side of me, like jailers, while I read. As if they were trying to make sure I didn't run away after I saw what was written there.

That must have stressed you out.

It was like watching porn.

Porn?

Emotional porn. His deepest shit was totally exposed in those emails. All his paranoia.

What was he afraid of?

Nothing rational. The tranquilizers he asked me to buy for him? He thought I bought different pills and was deliberately drugging him. And he thought that every guy I chatted with on the trip, not only you, was a potential partner in some intricate plot designed to steal something from him.

Crazy.

And you know what's weird? When he imposed a curfew on me, I couldn't feel sorry for him. When I'm kept on a leash and humiliated, the first thing I do is rebel. But the more I read, the more I realized that he knew something bad was happening to him and that, with his own hands, he was destroying his honeymoon with the woman he loved—and just couldn't stop it or ask for help.

What a mess!

Then I started to cry. Bottom line, since I landed, I'd been pretty cut off, mostly floating above and below things—I think that when you lose someone, a kind of pit opens inside you, and maybe you're afraid to look into it—and it was there, in front of the computer, with his two brothers breathing their . . . hostility onto me from both sides, that it finally sank in: That's it, it can't be fixed anymore, I won't have Ronen anymore. I won't have any of those small stickers we used to put on coffee jars, every morning a different sticker that began with the words "I love" and continued with small things: I love that you drink your coffee in one gulp as if it's water; I love that you come back in a minute after you leave the house to get things you've forgotten; I love that you switch radio stations because maybe the song you're waiting for will be on it— Is it okay for me to talk about him, Omri?

It's weird that you hardly talked about him before now, I thought. But I said, Of course.

Thank you, Mor said.

And . . . it's natural that his emails made you cry, I added.

They let me cry for half a minute, a minute at the most, and then they demanded to know—at some point, one of them pounded the table—what I had to say about what Ronen wrote. About his accusations. So I looked them in the eye and said that none of it was true. I didn't drug him. I didn't lock him in the room in the hostel. He was the one who locked me in. And I didn't cheat on him during our trip.

And what about kissing me in the hostel? I wanted to say. But I didn't want to sound like Ronen's brothers, so instead, I asked whether they finally left her alone.

It seemed like it, Mor said. But at the same time, they were pressuring the authorities in Bolivia to allow their own experts to reexamine the autopsy results.

How do you know?

Tell me, what's that disc? Why is your picture on the cover?

It's a disc of Camouflage songs. That's the band I used to play with. But—

No kidding, you have a group?

Had.

Play it. I need . . . to calm down a little.

The opening sounds of the first track filled the car and she leaned back in her seat and closed her eyes.

The drums came in and I thought: You can really tell that it was recorded before the divorce. I'm too unraveled to play that way now.

I looked at Mor. Her lips opened slightly as she listened. As if she wanted to drink the sounds, taste them.

Orna never gave herself over to music that way, I thought. Every single time I played her something new I'd recorded, she did a million things while she listened. She browsed through a magazine. Cooked quinoa. Checked her text messages.

At a certain point, when the piece became stormier, Mor began playing an imaginary keyboard slightly above her knee. And the movement of her fingers matched the rhythm perfectly, and I mean perfectly.

When the track ended, she opened her eyes and said, Wow, Omri, is that you on the drums? It was great. And, looking at me in a new way, added, You're really talented, eh?

Writing this now, I don't understand—why didn't I ask more about the autopsy? About why she was so stressed that Ronen's brothers wanted a second opinion if the only thing they might find out as a result is that Ronen committed suicide?

And why didn't I wonder why—if Ronen's brothers suspected her of cheating on him on their honeymoon—she chose to spend her time with me, of all people? She didn't have anyone else in the world she could lean on? What about all the girlfriends who were with her at the shiva? What about her family? What kind of corruption has she actually exposed that would make them cut her off?

Maybe we don't ask questions when we're afraid of knowing the answers. And maybe the explanation is simpler: I'm not an investigator and I don't have the instincts of an investigator. I'm just a guy hung up on a woman who pressed all the right buttons. That's how it is, when you press the right buttons, a person can go mad, fall into the abyss, become a partner in crime.

———

We listened to another few tracks on the Camouflage disc. Every once in a while, Mor would say: That's so beautiful. Or: Wow. Most of her praise came after the drum solos.

When the last track ended, she opened her eyes and said, Just explain one thing to me.

I thought she wanted to ask why the tracks on the disc were so long.

How could your wife divorce you? she asked, smiling at me.

I laughed.

I'm serious, she said. You're talented. Good-looking. A great fuck. What turned her off?

I kept one hand on the wheel and reached over to stroke her cheek with the other.

The traffic on the Coastal Road moved slowly. The fog was so thick that I could barely see the car in front of me. Only the yellow warning strip on the right flashed every once in a while.

Tell me, why did you even become a drummer? she asked.

When I was little, I used to spread frying pans and pots on the kitchen floor and drum on them with my hands, I told her.

I can picture it, she said. I mean, I can really picture you as a kid.

I can picture you too, I said. And I saw the same image in my mind's eye. Curls. Defiant expression. Lollipop.

In any case, I went on, after my dad took off, my mom bought me a set of drums, put them in my room, and said, If you're finally doing something, do it right.

What do you mean, your dad "took off"? Mor asked, and I thought, with Orna, it took me three months to feel comfortable enough to talk about my dad, and now, with Mor—

He disappeared, I said. Faded away. Did a cut-and-paste from our lives to a different life. Left behind a pair of leather boots that I used to smell sometimes to . . . make sure he'd existed.

And that's it?

Almost. He also left debts. Creditors would knock on our door and say that they were "friends of your dad," but my mom told me not to let them in.

What a story. Now I understand.

What do you understand?

A lot of things, she said. A lot. But instead of explaining, she began to stroke the back of my neck. Right on the comfort spot I have there. As if someone had leaked the location to her.

The Camouflage disc began to play again. From the beginning. Now, after Mor called me "talented," I thought I really did sound pretty talented. And for the first time since the divorce, I felt a desire to get our group together again. Or to form a totally different group. Not just to play with other groups. And actually, why not? Who was stopping me? I'm talented. I'm a great fuck.

If only we could drive forever, she said, and crossed over the handbrake to kiss-bite my neck and ask like a Girl Scout on an outing with her troop, When will we get there?

The GPS says fifteen minutes, I said. And pictured how, when we got into my apartment, I would pin her against the wall and cuff her wrists together with one hand and rip off her pants with the other—and then, as gently as possible, I'd go down on her.

I never imagined that, fifteen minutes later, someone else would be cuffing her hands. And mine.

The night I found Orna's emails and the guy she was fucking, I smashed her computer on the floor. Right in front of her. She shouted, Are you crazy? I'm calling the police! But I told her that if she called the police, I'd call the wife of the guy she was fucking.

So there had been no earlier interaction with the security forces.

They were waiting in civilian cars outside my apartment, and when we approached the entrance, they surrounded us. There was no point in trying to run. They handcuffed Mor. And then, to my surprise, they cuffed me too.

Mor managed to give me a last look, the look of a rabbit caught in the headlights.

Then we were put into separate cars.

There was also one absurd moment: They're apparently taught that they have to push the prisoner's head down before he gets into the car, defeat him even before the battle begins. But because of my height, they couldn't manage it, not even on the third try, and they had to ask me politely to get into the car. As we were driving, I asked, What are you arresting me for? And the cop sitting next to me put his hand on my shoulder, squeezed it hard, and said in an almost friendly tone, Shut your mouth.

Was the rabbit-in-the-headlights look also fake? I wonder now. The performance of a community drama theater graduate? Part of the clever plan designed to lead us straight into the arms of the police, in front of my building to boot, so they would think she and I were partners in something?

I'm not sure about it. Even now that I know what I know, I'd rather think of us more as two people caught in a situation that was a few sizes too big for them than as Bonnie and Clyde.

The Intelligence officer asked me if I had enemies in prison. I mumbled no, of course not.

The social worker told me over and over again, be strong. But didn't explain how.

Then they put me in a cell, and for twenty-four hours, no official person spoke to me. I drummed on the walls with my bare hands to keep from losing my mind.

They took me out once to be processed. They took my picture from every angle. They took a blood sample and a urine sample. And returned me to my cell. They brought other people into the cell twice. Then took them out after a while. They brought food three times. Inedible. Once there was even dessert—vanilla pudding.

The cell itself was nothing like the ones you see in TV series. It was much more depressing. A small barred window with murky light coming through it. A bunk bed. A mattress the thickness of a yoga mat. A toilet with a broken seat. A shower that was a hole in the wall. The constant smell of cigarettes. The constant jangle of keys. The constant sound of iron doors opening and slamming shut in what seemed to be a permanent rhythm that drove you crazy.

They'd confiscated my phone, so I couldn't read Liori's old texts to calm myself down. Instead, I tried to count the sheep on her sheep pajamas. To picture her wearing them—and count the sheep. I remembered how she would crawl into our bed on Saturday mornings, and even though her small body separated Orna and me, I felt as if it was actually joining us together. Suddenly I felt a strange yearning for Orna, not the now Orna, but the then Orna, who had been happy with me. And for the feeling that there was nowhere to rush off to because my entire world was with me in that bed.

The interrogation room didn't look like the ones you see on TV either. There was no naked lightbulb or Formica-topped table. Only binders. Dozens of binders.

The detective gave me a small bottle of soda water and a plastic cup (Of all things, soda water? I thought. Who am I, my dad?), and while I drank, he told me the news. First the bad news. Then the worse news.

The police in Bolivia had given the family's investigator permission to reexamine the pictures of the body and the autopsy results. Apparently the Bolivians' autopsy had been sloppy. Or the body had been so damaged that a new autopsy needed to be performed by an expert. In any case, the expert who reexamined the body found clear signs of a struggle and high levels of drugs in the blood—which raised the possibility that Ronen Amirov's death had not been caused by an accident, as the widow claimed when she was questioned in Bolivia. In the emails he sent to his family, he wrote about the affair that had developed during their honeymoon between his wife and an Israeli named Omri, and said he suspected his wife and that same Omri were planning to kill him, claim he died in an accident, and enjoy the money from the life insurance policy he'd bought before the trip. We have photographs of you, Omri, in an intimate situation with Mor Amirov, during the shiva, the detective said. In addition, you drove together to your apartment, also during the shiva. And most important: We've questioned Mor over the last two days. She denies that it was premeditated murder but is prepared to admit that there was a physical struggle between her and her husband on Death Road, and that you witnessed it. A struggle that ended with him falling into the abyss. Considering the date you returned to Israel, that is definitely possible. And I must say that the fact that...you and Mor Amirov had sexual relations when she was supposed to be in mourning for her dead husband raises a reasonable suspicion that the sex was your way of celebrating the success of your plan.

I reacted with silence. People use the phrase "shocked silence." But shock wasn't exactly what I felt. It was more like emptiness. The emptiness of a soccer stadium after the game has ended with a loss and all the fans have gone home, leaving their sunflower-seed shells behind.

What do you have to say about that? the detective wanted to know.

That I think I need a lawyer, I replied.

Of all the things in the world, the first thing I thought after the detective left the room was, How will I explain to Liori that she can't come to my place for the weekend?

She has this kind of face she makes right before she cries. A pre-crying face. A heartbreaking expression of misery that begins at her lips, rises to her nose, and scrunches her eyes.

If she hears her dad has been arrested, if one of her classmates hears it on the news... As it is, since the divorce—

So the first call I made wasn't to a lawyer but to Orna. While I waited, a picture of the three of us— which I couldn't bring myself to change—appeared on the screen, on a bike trip in the Agamon Hahula nature reserve. We look like a normal family. Smiling. Happy.

Orna answered after too many rings.

I said, I'm in trouble. I said, Accomplice to murder. I said, In Bolivia. I said, Of course I'm not guilty. I said, I'll get out of here in the end, but meanwhile, I have two requests.

Silence on the other end of the line.

Are you there? I asked.

Yes, Orna said. I'm just in shock.

The truth is, so am I, I said.

What did you want to ask for? she said. I could hear everything in her voice: impatience and disappointment and genuine concern and also a tinge of...how lucky I am not to be with this loser anymore.

Make up a story for Liori. Tell her I'm sick. Don't say jail. Let's protect her from all this shit while we can.

Okay, Orna said.

And my second request is, call your lawyer. And ask him to recommend someone who does criminal law.

Liori was the real reason I didn't keep following Mor and her husband on Death Road.

I caught up to them after a day. I'd rented the best mountain bike in La Paz and rode like a madman. I hadn't been in great shape since the divorce, so after a few hours, my muscles hurt. But I didn't stop to rest for even a minute. The pictures running through my mind fueled my motivation: That strange silence of Ronen's on the way to the ice-cream parlor. The look Mor gave me when they walked me to my hostel, a look that, in retrospect, I think was a distress signal. The shouts the señora heard coming from their room. The shattered glass on the floor. Something was wrong with those two—I pedaled faster—otherwise, why would she come to my room in the middle of the night? And why would she choke when you tell her that a trip is an extreme situation?

They were a curve away from me when I saw them the first time.

He was a few meters in front of her.

I hadn't planned what I would do when I caught up to them. And with a certain delay, it occurred to me that it might not be such a good idea to join up with a couple on their honeymoon a day after I kissed the bride. Who knows whether she told him. Who knows how he'll react.

So I just followed them, to see if everything was all right with Mor, far enough away so they didn't see me but close enough for me to protect her if she needed protection.

When it got dark and they stopped to set up their tent, I stopped too, turned around, pedaled a few hundred meters back and put up my own tent.

——

At night, I remember, I dreamt about Sha'ar HaGai, a spot on the steep, winding road to Jerusalem. I'm in the backseat of a car that someone is driving too fast on the downhill sections—maybe my father—and I ask him to drive slower on the curves so we don't fall into the abyss.

I woke before dawn so I'd be up before them and waited for them to set off. And despite the dream, I kept riding, maintaining a distance from them.

On Death Road, there really are these crosses on the side of the road in memory of people who had been killed there over the years. Every time I passed one of them, I said to myself that I was crazy. That there was no logic in what I was doing. But, I thought, for the fifteen years you were married to a logical woman, you acted logically. Maybe it's time you don't act logically.

On the third day, the visibility was really bad because of the fog. I tried to get a little closer to them, to ride a bit faster, but the road was all crumbly, and on one of the curves, I lost my balance, my bike skidded, and I fell. Flew right off it.

I grabbed on to one of the in-memory-of-the-fallen crosses and pulled myself up. I can't say that I almost slid into the abyss, or that my legs flailed in the air between heaven and earth, but there was something in that fall, close to edge—maybe it was the small cross I was holding on to, and the name inscribed on it—that made my heart pound for a long time after I picked up my bike. I was angry at myself. What are you doing, you idiot? You have a daughter. And you promised her that you're not doing dangerous things. Who do you care about more, your little girl or a woman you kissed once?

I got on my bike, turned it around, and started to go back. Not because of the police barricade, as I told Mor to avoid telling the truth. I just wanted to live.

I pedaled carefully, I could barely see anything in the fog. And I barely saw the guy coming toward me.

We both braked at the very last minute, handlebar to handlebar.

He cursed me in Italian. *Stronzo*. My mother's side of the family is Italian, so I answered him, *Vaffanculo*.

He laughed. And so, instead of killing each other, Paolo and I began to talk.

I told him that continuing to ride downhill in a fog like that was suicide.

He said this wasn't exactly a good time for him to die because his first book was coming out soon.

I said I this wasn't exactly a good time for me to die because I have a seven-year-old daughter who comes running to me every time I pick her up from day care.

We rode together to La Paz. Slowly. At night, we slept on the road in his scout tent. I told him about Mor and her surprise visit to my hostel room and about the kiss she gave me right before she left, and that somehow, even though we barely knew each other, I really cared about her.

Paolo listened and said, I would grab her husband, throw him into the abyss, and have sex with her, but don't listen to me, I'm a hot-tempered Italian. And then he said, Listen, that's not a bad story. Do you mind if I write it sometime?

So, in fact, you have an alibi? My lawyer asked, running his hand along his tie.

Theoretically, yes, I replied. If we manage to find that Paolo.

Do you know his surname?

No.

The lawyer curled his lip in contempt. As if the fact that I didn't know the Italian's surname was final proof that I was a nothing. I wanted to punch him out, that bastard. I really felt that the anger accumulating inside me was about to explode. But I couldn't. Because I needed his help. So I opened my fist and said, But I can tell you that he said a few things about himself.

Okay, the lawyer said. We'll try to work with that. But first, I have a letter for you.

A letter?

Your girlfriend's lawyer gave it to me. I have no idea how she managed to persuade him to pass a letter on to you. In principle, his license could be revoked for something like that. Tell me, what does she look like, that Moriah, to have such an effect on men?

Mor.

Her identity card says Moriah, it turns out. You didn't know she comes from a religious family?

She actually mentioned that. But I understood that she didn't really have any contact with them.

Well, it's obvious that she doesn't have any contact with them.

What does that mean? Why obvious?

From what I understood, when she was seventeen, she complained to the police that her father beat the hell out of her and her sisters. On a regular basis. But the entire family—the sisters, the mother—they all took the father's side. And denied it. Claimed she was making it all up.

No kidding, I said. And thought, So that's what she meant when she talked about "an employee exposing corruption."

So she's a super-pussy, eh? the lawyer persisted.

Not really, I said, annoyed that he was talking about her that way. And I thought, But she has a way of looking at you that in the first few seconds makes you want to pin her up against a wall, and in the next few seconds, she casts her eyes down with the shyness of a religious girl that makes you want to protect her forever from anyone who might want to pin her up against a wall.

Hi, my rock,

I'm writing to you because I have no choice but to take the risk.

I'm writing to you because my life has collapsed on me and I'm buried under the rubble and you are the only crack I can get any hope through.

Did you know that I was planning to start a non-profit organization after the honeymoon? I wanted to call it Stories from the Road. The idea was that volunteers in the organization would go on one-on-one trips with people in crisis and just listen to them. Like the suicide hotline—but on the move.

Now it looks like the only moving I'll do in the next few years is behind the walls of a prison.

My lawyer says that the sentence for manslaughter—even if the victim provoked it— can be as high as twenty years.

He says there are too many facts against me.

My past criminal record definitely does not help. (When my drama teacher dumped me in a text message, I bought a gallon of gasoline and tried to set his Ford Fiesta on fire. I'm not proud of it, but I don't regret it either.)

And when you add to that the business about the life insurance, and the bits of DNA under Ronen's fingernails, and the emails he sent to his family—it doesn't look good. My lawyer says the only thing that can help me in court is testimony that will unequivocally disprove the claims against me.

I'm writing to you even though chances are that at the moment, you think I'm a manipulative bitch. Chances are that you're going over in your mind everything that happened from the minute you arrived at the shiva and think that I set a trap for you and everything was planned in advance and carefully executed to involve you.

I totally understand if that's what you're telling yourself. You have good reasons for doing that. But I want to tell you a different story. Even if the chances are small that you want to hear it. And I want to tell it to you simply because it's the truth.

The truth is that I fell hard for you, Omri. I hadn't planned for it to happen, it's not something a new bride setting out on her honeymoon plans to happen. But that's what happened. And it was stronger than me. It was stronger than me from the minute I sat down on your bed in the room in the hostel, as if a hidden rope was drawing me to you and I couldn't fight it.

That's why I ran away from the shiva to meet you (what a lunatic I am).

That's why I had sex with you on the rock (a complete lunatic, but it was worth it).

That's why I turned my bike around and didn't go back to the shiva (I still couldn't leave you).

That's why I wanted to leave you at the gas station and go on alone (I realized that you were going to get into trouble because of me).

That's why I agreed to hole up in your apartment (I figured the police would find us, but I wanted to feel you one more time).

And that's why, deep inside, I really, really—

Deep inside, I hoped you'd come to the shiva, you know? That somehow, you'd find out about Ronen. And at the same time, I was afraid you'd come, but in any case, I thought no way, how in the world, and when you walked into the room, with that slight stoop of yours to keep from hitting your head on the doorjamb, I wanted to leap up and hug you, but I couldn't, after all, I was a widow. And I saw that you were disappointed that I didn't pay attention to you. I don't want you to think I didn't see you fiddling with your shirt and tying your laces even though they were tied, and undoing your ponytail and then retying it, and burying your head in our wedding album as if it really fascinated you. It was so endearing (I'm not using the word "charming," so you won't tell me off in your mind: I'm not charming!). There are no two ways about it, embarrassment looks good on tall guys. But the truth is that, with all the embarrassment, you didn't leave, you persisted, you remained sitting, steady, with your broad shoulders, and all that pulled at the thread of the feeling I'd had in your room in La Paz, that, in another life, you and I could—

So, while I spoke with my colleagues from the suicide hotline who were pretending they were my friends, I began to plan our meeting at the flat rock—

The thing of it is, Omri, there was another reason—apart from the hope that it would be good for Ronen—I was in a hurry to leave La Paz.

I wanted to get away from you.

When I fall in love, I feel a mild weakness, as if I'm coming down with the flu. Is it like that with you too, or is it the opposite? When you fall in love, do you become more focused?

I knew that, if we stayed in the city, I'd find myself sneaking off to your hostel every night.

I said to myself, What actually happened between us? Two conversations and a kiss. Nothing that should shake me like that. Nothing you can't leave behind. But I couldn't leave behind the touch of your warm hands under my shirt when we kissed, and I couldn't leave behind the feeling of stretching on tiptoes for a kiss, and I couldn't leave behind the feeling that I belonged in your arms, and I couldn't leave behind how I felt when we spoke: not like a slut, not like an idiot, but smart, funny, special. Do you understand? I couldn't get it out of my mind, I kept dreaming about you—yes, even then, even the night Ronen and I slept in the classroom while there was a torrential rainstorm outside—

It was as if I'd split into two Mors: One who really did everything I told you about in the third person on the rock—sang songs, tried to seduce, tried to forgive, tried everything to keep my marriage together. And the other—the embarrassing one I didn't tell you about—had already begun to empty her heart so there would be room for a new love.

And the more silent Ronen became with me, the more he cut himself off from me, the more he humiliated me, my thoughts of you filled more and more

space. *And picturing us together was what I did to*
keep from feeling hurt. To keep from feeling pathetic.

I didn't believe that my imaginings would become
reality so quickly. Absolutely not. Even when Ronen
flung me against the mirror after I punched him in
the chest (I didn't tell you everything, Omri, it's em-
barrassing to go from being a little girl who gets flung
around to being a woman who gets flung around),
and even when he was playing with his penknife
the morning of the fall and turned the blade in my
direction and said, "I don't know what I'll do if you
leave me"—I wasn't afraid things could get worse. I
thought I knew what Ronen's boundaries were, and
what the boundaries that lay beyond them were. And
I was sure that reading people was my superpower.

It wasn't until he started deliberately riding close
to the edge of Death Road, in the fog, and shouting,
Yes, I'm crazy, I'm crazy—

Only then did I understand that there were also
two Ronens: the at-home Ronen, whose actions I
could predict, and the on-a-trip Ronen, who was a
totally different person—

And only then did I shout, as I pedaled my bike,
I love you, Ronch, I won't ever leave you, watch out,
stop riding like that, please, stop riding like that—but
he didn't turn his head in my direction, didn't answer,

just pedaled faster, and didn't move away from the edge, just the opposite, he veered more to the right, to where the shoulder had started to crumble, and his wheels began to spray mud in every direction—

Then I rode closer to him. By turning the handlebars slightly. I knew exactly what I wanted to do, to grab his hoodie, pull him hard to the center of the road, knock him down, punch him so hard that he would lose consciousness, tie him to a tree with his bicycle lock, and call for help, the police, an ambulance, someone who would stop him from hurting himself until he could be hospitalized—

But it turned out that the on-a-trip Ronen had a different plan, because as soon as I got closer to him, he grabbed me by the sleeve and pulled me hard toward him—

Maybe he wanted to push me into the abyss, maybe he just wanted to scare me—how could I know? It all happened instinctively, in the fraction of a second—

I shook him off me roughly: I steadied the handlebars with one hand and slid my other hand under his, which was clutching my sleeve, and then, all at once, my hand jerked upward, releasing my sleeve from his grip and causing him to lose his balance for a second—

But there's a good chance he wouldn't have fallen if the other Mor, the embarrassing one, the criminal one, hadn't added a small, premeditated push on his chest with her free hand.

After the fall, there was complete silence.

I remember getting off my bike to look into the abyss, but I got dizzy and took a step back. I remember that my bike fell because I didn't lean it against anything. I remember that I walked to the beginning of the bend in the road to see if anyone had witnessed what happened, but there was only a flock of birds. And it moved away too. I remember that I tried to get close to the edge again. And got dizzy again. And sat down on the wet ground. And looked for my phone in my pocket so I could call for help, and then I remembered, shit, he had it. In the backpack that had just fallen into the abyss.

The rain kept coming down and the ground under me got so muddy that I felt myself beginning to sink into it.

And I didn't care if I sank into it.

I knew I was supposed to do something. Get up and act, exhaust every possibility. But for long minutes, I couldn't do anything. Except wallow in the mud.

I had no thoughts. None that were focused, in any case.

Just a profound, really bottomless alone-in-the-world feeling.

As if all of humanity had been annihilated and only I was left.

Or the opposite: From now on I would wander the world like Cain, a mark on my forehead, unworthy of being among human beings.

On the one hand, I don't think I've ever felt as alone as I did in those moments after Ronen fell.

And on the other hand, since there was no one there apart from me, I could choose, later on, whichever version of events I wanted to tell.

Do you understand now why I was so stressed when his brothers threatened to reopen the investigation based on what was written in his emails? And why I didn't want to get you involved?

If only the story of that honeymoon was about a husband who flipped out and a wife who tried everything to contain and salvage but just didn't succeed. That's what I tried to tell you (and myself) on the rock behind the monument.

But that's not the truth. Relationships are a jungle. Like you said. And the truth is that his wound opened my wound, which opened his earliest wound, which opened my earliest wound. Until I did what I did.

I leave my dark secret in your hands. (Do you have one too?) I'm not stupid. I know you can use this letter in court as evidence that will incriminate me. And I pray you won't do that, and hope that maybe, just maybe you'll agree to do something else. It's possible that you won't ever want to hear a word from me after you've read what I've written here, but still, if there's the smallest chance you will, and because my lawyer says that the issue is not what really happened but which side can tell the more convincing story in court, here's the story I thought of:

You followed us to Death Road because you were worried about Ronen's strange behavior. And about what the señora in the hostel told you. You caught up to us just as Ronen finally lost it. You saw us struggle. You saw that he was the one who tried to pull me into the abyss and I was the one defending myself. With everything I had. And you saw up close how I had to pry his arm off me so I wouldn't fall. Which caused him to fall. Of course, I'll tell them the exact same thing. My lawyer says that if all the small details in our stories match, there's a good chance we can convince the court that it was a case of self-defense. And after all, you know most of the small details from the story I told you on the rock in third person.

What do you say?

I know this is a big request. And if you agree to it, you're taking a risk. But I'm also taking a pretty crazy risk by sending you this letter. And I'm doing it in the hope that maybe you feel the same way I do: That love is not something you can plan. That it sometimes bursts into life in seemingly impossible situations. And if we deny what could happen between us, Omri, that would be running away big-time.

I had a moment, Omri, my love. In your car. I think it was a little after you told me about your dad. I suddenly had a kind of vision: the two of us going out for a walk in the early evening (is there a park in Ramat Gan where you can hear birds chirping?), your steps are big and slow, and mine are small and quick, so they match, and I tell you that today, for my work on *Stories from the Road*, I hiked along Yavniel Stream with a young widow and suddenly, while she was talking about her dead husband, I felt pain, really strong pain, about Ronen, and you put an understanding hand on my shoulder and weren't upset that I was talking about him, and then you told me about a call you received from Carlos Santos, the drummer, who said he was sick and wants you to fill in for him at the concert in Hayarkon Park, or about the new workshop you opened for high-tech teams, and it's so successful that "you're afraid we'll get rich"—

*I imagined you saying that. And me laughing. I
imagined us happy together.*

Yours,
Mor

So, what does she write? my lawyer asked, drumming his fingers on the table in three-quarter time.

I didn't say anything for a few moments.

The risk Mor had taken stunned me.

It was clear to me that she had recklessly put her fate in my hands, which would also make me put my fate in her hands. The tactic was transparent. But even so, it worked on me.

I felt it in my body. A kind of wave of wonder and compassion and desire to save her flooded my chest and spread to every part of my body, all the way to my earlobes.

I waited for the wave to pass.

And then I told the lawyer about Mor's suggestion. The gist of it.

He swallowed the harsh words he wanted to say about her—I could actually see them slide down his throat—and said, You don't really intend to consider it, right?

I didn't say anything.

Are you kidding me? he asked unbelievingly.

I didn't say anything.

Listen carefully now, he said. Are you listening? As your lawyer, I have to warn you that once you admit you were there with them, anything can happen.

I nodded.

Including being accused of perjury, the best-case scenario, or of being an accessory to murder, the worst-case scenario.

I nodded.

Including the fact that this woman, who . . . let's say she's not exactly Mother Teresa, can turn on you in her testimony and accuse you of being the one who pushed her husband into the abyss.

I nodded.

Okay. The lawyer sighed and raised his eyebrows in surrender. Whatever you decide to do, we have to find that Paolo.

It turned out that quite a few Italian writers answer to the name Paolo. Paolo Giordano. Paolo Pagani. Even Paolo Di Paolo.

But the Paolo we needed still hadn't published a book, he was only about to publish one.

What else do you know about him?

That he grew up near Lake Como. Moved to Turin to study writing. In some *scola*. He had a girlfriend. Who left him after he wrote an unflattering description of her mother in a story. And was stupid enough to let her read it. Ah, and he also had a serious tragedy in his family. Now I remember. At some point during the night, he said that all the Israelis he met in South America were on a post-army trip. And I didn't look at all like someone recently discharged, and I also remember that...I mentioned I have a daughter? I told him I'm on a post-divorce trip. He was silent, in a show of sympathy, and then said, divorce is shit. But at least it's better than being dishonest. I told him I didn't know what's better, I'm still trying to take it all in. And I'm still afraid it'll screw up my daughter for the rest of her life. "Screw up your daughter for the rest of her life?" he said with a disdain that hinted that his machete was larger. After a brief silence, he told me that when he was nine, his mother was astonished to learn that his father had another family. In Capri. Another wife, other children. He used to travel to Capri very often for business. But no one suspected. The bastard managed to live a double life for ten years. And if the smartphone hadn't been invented, it probably would have kept on working for him. When she found the texts he sent to his other wife, Paolo's mother spoke to her brothers in Sicily, and one night they grabbed the father, took him to a forest, and cut him in half at the waist with an electric saw. They tossed the bottom half into Lake Como, and the put the other half, with the head, into a large box and sent it by FedEx to his second family in Capri.

That must be what his book is about, the lawyer said. I once went to a writing workshop, and the instructor told us that in their first novels, writers tell the most powerful family story, and that's why the real test of every writer is his second book.

Terrific. But...how does all that help us?

You said that your mother's family is Italian? She herself speaks Italian? So tell her to get on the phone tomorrow and call all the book publishers in Italy and find out which one of them is about to publish a book that tells the story of a guy who gets cut in half with a saw. Or the opposite.

The opposite?

A woman who gets cut in half, let's say. The workshop instructor said that if we're afraid that the real people we base our story on might be offended, or worse, might sue the pants off us, we should do transformations.

My mother's silence after I made my request spoke volumes.

I could actually hear everything she would have liked to say.

For example: "How does a smart boy like you get into such a stupid mess?" Or: "That's what you had to inherit from me, my tendency to choose problematic partners?" And of course, the all-time classic that began in the days when my dad's women used to knock on the door: "*Si raccogliere quale che si semina.*" You reap what you sow.

But she didn't say all of that.

Instead, she wrote down in her trusty red pad all the details I dictated to her and located Paolo Accordi in less than forty-eight hours.

She caught up with him in bed. A pre-first-book-publication anxiety attack. But he remembered me and agreed to fax my lawyer his detailed testimony, signed by a notary public, stating that on the day Ronen Amirov fell into the abyss on Death Road, I was with him, and therefore, I could not possibly have been involved in the fall.

Okay, my lawyer said, his fingers drumming on the table in seven-eighths time. We have a pretty solid alibi. From this point on, you have to use your good judgment. If you even have any when it comes to that woman. In any case, my position is clear, right?

I nodded.

Don't tell me you're still undecided.

I didn't nod.

Okay—he exhaled a long breath of frustration—even if you decide to do something really stupid, not to mention colossally stupid, and lie for her in court, we should agree on the truth first.

Here, he said, taking a spiral notebook out of his bag along with a black Pilot pen. Write down what happened. Each event exactly as it happened. One after the other.

So I wrote for an entire night. Without stopping. And in the morning, I read it all, from the beginning.

Sometimes I thought the guy described on those pages was a complete sucker. And sometimes I thought he woke up to life after years of stupor, and is unwilling, rightfully so, to give it up.

Sometimes I was sure that Mor really did follow her heart through all of it. And sometimes I was sure she's the femme fatale of La Paz. That she planned all of it, or almost all of it, in advance.

But I didn't take into consideration one thing.

The world is divided into two kinds of people: those who have kids and those who don't. And only a woman who doesn't have kids can ask a guy who does to put himself at risk for her that way.

Liori—I said to myself before the lawyer came into my cell to hear my decision—is my story from the road now. I won't do a runner like my father did. I'll insist on being totally present in my daughter's life. And I'll love her until she reaches a safe haven. I'll make sure that her sensitivity isn't something people take advantage of. And I'll never, and I mean never, give her a reason to be ashamed of me.

They accepted my alibi. I was released from jail. I tore Mor's letter into tiny pieces. Even though she tried to pull me into the abyss with her, I didn't want and didn't try to get revenge. Seems like I'm just not the type. In my court testimony, I tried to paint as positive a picture of her as I could, and minimize as much as possible the importance of our relationship and its effect on the events in Bolivia. It's not clear how much it helped. Ronen's emails, which were presented to the court in their entirety, were a horrifying foreshadowing of what would happen on Death Road. Testimonies of people who knew him, played music with him, went to school with him, supported the claim that "he wouldn't hurt a fly" and definitely not Mor, the person he was so attached to. The autopsy results were inconclusive about which of them was the one trying to defend himself in the critical moments, on the edge of the abyss. Nonetheless, the defense couldn't offer a convincing explanation for the security-camera footage of the pharmacy showing Mor buying a different, much stronger tranquilizer than the one Ronen mentioned in his emails that he had asked her to buy. And the glitch in the brakes of Ronen's bicycle looked like damage that a woman who'd spent all her vacations in a garage was capable of causing.

Mor was convicted of manslaughter. And sentenced to ten years in prison.

With great effort and tight coordination—which reminded me of how synchronized we were once—we managed, Orna and I, to hide the whole business from Liori. Or at least I thought we'd managed. One night, before she fell asleep, she told me she didn't want to die. I said I was glad to hear it. Then she explained, in complete seriousness, that she visited the world of the dead and it's no fun at all there. Can I ask how you got there? I asked cautiously. And she answered immediately, On Death Road! And explained, as if this were a well-known fact, that you go into a kind of tunnel and when you come out of it, you're already there.

There?

In their world, Daddy. Of the dead.

For the first few weeks after the sentence was handed down, there were some media reports about "A Deadly Honeymoon," and when I occasionally googled Mor's name ("Occasionally?" Who am I kidding. Three times a day, like prayer), it would appear, and under it, an article written several years earlier about the new ERAN suicide hotline for youth in distress. She's pictured there, saying, "In my conversation, I try to reach the moment when my loneliness meets theirs. I have to connect to the lonely girl I was in order to help them." And also, "Someone who grows up in a happy family doesn't understand how miserable a family can make you."

Under the ERAN suicide hotline entry, in the local news site of the town of Ma'alot, was an old article about *Hamlet*. It was actually a review—the name of the reviewer doesn't appear—of the play put on by the community youth theater. The anonymous reviewer thought that, with all due respect to the attempt to be original, there's no way that Hamlet was a curly haired girl, because after all, that takes things completely out of context, and if Shakespeare knew what a laughingstock they made of him in Ma'alot—that's what it said—he would turn over in his grave. Under the text was a blurry picture showing Mor on the stage, brandishing something that looked like a sword.

At some point, I stopped googling her. In an attempt to forget her.

I went out with women, even slept with a few of them. But I was always outside of myself, watching. And I always got dressed very quickly afterward. Which made me understand how rare the bubble was that Mor had created around us when we were together. During the first moments of morning, before wakefulness took over, and during the last moments of night, before sleep anesthetized me, she would appear on my internal screen, wind a curl around her pinkie, and ask, "How are you?"

I thought to myself that this doesn't have to be either/or. That either Mor is a deadly Jezebel or she's just unlucky as hell. Either she really liked me or she used me. Totally good people and totally bad people exist only in TV movies. Real people are both. And that's why it's possible that she really fell in love with me in La Paz and also tried to use me to stay out of prison. There's no contradiction between the fact that she lied to me quite a bit and the fact that there was a magnetic attraction between us.

I thought about the fact that, in Orna's eyes, especially in the last few years, I always saw what I wasn't. And in Mor's eyes, I saw what I was. And after all, with time, a man becomes what people see in him.

In the end, I went back to teaching at the conservatory. I put together a new group. I started running open workshops on a roof I rented in downtown Tel Aviv.

And all in all, how much time did we spend together? A sweet hour in La Paz. And another sweet day in Galilee.

I kept remembering how she rested her head on my shoulder, and I said to myself, a woman who does something like that is forming a bond with you. And you, you went and broke it. Or maybe you were overcautious and lost the kind of love that comes only once in life.

I didn't share these thoughts with anyone. Just like at a shiva, everyone tries to comfort the mourners with the phrase "I'm sorry for your loss," my mother, my sister, and all my friends tried to comfort me with exactly the same opinion of Mor: "Good riddance."

Nevertheless, I used to walk along the street and imagine her all the time.

Imagine that she's on a furlough from prison and I meet her completely by accident.

Imagine the tiniest details in the scenario: What she's wearing—tight pants and a soft shirt. Her hair— loose, not pulled back. The silver strands—silver. Her walk—light and bouncy, like in La Paz. Her large earrings bouncing along with her. Her smile when she sees me walking toward her. Happy. Her expression when she's already come close to me. Innocent, like a religious girl.

But I don't buy that innocence. Absolutely not. And before she can hug me or say, "Hey, my rock, how are you?" or anything else that would make my defenses crumble—I slap her beautiful cheek. It's not a hard slap. It's not meant to hurt her. But it's a slap. Which she deserves for trying to get me into trouble. And she rubs the spot on her cheek. Not surprised. Not offended. Not angry. And she says in a cold voice, "You see, Omri, you're like that too." And so the final memory I have of her is an ugly one, and it's much easier to move forward with that kind of memory than with the memory of her head resting on my shoulder and her mouth saying, "I'm totally lost, Omri."

Or than with the note I received from her exactly one year after she went to prison.

There was no name on the back of the brown envelope the clerk handed me, and even when I recognized what was waiting for me inside it by running my fingers over the outside of it—I didn't realize it was from her.

I thought it was a gift from one of my former students who wanted to boast about his new disc.

So I didn't open the envelope until I got home.

Inside was *Run, Kid* by Knesiyat HaSechel. Without any gift wrapping.

On the back of the disc, the song "Let Love In," was underlined in yellow marker.

The song opens with eight drumbeats. Slow drumbeats, tribal-sounding, that you can imagine as part of some ancient ritual. Then the acoustic guitar comes in with some innocent strumming that might make you think, if you don't know the group, that this is a quiet song, but a few seconds later, the soloist's voice bursts out, always sounding as if it's erupting from a scar in his throat.

You're most beautiful when you're drunk
And you can't tell right from wrong
Not even beauty
You're most lost when you know what you want
And so am I
I went to the desert too
To kill the devil
And we came back together,

Friends.

Let love in, let love in, let love in, let love in.

didn't notice the small note between the disc and the envelope. It fell onto the floor, and only when the song ended and I got up to turn off the stereo did I see it.

A simple yellow office note with only four words on it: *Don't wait for me.*

didn't understand how the hell she knew. After all, that song had been playing in my mind when we were together, and I never said a word about it to her. I'm one hundred percent positive that I didn't say anything. So what are the chances?

I searched YouTube for the song, hoping to find a clue, and all I found was a low-budget clip. The soloist is standing in a yellowing field. In the background is a city that from a certain angle looks like a small town and from another angle like Tel Aviv. He moves closer to the camera and hurls the first sentence at it, *"You're most beautiful when you're drunk,"* and then moves away, as if he were afraid of what he said, and then he comes closer to the camera again, as if he wants to fix things, add a critical detail, and hurls the second sentence, and between sentences, there are occasional short cuts to a girl in a bikini who is underwater, diving, somersaulting, deliberately blurred most of the time. At 1:56 minutes, she opens her eyes and directs a vulnerable look at the camera. And then she disappears and doesn't come back, and in the minute left in the clip, the soloist continues to move toward and then away from the camera, trusting and suspecting, until right at the end, he raises his head and shouts to the heavens: *"Let love in, let love in, let love in, let love in."*

I watched the clip over and over again, and over and over again, I had the frustrating feeling that Mor had hidden a message for me in it. A truth behind the truth that evaded me.

And that the person who asked me not to wait for her knew, in fact, that I would wait for her. Outside the prison gates. The day she's released. With the disc already loaded in the car stereo. I'll just have to press Play.

FAMILY HISTORY

The lawyer suggested that I write my version of the events.

"Try to stick to the facts," he said. "The committee isn't interested in feelings."

Outside my window, evening is turning into night. The house is empty. There are no children's voices coming from the living room, no water flowing over Niva's body in the shower. Schubert sonatas are playing in the background, the volume low.

If I have to confess, this is the time.

At first, she was just one of the many doctors doing their residency. Perhaps a bit better-looking than most. Perhaps a bit brighter than most. But I didn't give her special treatment. It occurs to me now that once, I even rebuked her. The entire group was standing around a patient's bed and I asked Liat to give a brief summary. She spoke clearly, confidently. And that itself put me off.

"A forty-five-year-old man who arrived with chest pains that intensified when he moved and exerted himself. No risk factors for ischemic heart disease. CRP slightly elevated. EKG with no signs of sharp ischemia. Most likely differentiated diagnosis: pericarditis." The treatment she recommended: a high dosage of aspirin and . . . colchicine to prevent reoccurrence. She added the colchicine with a tinge of self-satisfaction in her voice. She reads articles! She's au courant with the latest word on the subject!

Good, I said as I read the medical file on the computer. Very good, Dr. Ben Abu. There's only one thing you forgot to mention: The patient's father died of a heart attack at the age of forty-nine, which means that there's a family history, which means that saying "no risk factors" was . . . how shall I put it, a bit irresponsible on your part.

Tell me please, I asked the patient, do you live in a one-family house? An apartment building? With an elevator? Without? And how many steps do you climb to your apartment?

Twenty-five, he replied. Actually, thirty.

And has it been more difficult to climb them during the last two weeks?

In fact it has been, he said, I had trouble breathing.

What is the first thing a doctor must do? I asked the residents, rhetorically. Eliminate anything that might kill the patient! And then—after a dramatic pause during which they could imagine the pathological repercussions of the mistake that almost happened here—I stared right at Liat and added: I would have expected a resident to know that. First-year students know that.

The words, "But Dr. Caro," were on the tip of her tongue, and I could see her stopping herself from saying them at the last minute. I could see how the full sentence—"But Dr. Caro, elevated pain during changes in position does point to pericarditis"—slid slowly down her throat, as her face turned the purple shade of someone who has just been publicly humiliated.

My eldest daughter, Yaela, who had been an officer in the military Center of Communications and Information, always says that hospitals are even more hierarchical than the army. There's something in what she says. A resident wouldn't be so quick to dispute the diagnosis of a senior doctor decades older than her. And wouldn't be so quick to file a complaint against a senior doctor. But I'm getting ahead of myself.

'm trying to recall the moment when Liat first stood out from the crowd and became an object of my attention. I think it was when I heard her humming Schubert's Sonata no. 664 in A Major to herself. She was standing at the nurses' station, typing out instructions for them. I had walked over there to find out what was happening with a CT referral for a patient and I heard the melody I love coming from her, ta-ta-tam, tam-ta-ta-ta-tam.

Maybe I shouldn't have spoken to her at that moment. But curiosity got the better of me: Why is a young woman like you humming that forgotten piece of music? I thought I was the only one who listened to it anymore.

She pushed her hair behind her ear, blushed slightly, and said, I don't know, Dr. Caro. I was switching radio stations this morning. On the highway. And suddenly landed on *The Voice of Music*. Where that melody was being played. Schubert, right?

Yes.

And it was so . . . beautiful that I just couldn't change stations.

Especially the motif you were humming, I said and nodded. It . . . makes me cry every time I hear it.

Yes, she agreed, and looked at me as if she were impressed. Then she pushed her hair—which had come free in the meantime—behind her ear.

My love affair with Niva also began because of music. Because of King Crimson's first album, to be precise.

We were studying for an anatomy exam in the dorm room of a girl from our year, Michal Dvorski. This was our plan of study: After we finished going over a subject, we would take a break and each member of the group in turn would choose a record to play from Michal's collection. A record rotation, you might call it.

When it was Niva's turn, she chose *In the Court of the Crimson King*. I recognized it right away from the red cover that had a drawing of an open mouth on it.

No one was happy with her choice. Cries of protest filled the room. At the time, all anyone wanted to hear was Abba or Bon Jovi. But I defended her right to place the needle on a different, more complex kind of music and announced to everyone there that the freedom to choose music based on personal taste is anchored in the French Revolution, whose slogan—liberty, equality, and free music choice—was well known.

And so it was that we first bonded as a minority defending itself against the tyranny of the majority.

Niva wasn't one of the beautiful girls in our year. And until she placed the needle on King Crimson, I had thought she was pretty reserved. She walked with a slight stoop and was always buried in a too-large sweater. But when she chose that dramatic, theatrical music, I wondered whether, under that sweater, there might blaze a fire that only the Liliths of the world possessed. When the study session ended, I made my way slowly over to her, hesitant because of the many disappointments I'd had with women before that moment, and asked if she wanted to go with me to see the new James Bond movie.

In reply, she gave me a warm, genuine smile and said she didn't like James Bond.

I think the second time I noticed Liat's distinctiveness was at the coffee cart.

We both arrived there at the same time, which was not a usual time to be hungry, and for an amusing moment, we were like Barak and Arafat entering the talks at Camp David: Each one of us insisted that the other go first—

Until, finally, she surrendered with a smile and placed her order.

In addition to coffee, the coffee cart offers cold drinks and a small selection of sandwiches. Among them was one that I especially liked: avocado and feta cheese.

Since it wasn't a very popular choice, they only made two of them. And then, to my surprise, I heard Liat order one, along with a bottle of red grapefruit juice. I waited patiently for her to receive her order and then I also asked for an avocado and feta cheese sandwich along with, as always, a bottle of red grapefruit juice.

We stood across from each other at the cart, holding our identical orders. It was obvious that one of us would have to comment on the growing number of tastes we had in common, but I didn't think it would be her.

So what's your favorite *smell*, Doctor? she asked. Getting right to it, skipping all the intermediate steps that occur between people who aren't really close, and ignoring the fact that I had only recently rebuked her in the presence of her colleagues.

My favorite smell? I said, pretending to be undecided even though my reply was clear: The smell of guavas.

She nodded in approval. And the smell you can't stand?

The smell of newspaper.

Every newspaper?

Especially *Haaretz*.

I don't believe it!

I really like the contents, I explained, and it's the only paper that publishes a survey of jazz albums I can talk about with Assaf, my son. But recently, I took out a subscription to their site and my problem was solved.

Me too! she said in astonishment. She thought for several seconds, and finally, raising a finger for each item, she said, Schubert. Guavas. Grapefruit. *Haaretz*. Avocado and feta cheese. How about that?

———

n the end, Niva suggested that, instead of the James Bond movie, we go to see Habrera Hativeet perform. The band was appearing in a tiny, now defunct hall on Bezalel Street. A couple of their songs were already being played on the radio, but the group hadn't released an album yet, so there were only a few more people in the audience than on the stage. Niva said, I hope you'll like this. It's not for everyone. She was wearing corduroy pants and a green flannel shirt that matched the color of her eyes. I didn't know if I should compliment her, whether she would be pleased.

Very few musical experiences can be compared to discovering a new continent. But that was how I felt during Habrera Hativeet's performance—as if I were hearing something the likes of which I'd never heard before. Of course, you could probably find explanations for that in music theory: the Arabic musical scales that are so different from the Hebrew ones; the irregular musical patterns. And of course, you could base your argument on heredity and claim that the hot Sephardic blood flowing through my veins was aroused when Shlomo Bar performed. After all, both the Jews in Morocco and the Jews in Hebron are descendants of the Jews who were expelled from Spain during the Inquisition. But I wasn't thinking of any of those things during the performance. Habrera Hativeet's music set into motion entire parts of my body that had never been activated before, and when the band opened their encore with "Dror Yikra," I even stood up to dance. I, who was a wallflower at every party.

When the performance was over, we went out into the cold Jerusalem air and Niva suggested we go to Agrippas Street for some hot soup. I agreed, even though a quick mental calculation made me think that I might not have enough money in my pocket to order a bowl for myself.

As we passed Talitha Kumi, she put her arm through mine for the first time. And right before Davidka Square, we stopped to kiss.

I want to be precise about the kind of desire I felt for Liat at that point. It's important to be precise. Even more so because of the accusations against me.

It wasn't sexual desire. Absolutely not. The symptoms of sexual desire in a man are quite clear, and I know them very well after my years with Niva. When she moved close to me, her intentions clear, and kissed the bottom of my neck, my pulse would quicken and my breath would dry up. Desire grew inside me. Since that first kiss near Davidka Square, and throughout the years and the pregnancies and the anger and the hurt, Niva had aroused in me almost chronic sexual desire.

151

I'm not trying to portray myself as a saint here. And certainly, throughout the years, I've been attracted to other women. Nurses. Colleagues. Patients' relatives. Sometimes, after Niva fell asleep, I would allow myself to imagine fingers unbuttoning an unfamiliar blouse, a hand sliding under a short skirt. But I swear: It never went beyond imagining. During all the time we were married, I never had sex with another woman even once. Maybe it's the education I received, which was pretty conservative. And maybe the knowledge that Niva would never forgive me, that, in response, she was capable of taking Yaela and Assaf and leaving me.

In any case, after she became ill, that kind of desire died in me. I was completely focused on treating her, or more precisely, on being with her to the inevitable end.

I wanted to be with Liat too. Residents are always rushing around, and every time I saw her hurrying—from the nurses' station to the on-call room, from the on-call room to the X-ray department, from the X-ray department to the seminar room—I felt a strong urge to go with her, to walk at her side, to match my steps to hers.

And she aroused another urge in me: To know as much as possible about her. What kind of apartment does she go home to at the end of the day? Does she have a partner or is she alone? And when she goes out in the evening, does she wear black New Balance sneakers? What kind of exercise does she do to have such a good figure? Does she have a picture in the locket she wears around her neck? What does she have in her bag that she doesn't want anyone to know about? What is the rest of the tattoo whose edge sometimes shows between the hem of her pants and the top of her socks? What does she read before she goes to sleep? Does she wet the tip of her finger with her tongue when she turns the page?

Of course, I couldn't satisfy all that curiosity directly. It's improper for a senior doctor to harass a young resident with such invasive, personal questions. So I made do with our daily conversation at the coffee cart, which she always began in the middle.

Did you notice how much Albert in room eighteen looks like Rabin? And the guy in the room with him—an exact copy of Yigal Amir?

Did you hear what happened to the bottles of Septol that disappeared? The alcoholic in room twelve drank them.

You won't believe what happened in the emergency room this morning. A guy showed up with a toilet brush stuck in his . . . rectum.

After the anecdotes came the professional matters and questions about my views on them. I enjoyed how naturally she moved from the humorous to the serious, and I tried to make my replies worthy of the look she gave me.

Don't you ask yourself sometimes what's the point of what we do, Dr. Caro? When you get right down to it, in most cases, all we do is get our patients a postponement.

Did you know, I replied, that Leonard Cohen was able do his last, mythological world tour only because of the "postponement" his doctors got for him?

And don't you find the smell of death in the department hard to take?

In the end, you get used to everything, I said.

So tell me, when did you realize that you wanted to be a doctor?

There wasn't any specific moment, but apparently... the fact that my twin brother died of leukemia when we were seven affected my decision.

Wow. I'm... sorry to hear that. Were you identical twins?

My mother didn't cut his bangs just so she could tell us apart.

What was his name? Is it okay to ask?

Shlomo.

Do you remember anything about him?

He... didn't like to go the bathroom alone. Even at home. And he always told me, "Keep watch at the door."

And he wore only Hapoel Jerusalem shirts, all the time, even when he went to sleep.

Wait a minute...if that's the case...why didn't you become a pediatrician?

It put me off. I'm not sure I can explain why. It just put me off.

And...sorry for the question. How come...at your age...you're still running around in the internal medicine department? After you completed your specialization, why did you come back to the department?

First of all, because of the variety of cases. Second, because I can teach in the department, help train residents. For example, someone like you—from the earliest stage to the moment you yourself can teach young residents.

Never thought of that. And...tell me, Doctor, the fear that I've made a mistake, the way I torment myself after every shift, wondering whether I might have done things differently, does that get better with time?

No.

From time to time, Liat and I discovered—or to be more precise, reveled in the discovery of—other things we shared: Independent, secret attempts to translate Leonard Cohen's songs into Hebrew because the official translations didn't do it for either of us; a weakness for science-fiction and fantasy books, especially Frank Herbert's Dune; high sensitivity to caffeine; severe flat feet that required us to wear New Balance shoes; fear of elevators; an unusual affection for descending escalators, for that instant when you place one foot on the first step and your body moves forward, as if it is about to fly off. Or plummet.

I have no doubt that Liat felt me watching her, and, compared to the way I treated the other residents, I tended to favor her. In the soft way I spoke to her. In the way, after the colchicine incident, I avoided criticizing her in the presence of her colleagues during rounds. In the way my neck grew red whenever she stood close to me. Too close.

Obviously she believed I did all that because I liked her as a woman. Small feminine gestures she made when I was around—fingers toying with her locket chain, a look that went on for a second too long—made it clear that she had come to that conclusion. And to tell the truth, you can't blame her if that truly was the conclusion she had come to. Because what other conclusion could there have been at the time? And how could I have explained her mistake to her when I myself didn't fully understand where my feelings were coming from?

One night, I couldn't resist and googled her.

There were only a few relevant results. Three, to be exact.

The first was her picture after she won the national orienteering championship. She was wearing a yellow tank top with narrow straps, a gold medal lying on her breasts, and was smiling a half-proud, half-exhausted smile.

The second was an article on an NGO called Running for Life, in which young people who have recently completely their army service coach at-risk kids. Liat was interviewed as one of the volunteers and quoted as saying, "We believe that anyone who learns orienteering in the field will be better at navigating through life." And she also said, "The minute they step into the fresh, open air, they begin to smile. It's amazing to see how such a simple activity has such a strong effect."

The third result was Liat's Facebook page, but only people with a Facebook account could get into it. Niva would certainly have been amused by how quickly and easily I abandoned my principles and joined the social media network that, in our arguments, I had called "a colossal waste of time" and "a pale substitute for a real social life."

Within five minutes, the profile of Paul Muad'Dib, the name of the protagonist of *Dune*, was active, and a moment later, I was already logged on to Liat's page, where I found a treasure.

Photographs of Liat taken in various and sundry places in the world—I had the impression that she was overly fond of Latin America—her chestnut-colored hair pulled back in a different way each time, once in a single thick braid, once in dozens of very small braids, once in a tight bun on the top of her head, once in a spectacular braid-crown à la Yulia Tymoshenko. Interspersed between the photos were short, surprisingly honest texts, a kind of virtual diary, which I read avidly. Two of them touched me so much that I copied them into a new document on my computer so I could read them again whenever I wanted. The first had apparently been written on the anniversary of her father's death:

> *My dad taught me not to lose my bearings. My dad taught me that mathematics is actually philosophy. My dad taught me that, more than anything, shoes have to be comfortable. My dad taught me that the person who has the most fun is the victor. My dad taught me how to tie my shoelaces in a special knot that never unraveled. My dad taught me that saying you're sorry is nothing to be ashamed of. My dad taught me that above all, more than anything, you're allowed to laugh. My dad taught me that telling the*

truth is important, but not hurting another person is sometimes more important. My dad taught me that loving means being hurt. But that's no excuse not to love. My dad died ten years ago, and I miss him more with every day that passes.

Reading that, I couldn't help thinking about what Yaela and Assaf would write about me. What they would say they had learned from me. If they had, in fact, learned anything from me.

The second text I copied and pasted was written after Gilad Tal, an intern in her previous department, had committed suicide:

Why is it that in nine years of studying, barely one week is devoted to the emotional aspect of the profession? What angers me the most are the people who were "shocked" that Gilad committed suicide. I'm shocked that you're shocked. If you put such intense emotional pressure on people for such a long time without offering any support, it's clear that there are those who will commit suicide. Gilad's blood is on your hands!

My Niva felt the same way you do, I wanted to tell her the next day at the coffee cart, but kept silent. So as not to reveal the fact that I was secretly reading her Facebook page.

And obviously a much longer time would have passed before we spoke about or acted on what was between us if it hadn't been for another powerful urge that Liat aroused in me: to protect her from pain and from anyone who might try to hurt her.

The medical profession is considered to be a secure one that exempts its practitioners from financial worries, every Jewish mother's dream. But people forget the long years of study and internship during which students receive very little recompense or none at all. So how is someone not born with a silver spoon in his mouth supposed to get through those years? Someone whose father, for example, was still sitting shiva for his dead twin brother, and whose mother was forced to support the family by working as the secretary of the Broadcasting Authority orchestra and cleaning the houses of Jerusalem's well-to-do in Rehavia to make ends meet, a mother who taught her children how to combine the leftover pieces of soap into a single bar, who cut off the tips of their shoes so they could wear them in summer, and sat for hours, erasing everything they'd written in their school workbooks so she could sell them for a few pennies to Moshe Chai New and Used Books on the pedestrian mall.

After a month of dating Niva, I was bankrupt.

Until then, the two jobs I held down—cashier at a movie theater and night watchman at the Supreme Court—enabled me to pay back my student loans and live a student's modest life. But Niva had a fierce desire for culture. And I had a fierce desire for Niva. So I found myself paying for theater tickets at the Khan, concerts at the International Convention Center, lectures at the Writers' House, and guided tours at the Israel Museum. And after nourishing our minds, we had to eat something, right? Otherwise the experience was not complete. I had no choice but to pay, my stomach in knots, for pastries at coffeehouses and meals at restaurants.

To be fair to Niva, she always offered to pay for herself, but I always rejected her offer out of hand, even though I knew her parents were wealthy and even though I knew they wouldn't have allowed her to hit rock bottom the way I had. One Sunday morning, Geula, my bank manager, told me that if I continued spending at the same rate, she would have to block my account, and added that if she hadn't known my mother from high school, she would have done it already, with no warning.

That same morning, when I reached the medical school, I saw a small ad on the bulletin board at the entrance. Alongside the notices of canceled classes and changes in the exam schedule was an ad with a phone number on tabs you could tear off.

ospital visiting hours are from twelve to two and four to seven. But in reality, patients' relatives are there all the time. In the rooms. In the corridors. Knocking on the door of the on-call room. Completely surrounding the counter of the nurses' station. Pulling on your sleeve. Standing in your way. Demanding attention. Demanding a second opinion. Shouting: Nurse! Or: Bro! Bro! Talking on the phone. Talking to each other. Talking and talking, mainly to drown out their anxiety about the fate of their loved ones.

I didn't do a psychiatry residency. But I think that an additional category related to patients' families should be added to the *DSM*, the bible of mental disorders. I want to be clear: I'm not writing these things disdainfully. I myself was at Niva's side for six months in the oncology department. (Yaela came twice for brief visits, Assaf made do with Skype conversations. Maybe we hadn't made the seriousness of the situation clear enough to them. Maybe we ourselves hadn't wanted to acknowledge the seriousness of the situation. And maybe, as Niva claimed, we had done too good a job of teaching them self-realization.)

One way or the other, the anxieties involved in being at a patient's bedside, the long days spent mostly waiting, the frustration you feel when the doctors' need to prioritize certain actions over others clashes with your expectation of immediate response—I experienced all that personally. And that, along with life in this country, which is also characterized by chronic stress, is a cocktail that can unnerve anyone. And cause him to argue, refuse, and even shout—

But the shouts coming from the nurses' station that day made me cut my rounds short and rush right over there. Something in the tone was unusual, unrestrained. And perhaps a sixth sense set off an alarm in me.

Liat was bent back over the counter and a man of about thirty was holding her by the collar of her shirt and shouting such vulgar curses at her that I find it hard to repeat them. But I'll do it anyway.

You bitch, he screamed, you fucking whore. My mother's been here since this morning and they keep telling us "Soon," so either you go over to her now or I'll fuck you. Here. On the desk.

Liat froze. The athletic, sharp-tongued girl froze. (The way assertive, self-confident Niva had frozen once when her commanding officer, damn him, locked the door to the war room they'd just entered. A kind of instinct. Biological. Despicable. If only natural selection would make it extinct someday.)

I grabbed the guy by the shoulders and, with all my strength, pulled him off Liat. I hadn't been involved in a fight for years, not since the big brawl after the soccer derby in Katamon in 1974. Then, facing the Beitar fans, and now too, facing that guy who stood in front of me, his fist raised to punch me, I felt a surprising emotion: the joy of battle.

But back then, I'd been twenty-two, a veteran of that hellish battle for the Suez on Yom Kippur, focused and furious and looking for trouble, and now I was sixty-eight, soft-boned and ham-fisted, still bowed by Niva's death.

Liat was tending to my wounds—one above my right eye and one on my left cheek—in the treatment room. We were sitting in office chairs between an equipment cart and a bed, so close to each other that I could smell her breath and her perfume. My pulse was elevated. Extremely elevated. And I hoped she couldn't hear it. We didn't speak. We didn't exchange a single word the entire time she was working on me, I because my tongue was stuck to my palate, and she because she was totally focused on sterilizing and then carefully suturing.

I thought: I haven't been touched this way since Niva died.

And I thought: Someone who isn't touched with tenderness becomes tough inside.

And I also thought: If she leans over a bit more, her right breast will touch my left shoulder.

When she finished, she moved back and examined my face, satisfied.

Very impressive, she said, then looked right at me and asked: Tell me, weren't you scared? He was pretty... scary, that thug.

"I must not fear. Fear is the mind-killer," I quoted from *Dune*.

"Fear is the little-death that brings total obliteration. I will face my fear. I will permit it to pass over me and through me. And when it has gone past I will turn the inner eye to see its path..." she continued the quote and hesitated as if to allow me to complete it—

"Where the fear has gone there will be nothing. Only I will remain," I said.

And then, before I had the opportunity to respond, she leaned over, kissed me softly on the cheek, added, Thank you, and left the room.

———

There had been pornographic magazines in that small room. *Playboy*, *Penthouse*. But even as a teenager, I'd found it difficult to understand the magic that pornography held for my friends. Why should a woman I don't know arouse me sexually? Furthermore, how can any person with eyes in his head ignore the fact that most of the women pictured in those magazines are exploited. You just have to see the hollow, forlorn looks captured by the camera to know that.

I always preferred to close my eyes and see images in my mind's eye. That's what I did at the sperm bank. I pictured Niva in the shower. I pictured the water sliding over her curves, stopping for a moment in the clefts of her body, then resuming its flow along the secret channels. The cup filled quickly.

Back then, they paid five hundred liras for a standard donation, one thousand for a doctor's donation. A huge sum at the time. The tests they conducted before the donation were comprehensive. At every stage, a different functionary told you again what the conditions were to make sure you understood the practical ramifications of the act:

1. The donor has no right to receive information about the identity of the women who

will receive his donated sperm. Their identities will remain concealed.

2. The name and identity of the donor or any other information regarding him will not be given to anyone and will remain confidential.

3. The donor has the right to withdraw his donation only before it has been used.

I never told Niva about donating my sperm. There were times when it was on the tip of my tongue, but something stopped me. Maybe I was afraid she wouldn't understand it if I told her that I did it not only for the money but also for my dead brother. Maybe I was afraid of how she would react. And maybe we sometimes prefer not to tell others what we've done because that would make it more tangible.

It's important to mention that the secret I kept from her didn't taint our relationship or drive a wedge between us. Secrets are woven into the fabric of all happy families. But there were nights—especially after our chicks had relocated from the nest—when Niva tossed and turned in bed. She would try to sleep with the pillow, try to sleep without it, and would finally give up and turn on a small light. She would get out of bed, pour a glass of water, and drink it. Then she would walk into the living room and pull out an album, browse through pictures of our kids and silently blame me for the fact that they had chosen to live far away from us. On those nights, as I waited for her to return to our bed, silently blaming her for exactly the same thing, the thought—the question—flashed through my mind: Is it possible that I have another child in the world? And if so, where is he now? Who is watching over him?

And then Dr. Danker began pursuing Liat. I knew him and his unscrupulous methods well. That's why I noticed it even before she did. So I wasn't surprised when, a few weeks later, Tami, the department's head nurse and chief gossip, told me with a smirk that they'd begun dating.

I couldn't stand by and do nothing.

Dr. Danker, who bore a slight resemblance to the coffee model George Clooney, had breezed into our department eight years earlier after his glorious return from a period of research in a university hospital in Boston and, ever since, had been personally responsible for a string of brokenhearted women in the department: nurses, interns, residents. The pattern repeated itself: It began with a charming display of patronage—assistance in preparing a presentation for the journal club, saving the chair next to him at morning meetings, hot croissants at the Aroma Café adjoining the hospital, and free tickets to performances at the Zappa Club (his cousin was the manager of ticket sales); it continued with joint lunches, during which he would tell his companion that, although he felt ready to be a father, he wasn't prepared to compromise about his choice of a mother because he couldn't help it, he was a romantic. That led to several weeks, months at the most, of a passionate relationship during which the victim would come to work wearing a scarf to hide the signs of sucking he'd left on her neck. Then, abruptly and pitilessly, Dr. Danker and his lab coat—on which he wore his medal of valor from the second Lebanon war—would move on to the next girl, leaving the previous one to bleed on the side of the road.

A few months ago, one of those previous ones arrived in the department with a spray can of tear gas and chased him down the corridor. With great valor, he locked himself in the on-call room and didn't come out until the security people had removed her. He didn't even have the simple decency to open the door and talk to her.

And I still haven't mentioned his most insufferable trait: the tendency to boast about his conquests to his male colleagues on the smoking balcony behind the department kitchenette, for the most part, totally nonacademic descriptions he forced them to listen to.

"And then she takes the picture of her husband and kids that's on the desk and turns them around so they won't see."

"I couldn't believe it. The head of my department!"

"She suddenly screamed when we were in the middle of doing it, and I thought it must be hurting her, so I stopped, but then she whispered in my ear, in the original Queen melody, '*Don't stop me now, I'm having such a good time.*'"

I was horrified at the thought that soon he would be describing his exploits with Liat the same way, so I decided to take action.

I copied her phone number from the list that was posted on the wall near the department office, and when I got home, I charged Niva's phone and used it to send a text message to Liat. And then another one.

In retrospect, considering what happened with those messages and the way they were used against me, I admit that maybe it wasn't the smartest thing I could have done. But at the time, it seemed to be my only choice. They were supposedly written by a woman who had suffered in the past from Dr. Danker's heartlessness and now, in the name of sisterhood, wanted to warn Liat away from a similar fate. Interspersed in the warning were kind words about Liat:

Beware of Dr. Danker. He is a poisonous man.

Someone like you, who is both intelligent and good-looking, deserves someone who will truly appreciate you.

You deserve more.

A few weeks later Liat didn't show up for our regular rendezvous at the coffee cart. At the lunch break, she went to the shopping center with Dr. Danker, and they came back holding hands.

All my efforts to stop the train speeding straight toward the abyss failed. I felt that my body couldn't contain my mind, which wanted to scream out my concern.

Naturally, I wanted to talk to Niva about it, the way I used to talk to her about so many concerns I had during the years we were together. We had a kind of ritual: We would wait until the kids were asleep, first Yaela and then Assaf. Her regular breathing always came before his. We would wait another half an hour, to be on the safe side, before I said to her, Put on some music. From my tone, she guessed which album would provide the most appropriate background music for our conversation. She would take it off the shelf, drop the needle on it, and lower the volume. And listen.

The records are still lined up on the shelf in the living room, arranged by musical style, alphabetically within each style. The phonograph is in good working order. I dust it every Friday. But the needle that read the music in my soul and gave meaning to my life is gone.

Every corner of this apartment reminds me of her. The island in the kitchen was her idea. The tall chairs around it—she chose. Also the pictures on the wall, except for the one of a boat, which we chose together in Greece. She used to comb her hair in front of that mirror. Until she didn't anymore. She used to make Saturday's stew in that pot. Until she didn't anymore.

Isn't it hard for you, Dad, to live that way, in . . . a shrine? Yaela asked me during one of our last Skype conversations. Don't you think about moving?

You don't understand, I told her, I don't want to forget Mom. I want to remember.

The children arrived in Israel two weeks before she died.

I picked them up at the airport.

Yaela was the first to arrive. From London. We hugged for a long time, then went to sit in a café in the arrivals hall and waited for Assaf's plane from Montreal to land.

Dad, she said, you look terrible. What's that beard?

I thought beards were back in fashion, I said. And she shook her head slowly, as if to say: Since when do you care about fashion.

I brought her up-to-date on the situation. Actually, I'd brought her up-to-date on the main things earlier, on Skype, but now I added and specified and didn't spare her the prognosis. When I finished, she began to cry. I was surprised. Of our two children, Assaf was the crier, while she had been endowed, since childhood, with her mother's self-possession. I remember that we once took them both to a *Star Wars* movie. Not exactly *Schindler's List*, but Assaf cried during the movie anyway, afraid of what Princess Leia's fate would be, while Yaela took advantage of the crisis to appropriate the popcorn for her exclusive use.

From an early age, that girl knew how to manage. From an early age, she volunteered to stay at home and watch her little brother when we went out to a concert or a play.

When Assaf came back from the Far East and his dark period began, Yaela was the only one who could get through to him. Niva and I were excluded from his room on the grounds that we stressed him out, and she was the one who sat on his bed and listened, day after day, for many days, listening so patiently to the existential theories he developed that he agreed to share with her the anxieties they covered over. She was the one who initiated contact with Balance Village. She also brought his saxophone to the village and persuaded all the professionals there that music was the only thing that would move him toward life. And she went there with me twice a week to listen to him play. (Niva didn't come along. She said the place aroused an inexplicable antagonism in her, but I thought she was simply ashamed of her son. That that was the issue. And although I didn't say to her, What kind of mother are you, I thought to myself, What kind of mother are you.)

Yaela graduated from high school with honors. In the army she was an officer. The computer studies department in the university she attended offered her a direct track to a doctorate, and the postdoc in London, which was supposed to take two years, became permanent when the university made her an offer she couldn't refuse.

And now that intrepid little girl, who had become my strong-minded young woman, who had become an impressive woman in her own right, was bawling like a baby in a café in the airport arrivals hall.

I reached out and stroked her hair. I wasn't sure I was doing the right thing. Whenever she had sought comfort over the years—mainly for unrequited love—she'd found it with her mother. But now she moved her head toward me, a sign that my caress was welcome, and only a long minute later did she shake me off, wipe away her tears, and say, What about Assaf? Are you sure he got on the plane? It would be just like him to miss it.

A few moments later, Assaf came walking toward us in the stream of arriving passengers, a rectangular case holding his saxophone slung across his shoulder, as usual, and no smile on his face, which was not usual.

We drove home in silence.

At that point, the doctors had admitted to me that there was nothing they could do, so Niva lay in our bedroom. In our bed.

We spent the last two weeks of her life, the four or us together, like we used to be.

It was our family's shining moment. And our most terrible. We laughed a lot. We roared with laughter. We lay in the living room the same way we used to lie on the ground on family trips. Back then, we used to call it "a pile of us on the grass." We would spread a thin blanket on the ground, let's say on the Carmel or on the lawn near Ben-Gurion's grave, and lie down in such a way that we formed a square—or a rectangle, depending on the age of the kids. Each one rested his head on someone else's thigh and each one stroked the hair of the one whose head was on his thigh. Now, we stroked Niva's bald head. And we played Scrabble and Monopoly. And Assaf occasionally played his saxophone for us. And we ordered takeout because Niva had been the cook at home, but now she wasn't. During the really final hours, we went into the bedroom separately to say goodbye to her, but she was so groggy that it was already too late for soul-searching conversations, and we all regretted that we hadn't had them earlier. And then: I gently remove her wedding band from her cold finger and put it on my own finger, above my ring. And then: the funeral. Someone presses the Play button on "The Last Summer," the song she'd asked us to play at her grave. *"So remember that you promised not to cry because the skies are big and the tears are small."* A sob pushes its way out of my chest. And then: the shiva. The three of us on the couch. Yaela on one side of me, Assaf on the other. A united front against all the visitors and their banal words of consolation, their banal awkwardness, their banal words of praise, and the banal expectation that they'll hear a story, but what kind of story can you tell here except that once upon a time, there was a much loved woman and now she's gone. After the visitors go, the three of us flout all the rules and watch Harry Potter movies. A different one every day.

On the eighth day—I'm sure they must have discussed it earlier, consolidating positions, and not including me—we ate a breakfast consisting of leftovers from the shiva and Assaf told Yaela about an important performance he had to prepare for, and Yaela told Assaf about students waiting for private meetings with her.

They spoke to each other, but it was clear that, in fact, they were speaking to me.

So I asked, When are you thinking of flying back?

And they said, Tomorrow.

I choked back the why-so-fast shout. And the don't-leave-me-alone shout. Instead, I asked matter-of-factly, When tomorrow?

At noon, they replied.

Then we spent the entire day restoring the house to its former order. Even though it was clear that the house would never be restored to its former order. In the evening, we watched the last of the Harry Potter movies in the series, *Harry Potter and the Deathly Hallows*, and at night, I dreamt I was walking in Jerusalem looking for the Pargod Club and not finding it. The knowledge of its location is right on the edge of my consciousness, but I can't grab hold of it. I wander the streets of the city in the blazing sun like a weirdo, like someone suffering from Jerusalem syndrome. Every once in a while, I stop someone and ask if they have any idea how to get to the Pargod Club, but people ignore me and back away from me as if I were a leper, until finally, on the corner of Hillel and King George Streets, a man in a doctor's white coat puts a hand on my shoulder and says, Don't waste your time, Caro, they closed Pargod. When I hear that, I fall down. Dead, like a soldier hit by a bullet. I lie on the sidewalk in the center of the city, my limbs outspread. And no one comes over to help me or find out what happened.

When I walked into the living room, I saw that Yaela and Assaf were already awake and had packed their things and put the suitcases, side by side, near the front door. Now they were sitting in the kitchen reading the morning newspaper.

Yaela looked up and asked, How did you sleep, Dad?

Very badly, I said. And she asked, Coffee?, in the same tone of voice Niva had. And we drank coffee. As if it was just another morning. And we read the paper together, as if it was just another morning. Finally, Yaela looked at her watch and said, We have twenty minutes. And Assaf said, That should be enough. They stood up. She took one of my hands and he took the other, and they pulled me after them to the bathroom and stood me in front of the mirror so I could see the horror with my own eyes. Then, with the help of an old-fashioned razor and shaving cream, they shaved me cleanly, with infinite gentleness.

Then I drove them to the airport. All the way there, I wanted to say, Please don't go. I don't know how to be alone. But the words didn't come out of my mouth, and deep inside, I knew that even if I managed to say the words, they would leave.

What I knew in my heart would happen, happened. One morning, Liat returned to the coffee cart, her eyes red from lack of sleep, or perhaps from crying, her face pale and a scarf wound around her neck.

I restrained the urge to put a consoling hand on her shoulder, and as always, I let her order first.

But not as always, she ordered only red grapefruit juice. And passed on the sandwich.

To the question in my eyes, she responded with a firm, I have no appetite.

We didn't say anything for a long moment. I silently and vigorously cursed Dr. Danker and imagined myself choking him to death with the tube of my stethoscope.

Finally, she said, There's something I don't understand.

When I nodded for her to go on, she said, What do doctors do on the days they're unable to be doctors? On the days when life is just too big for them?

They go to work, I replied. And saw immediately that she was disappointed at how unequivocal my response was. As if she had expected a mellower answer from me. So I added, It really is a profession that doesn't leave room for self-pity. But that has its advantages as well. My wife died a few months ago and—

I'm sorry for your loss, she said, her eyes widening, I didn't know.

And at the time, I went on, we were going through some difficult days with our son. With Assaf. When he came back from his big trip. We actually feared for his life. My parents died a week apart. First my mother and then my father. It was shortly after we came back from my postdoc in Toronto, and I didn't...I don't want to think about what I would have done during that entire period if I didn't have to go to work every morning.

I can imagine.

Obviously, I would have gone off the rails.

We were silent again. She seemed to be weighing my words. Finally, she took the last sip from her juice bottle and signaled that we should start back to the department. As we walked, she said, This place is suffocating me, Dr. Caro. Suffocating me. I love our work, but I can't stand the environment. You know what I dreamt during my night shift this week, when I finally managed to fall asleep for a minute or so? That we're on rounds and all the residents are standing around a patient's bed discussing the indications and contraindications related to her condition, and then the camera of my dream zooms in on the bed and I see that the patient is me, I mean, everyone is discussing *me.* Do you understand? What I really need to do now is leave everything, get on a flight to Bolivia, and do the Takesi trek again. Have you heard of the Takesi trek?

In Bolivia. Wasn't some Israeli killed there recently? On his honeymoon? Are you sure that—

Ah, no, that was on Death Road. On a bicycle trip. I'm talking about the Takesi. Icebergs, lagunas, jungles. You do it on foot! I mean, you take a taxi to the foot of the mountains, and from there, you start climbing to the Andes—at some point, the dirt road turns into an ancient Incan trail—and continue walking until you reach a small village. There are no hostels there, so you sleep in one of their school classrooms—

She continued to describe the trip, and I continued to nod and imagine her in shorts, picturing her gemelli muscles bulging from the effort of such a steep climb, until we reached the automatic doors of the department. Then I touched her arm—grazed it, to be precise—and said, If you need a sympathetic ear, Liat, I'm here.

Thank you, she said, looking at me gratefully, trustfully, and said again, Thank you. And also said, What would I do without you.

Nonetheless, I was very surprised when I reached home that evening.

———

thought it was kids asking for donations to some charitable organization who were knocking on the door.

Except for people asking for donations, no one had knocked on my door in the months following Niva's death.

Friends did call occasionally, but they never came to visit. Perhaps they were waiting for me to invite them. Or were afraid my sadness was contagious. And perhaps they had always enjoyed seeing us because of Niva, not because of me.

I opened the door—and Liat was standing there. Now it was already clear that she'd been crying. The light makeup she always used was smeared in the corners of her eyes, her cheeks glittered with tears, and she held a stethoscope in her hand.

You forgot this in the department, she said. And I saw that you have community clinic tomorrow, so . . .

Thank you, I said and took the stethoscope from the hand she extended and added, What would I do without you, Dr. Ben Abu.

She smiled and said, Okay. It was the goodbye "okay" of someone who is planning to retreat, but she didn't retreat, and a moment later said, I don't want to bother you and your family—

I'm alone here, I said.

"Humans are almost always lonely," she said.

Indeed, I said and smiled so she would understand that I recognized the quote from *Dune*, and said, You're invited to come inside, Dr. Ben Abu.

You're sure it's all right? she asked and pushed a strand of hair behind her ear.

Certainly, I said, certainly. And I wondered, How does she have my address? Then remembered, the list of staff names and numbers at the secretary's desk. I suddenly felt embarrassed: She was used to seeing me with my doctor's coat on, and now, there I was, wearing my home clothes, just an old man in a tracksuit and slippers with sunspots on his cheeks.

She walked in and looked around the living room.

Wow, she said. So many records.

Yes, I boasted. That's the collection that Niva and I cherished.

She stood in front of the shelf and browsed through them.

Quite an eclectic collection, I acknowledged. We were people who loved—both Schubert and Dudu Tassa.

It's nice that you remember.

A good memory is critical to our profession, no? Niva always...she insisted that we shouldn't settle for listening only to the music we heard when we were young, and always...she always looked for new voices.

Is that her? she asked, standing in front of the photograph near the TV.

Yes.

Impressive.

I agree.

And she had . . . she has laughing eyes.

Right.

Where did you meet? Is it . . . okay if I ask?

At school.

What, she's a doctor too?

No. After university, she joined a pharmaceutical company. She claimed that a resident's working conditions were slavery and no one should agree to that abuse.

No kidding. She was ahead of her time.

Besides, she wanted to be the one to develop the drugs, not the one who prescribes them.

She was right.

Liat, would you . . . like something to drink? Tea? Coffee?

Do you have any alcohol?

Ah . . . yes . . . of course. What would you like? Wait. Don't tell me. I'll tell you. Red grapefruit Campari.

She sat down on the couch and I went to mix her drink. I noticed that my steps were lighter than usual. A fossil coming back to life.

I returned with two tall glasses, one for her and one for me. But after she drank almost all of hers in one swallow, I gave her mine too. And went to mix another two.

I'm sorry, she said, smiling in embarrassment when I came back, once again pushing some strands of hair behind her ear. I needed that, she said.

I sat down on the couch, as far away from her as possible.

Do you want to tell me what happened? I asked, pretending I didn't know what happened.

She sipped her second drink for a while, then began to speak. Tickets to the Zappa Club. Help in preparing presentations. An apartment in a high-rise. Declarations of love. Talk about having children together. Even about what their children would look like. And the thing was that a voice inside her was constantly saying that she must not succumb completely to Dr. Danker. There were also text messages. (But this is really just between us, okay?) Some woman sent her a text from an unknown number. Tried to warn her. Wrote that Dr. Danker is "a poisonous man." What would any normal girl do when she receives texts like that? Protect herself. Take things slower. But not her. She's screwed up. Only attracted to men who are bad for her. It's always been like that. Maybe it's because her dad died when she was fourteen. And maybe not. Maybe that has nothing to do with it. Maybe she should have studied psychology instead of medicine so she could understand herself. But what does understanding help if you can't change? Right, Dr. Caro?

You can call me Asher.

Right, Asher?

I didn't say anything. I had the feeling that she didn't really need an opinion now. Then I got up, went to the classical music shelf, took out a recording of Schubert sonatas performed by Radu Lupu, put it on the phonograph, and dropped the needle on the beginning of the third track. Meanwhile, she finished my glass as well.

The first sounds of Sonata no. 664 in A Major filled the room, and her eyes lit up: Isn't that . . .

It is, I said, and sat down.

We listened to the music. Her eyes were closed. My eyes were open, looking at her closed ones.

How beautiful, she said when the sonata was over, and a tear glistened in the corner of her eye.

Pure pleasure.

It's as if the music . . . presses the Play button of our most . . . secret emotions. Don't you think so, Asher?

Definitely, Liat.

Maybe we should leave everything and open a healing-through-music start-up together?

Now that's an idea! I said, trying to sound like a Ha-Gashash HaHiver comedy sketch. And when she didn't smile, I realized she wasn't familiar with it.

I...I'm so tired, Asher. Her voice suddenly shook, and her head slowly fell back. My tiredness is...really...really bottomless. Is it all right if I close my eyes for a minute?

Certainly, I said. But wait a second. I'll get you a pillow. So you'll be comfortable.

I went into Yaela's room and came back with a pillow, fluffed it up, and handed it to her. She put it on her lap and closed her eyes, then took off her New Balance shoes, released her ponytail from its rubber band, stretched out on the couch, and put the pillow under her head.

Her honey-colored hair spread out on it like a fan, asking to be stroked.

Oh, Asher. She opened her eyes for a minute, and her face suddenly looked very pale in the frame of her hair. Listen, I feel really awkward about this, it's just that, suddenly, I'm a little...dizzy. It must be the Campari. I'll just lie here for a few minutes, and then I'll go.

It's fine, make yourself at home, I said and went to get her a blanket.

I was always the "tucker-in" of the family. When they were kids, Assaf and Yaela always asked for Daddy to tuck them in, and I developed a special technique that included shaking out the blanket and lowering it slowly, gradually, lightly brushing them with it, until it landed softly on their bodies, then gently pulling the edge of the blanket to their necks, and, finally, stroking their heads with spread fingers that made their way from their forehead to the top of their head. Twice.

And that's what I did this time as well. Shake, lower, pull, and, finally, my hand automatically reached out to stroke Liat's head.

I think she said, Nice, after the first stroke. I'm not one hundred percent sure that's what she said because her voice was very low. And her eyes were closed. But she didn't move her head away or let me know in any way that my touching it was unwanted. So I did it again.

Then she changed position. Perhaps out of politeness. Perhaps not. But the change was so sudden that my hand fell from her head to under her collarbone and into the opening of her shirt. And I think, I mean it was possible, that my pinkie brushed against the curve of her breast.

I immediately pulled my hand away.

But she opened her eyes and sat up as if she'd been bitten by a snake, and said sharply, Why did you do that?

And she said, Do you think…

And also, I don't believe it, I thought that—

It was an accident, I tried to explain.

Yeah, right, she said, her eyes blazing. Tell me the truth, Dr. Caro, why are you so nice to me? Why have you been devouring me with your eyes from the first day I arrived in the department? Why do you speak to me differently from the way you speak to the other residents?

I don't know, I said truthfully.

Nat-u-ral-ly. Naturally you don't know. Her smile was so bitter that it looked more like a grimace and she pulled her bag off the back of the couch so hard that it fell onto the floor. She bent down to pick up her wallet and sunglasses and a box of Nurofen, which had fallen out of it, threw them back inside, stood up, and walked toward the door—

Wait a minute, Liat, I said and grabbed her arm.

Don't touch me, she said.

Please don't drive in this condition, I insisted. You drank a lot. Let me at least take you home.

I said don't touch me, she said, shaking me off. And she went out onto the landing, slamming the door hard behind her.

imagined an accident. I imagined an accident on the Ayalon Highway. I imagined an accident on Namir Road. I imagined an accident at the Azrieli intersection. I imagined a smashed-up car. I imagined a car going up in flames. I imagined a phone call from the head nurse. I imagined a funeral. A funeral again. I paced the living room diagonally like a detective trying to solve a crime he himself had committed. I went over to the kitchen drawer where we kept medications to take a tranquilizer. And changed my mind. There are things that a pill cannot tranquilize. I went back to the living room. I touched the couch, which was still warm from the heat of her body. A hair from her head lay on the pillow. Light brown, honey-colored. I picked it up and ran it through my fingers. Then I held it between my thumbs—the way I used to hold blades of grass to make the sound of a trumpet to entertain the kids in Yaela's kindergarten, and then the kids in Assaf's kindergarten, which is why Yaela and Assaf chose me, not Niva, to be the parent on guard duty at the kindergarten gates when it was our family's turn.

I blew on the hair and then brought it to my nose. And inhaled. It seemed to have retained Liat's scent. I went back into the kitchen, took one of the plastic bags I used to wrap the sandwiches I made for Niva to take to work every morning, opened it, and very carefully placed the hair inside. I didn't think of using it as evidence. How could I have known. I wanted to keep something of her for myself. In case there was an accident on Ayalon Highway. Or Namir Road. Or the Azrieli intersection. In case her car veered out of its lane. Or crashed into a wall. Or ran a red light at an intersection just when a truck was driving into it. Image after image raced through my mind until I couldn't bear it any longer and sent her a text.

> *Dear Liat, I apologize if I hurt you. Could you please send me a sign that you've reached home safely, I'm worried about you.*

But I was so upset that I didn't notice I was sending the text from Niva's phone instead of mine.

Ron Goldberg was in our class at the university. He was also with us in Michal Dvorski's dorm room when Niva decided to play King Crimson and was one of the most vociferous supporters of her choice.

In general, Ron Goldberg stood out for being vociferous. He always raised his hand in the middle of a lecture to ask a question—which was intended more to announce that Ron Goldberg had come to class that day than to clarify a point in the material we were studying.

He didn't always come to class. He used to copy during semester finals. He bought his papers from previous years' students, and he spent most of his time in Tel Aviv, because "Jerusalem has been dead for two thousand years already. How can you possibly love it?"

Behind his back, we called him Gasbag Goldberg. And we wondered: Who would ever put a scalpel in his hand?

That's why you could say we weren't surprised when, during his residency, he did a degree in health systems management and then went into the administrative side of medicine, where his vociferousness and ability to identify the centers of power helped him go from promotion to promotion, until a year ago, he was appointed director of the hospital where I work.

Asher Caro! he shouted happily at me in the department corridor several days after his appointment, and when he shook my hand, added, Who would have believed it?—giving me an arrogant look that said: Who would have believed the time would come when I control your fate, when I make decisions related to your professional future and can cut your salary and work schedule with the flick of a signature.

It was at Niva's shiva that he actually surprised me. He didn't make do with one visit, just for the record, but came twice, bringing a dish his wife had made both times. And he showed an interest in Yaela and Assaf. Genuine interest, not just the obligatory question or two. Both times, he sat in the living room for more than an hour and listened more than he spoke. And when he did speak, it wasn't about himself and his achievements but about Niva. Your mom, he said to Assaf and Yaela, was the most impressive girl in our year. There was something regal about her. I don't need to tell you. We all were a little in love with her. But she decided on your dad in our third year and that was that. No one else had a chance.

When I walked him to the door at the end of his second visit, he put a hand on my shoulder and said in an intimate tone that was very different from the one he used in his occasional media interviews: Whatever you need, Asher. If you need time off, if you need help of any kind, don't hesitate to ask me.

Thank you, I said. And I truly felt grateful. And surprised: After all these years, it turned out that Gasbag Goldberg had another side to him.

Three days after the incident with Liat in my home, I was summoned to a meeting with him.

I didn't connect the two things. It never occurred to me that they might be connected.

I was in the community clinic on the day after Liat's visit, so I didn't see her. The day after that, I didn't see her at the morning meeting and I heard from the mouth of the Head Gossip that although she hadn't felt well during her shift, she had insisted on continuing to treat her patients but was given exceptional permission to not stay for the meeting. Another case of a resident dumped by Dr. Danker has entered the statistics, added the Head Gossip with a smirk.

I missed seeing Liat at the coffee cart. I missed her very much. And I was concerned for her well-being. But on the other hand, I felt relieved by her absence, which continued for the next few days. I didn't know how I should behave when we met: Should I avert my glance like someone who has transgressed against her? Or perhaps the opposite, I should look her in the eye and explain that stroking her head was an innocent gesture and the texts I sent her over the last few months were sent only out of genuine caring.

Only once in all those months we worked together had I seen Liat angry. She was furious at a surgeon who she felt had avoided seeing a patient of hers, and the scene was quite dramatic. Would her blazing eyes and going-for-blood tone be directed at me now if I tried to explain?

In the evenings, I wrote texts to her.

I'm sorry if I hurt you, I wrote to her.

Red grapefruit juice isn't as good when you drink it alone, I wrote to her.

When Niva was a soldier, her commander locked the door of the war room behind her, I wrote to her. *Someone who saw how such an experience is burned into a woman's soul could never... do you understand?*

I didn't send any of the texts. I was afraid of how Liat would respond. And no less afraid that she wouldn't.

Over and over again, I relived in my mind those moments near the couch—fluffing the blanket, tucking it in around her body, reaching out to stroke her head, her sudden shift of position—and over and over again, I tormented myself with the question: Did the hand that fell into the opening of her shirt desire to fall?

No, I answered myself over and over again. I felt no desire at those moments. I did not imagine myself leading her to my bed later that evening. On the contrary. I felt serene. As if everything that had happened—the couch, the head on the pillow, spreading the blanket, the soothing caress—that was the ideal. There was no possibility of anything more. Or anything less.

I hoped that after she had some rest, Liat would get over her anger at me and realize that my intentions were indeed pure and begin meeting me at the coffee cart again.

Close the door behind you, Ron Goldberg said. In an ominous tone. Then he pressed a hidden button and asked his secretary not to put through any calls to him.

But even then I couldn't guess what kind of storm was about to break over me. I assumed he wanted to offer me early retirement because of the budget cuts imposed on us, just as they were on the entire health system.

Asher, Asher, he said, and sighed, you've put me in a very uncomfortable position.

The fish in his famous aquarium were motionless.

What is this about? I asked, leaning forward in my chair.

He flashed me a look that said, You don't really believe that I believe that you don't know what this about, then took a pipe out of his desk drawer, lit it—in violation of all the nonsmoking regulations in effect throughout the hospital—sucked on it, and only then pointed to the only piece of paper lying on his huge, empty desk.

A police complaint for sexual harassment has been filed against you, he said. The name of the complainant is Liat Ben Abu. She's a resident in your department and works closely with you. Is that right so far?

Yes.

According to her, you met alone in your home, you made her a drink, and then touched her intimately without her consent. Do you confirm this description?

That's not the whole picture.

She wasn't in your home?

She was.

And what she describes didn't happen?

Not exactly that way—

Okay. We'll get back to that. And what about the texts?

What texts?

There's a screen photo here showing texts she claims you sent her from an unknown number. Among other things, you wrote that she is "a feast for the eyes" and slandered another doctor in the department in an attempt to persuade her not to see him. Do you deny that too?

I don't deny it. I did send those texts from Niva's phone. But it was absolutely not my intention to harass her.

What then?

I didn't say anything. I didn't know how to say it. One of the fish in the aquarium turned and gave me an accusing look.

Ron Goldberg sucked on his pipe again and said, Asher, Asher. After a moment of silence, he continued, Just between us, I believe you. Niva died. Naturally, you're lonely. I saw a picture of the complainant. Ugly she's not. I can understand how a woman like that might confuse you. But times have changed, Asher, times have changed. Once you could get away with such things. Today she can post something about you on Facebook— and you're screwed. You're screwed and so is the hospital. Do you understand?

He stopped and waited for me to nod in confirmation.

I didn't nod. I felt that a nod might be interpreted as agreement to his theory. And that made him lean forward abruptly and raise his voice by half an octave.

I don't think you understand what's happening here, Asher. This whole meeting wasn't supposed to happen. Not like this. Our legal adviser was supposed to be here to document every word that comes out of our mouths. But because we know each other and because of my affection for Niva, may she rest in peace, I decided to bend the rules and let you tell me your version face-to-face before the wheels of an official investigation begin turning. To hear your version from you face-to-face. To see if there is a way out of this. Do you know that she asked for time off without pay? Do you know what a mess you've gotten us into? At the very least, I expect you to be honest with me.

I am being honest with you.

So what happened there? What's your explanation for what she describes here? The meeting at your home? The texts? Touching her breast?

It wasn't . . . none of it was . . . I began, and stopped. I couldn't find the words.

Ron Goldberg gave me an I'm-all-ears look.

It wasn't a man-woman thing, I finally said.

He sighed. So what kind of thing was it, Asher? I don't understand.

It was ... more ... paternal.

Paternal? Ron Goldberg repeated, as if he wasn't sure he'd heard right.

Yes, I said.

R on Goldberg's three secretaries watched me as I walked out of his office. I thought there was contempt in their eyes. I thought they already knew.

I walked along corridors I had walked along thousands of times, and suddenly they seemed hostile. The pictures on the walls—Israeli flowers and white-peaked Alps—appeared to be ridiculing me with their beauty. The signs pointing to the exit seemed to be directed specifically at me. As if they were expelling me personally from the hospital. A doctor from oncology, one of the ones who treated Niva, strode toward me from the end of the corridor and stopped when he reached me. How are you, Dr. Caro? he asked. Terrible, I wanted to say, but instead, I gave him what had been my standard reply over the last year, Critical but stable, and continued walking. To keep a conversation between us from developing, God forbid.

The word "paternal" that I myself had said, or more precisely, blurted out, reverberated in my mind, as if the scratch on my internal record was located there. Paternal. Paternal. Paternal.

As I walked along the corridor—which was growing longer, as if it were connecting parts of my life and not two departments—I imagined the conversation I would have had with Niva now.

I imagined telling her that I hoped she knew there was no other woman but her. And that she understood I would never force myself on any woman.

I imagined asking her forgiveness for embarrassing her this way up in heaven.

I imagined telling her it's possible...I mean, the possibility occurred to me...although it's a remote possibility...but even so...

I imagined telling her who she is.

I imagined Niva giving me her give-me-a-break smile, which didn't move beyond her lips, the thinnest of smiles she reserved for the prime minister's pompous speeches or the excuses Assaf used to make up to stay home from school. I imagined her saying, Give me a break, Chicken Little, what are the chances.

Chicken Little, that's what Niva would call me affectionately whenever, throughout our life together, I was afraid about something that might happen. She was the only person who could reassure me. Every time I was afraid, as a resident, that I might have made a fatal mistake on one of my shifts that would lead to disaster. Every time Assaf closed himself in his room for hours during his dark period. Every time one of my Suez terrors woke me in the middle of the night after I heard a military analyst on the evening news speak about signs of war.

Come to me, my Chicken Little, she would say and cradle me in her arms, caress my heart that was pounding through my chest, and whisper, It'll be okay, my Chicken Little. You worry too much.

Across from the waiting room in the office of the lawyer Ron Goldberg had recommended I speak to so I would be prepared for the committee was a conference room. The bottom half of the wall was glass, so I could see the shoes and pants of the people sitting in it, and to my surprise, I could also hear them. I didn't like that. What if they could hear me? They were talking about some plea deal meant to keep their client out of prison, if I understood correctly. They kept repeating the word "prison"—and every time they did, chills ran down my spine.

A minute later, a young man came out of the room, walked up to me, shook my hand, and apologized for the delay.

To my relief, he didn't ask me to come into the conference room but led me down a long corridor to a side office.

I thought to myself as we walked: He's too young. Even younger than Yaela.

I thought to myself: At your age, everyone is too young.

He sat down behind a desk and invited me sit across from him. Diplomas in brown frames hung on the wall behind him. Among the professional diplomas was one that didn't belong, a certificate saying that he had passed a skipper course.

He wanted to know exactly when the committee was meeting and asked me to tell him the whole story in my own words.

I told him. And occasionally he would stop me to clarify a detail.

Although his questions were neutral, and he nodded almost empathetically, I thought I sounded unconvincing, suspicious.

Only toward the end did I tell him about the possibility that had occurred to me. But I qualified my words, saying that the likelihood was slim, very slim.

If you have a way to do it, you need to check it, he said. And stroked his tie from the top to the bottom.

For what reason?

What do you mean, "for what reason"? A smile appeared in the corner of his mouth, and I wasn't sure whether he was amused by my choice of words or by the fact that I was asking the question. Two theories will be presented to the committee, Mr. Caro: One claiming that you're an old lecher who can't control his urges, and the other that you are a doctor with much to his credit, a pillar of the community, whose paternal concern for a young resident your daughter's age was misinterpreted by that resident. And it's clear that if the DNA tests prove—

I understand.

Do you even have a way of checking it? Don't you need a saliva sample from her for the test?

A hair can be enough.

Sometimes, when Niva and I were sitting in one restaurant or another, the waiter would suddenly appear at our table with an expensive bottle of wine we hadn't ordered and explain: The people at the table over there asked me to bring you a bottle of our best wine.

When we looked up, we saw people on the other side of the restaurant waving at us, or placing their hands on their heart in gratitude, and often one would stand up and walk over to us, take one of my hands between both of his, and tell Niva how my diagnosis or treatment saved his life, or the life of a loved one, and how he would never forget my warm and caring attitude.

I appreciated those moments, and was particularly happy when Yaela and Assaf were there to witness them. Niva set the tone in our home, and now I'd happened upon a chance to show my children that in the world outside their home, their father is known and appreciated.

Each one reacted in their own way. Yaela would watch the gushing people in amusement, while Assaf would avert his eyes in embarrassment. I, for my part, really overflowed with humility, bowing my head in the face of the flattery and lacing my fingers together in embarrassment as I mumbled an ongoing Thank you, thank you with all my heart, but really, there's no need to exaggerate, I was just doing my job.

treated Aharona Elbaz's mother three or four years ago. She came to the emergency room with stomach pains. Her physical examination yielded no findings, and if it hadn't been for me—I asked for a blood test for gases and lactose acid, which enabled me to locate the clot that was blocking blood vessels in her intestines and send her for emergency surgery—she probably would not be with us today. Between the procedure and the recovery, Aharona told me about the company she had founded,

Genetics, which enables its clients to discover their ethnic origins and, consequently, to find other clients with a similar genetic makeup.

Unintentionally, we became a center for locating relatives, I remember her telling me. And I also remember her pointing out that many people discover "surprise relatives"—half-sibs and quarter cousins who had never appeared on their official family tree.

Later, I saw her name in the financial newspaper *The Marker* as someone who had successfully launched Genetics on Wall Street. A link appearing on the bottom of the item led to the personal story of a journalist on the paper who did the Genetics check and discovered, to his shock, that apart from his Polish roots, he was also eighteen percent Mongolian. Did my great-grandmother's grandmother have a thing with a craggy Mongolian soldier? the journalist wondered, and ended with: The family as an amalgam.

I called Aharona Elbaz. Her secretary answered. I left a message that Dr. Caro would like to speak with her. I went to the kitchen, got a damp rag, took one record after the other off the shelf, dusted their covers, and put them back in place. I thought to myself: I can still change my mind. I thought: It's possible now. From the minute the doubt has taken root, a person wants to reap certainty. All those nights you lay on your bed wondering whether it's possible that your third child is walking on some street now, and whether streetlamps were lighting his way in the dark—

Aharona Elbaz called me back. She said she was sorry about Niva's death and apologized for not coming to the shiva. I asked how her mother was. She said, Thanks to you, Dr. Caro, a lot better. I said, I need your discreet help for a friend. She asked what it was about, and I told her. In general terms. She said, For you, anything, Dr. Caro. But it would help me a lot if you could also give me a blood sample from the girl. I said that, at the moment, that was impossible, and she said, Genetics relies only on blood and saliva tests. It would mean finding someone from police forensics or from academia who can extract DNA from a hair for us. How important is it to . . . your friend? Very, I emphasized. And she said, So send me her hair and a blood and saliva sample from him, and I'll try my best. Keep in mind that it could take a few days.

continued to go to work while I waited for a phone call from Aharona. I saw patients. I made diagnoses. I recommended treatment. Yona, an eighty-five-year-old man with a pacemaker, totally lucid, touched my heart in particular. Because blood wasn't circulating to his right leg, all the toes had to be amputated, but there were problems during the amputation and he came out of it with shortness of breath, strong pain, and fever. The surgeons opposed surgical intervention, but I had the feeling that surgery was exactly what he needed even though there was a clear danger that his heart might not withstand the anesthesia. I made the decision along with him. My voice did not shake. My focus did not waver. Afterward, I continued from bed to bed to bed.

Liat didn't come back to the department. The number of days she was absent piled up, and the Head Gossip said that she had asked for vacation without pay for "personal reasons," and hissed into the collar of her white coat that one day, Dr. Danker would pay for all the suffering he caused women. It will come back at him like a boomerang.

I wondered how long it would take for the real reason for Liat's absence from work to leak from Gasbag Goldberg's office to the hospital departments. How long it would take for her complaint to become the corridor conversation and my name to be whispered along with the words "Who would have believed."

At home, my thoughts attacked me like viruses. Maybe I'd had a moment of confusion, I flogged myself. Maybe something inside me came undone when she undid her ponytail and lay down on the couch? Maybe the hand that dropped onto the opening of her shirt had done so intentionally? Not to mention the pinkie. And what will happen when Yaela and Assaf hear that their father has been accused of such a thing? How could I bear the shame? And what do I want the results of the test to be? What am I *really* hoping for?

None of the records I put on the phonograph during those days of waiting was suitable.

Schubert was too sad.

King Crimson too dark.

Led Zeppelin too coarse.

Chopin too soft.

A person knows he is in genuine distress when no music can get through to him.

Instead of music, I followed Roger Federer's progress in the French Open tournament from one stage to the next. Niva liked watching him and claimed that the way he played tennis bordered on art. Besides, she would add, that same spark of laughter in her eyes, he's a hunk! I watched Federer hit the yellow ball on live TV and tried to summon up the same enthusiasm Niva had shown when he won a point against his younger opponent, but the entire time, I couldn't shake the dismal feeling that this was a chronicle of a defeat foretold. That at some point, like every tragic hero, Federer would be defeated by his limitations, first and foremost, the limitation of his age.

A few minutes after his victory in the semifinal, the call from Aharona Elbaz came.

can ask them to run the test again, she said.

But the chances of error are small, she said.

Either father or brother, she said.

In any case, I assume that for your friend, this will be a shock, she said.

Tell him to take a few days to plan his next steps, she said.

It's a momentous decision, she said.

I'll send you what the analyst sent me, she said. For an official Genetics form, we would need a blood or saliva sample. I'm here, so let me know if you want an additional test.

had skipped down the street after the doctor told us that Niva was pregnant.

It had come after two years of failed attempts. The air between Niva and me was dense with feelings of defeat and two accusations that were never spoken aloud. It's your fault, she didn't say. It's your fault, I didn't say.

I could already see in her eyes the doubt I'd seen in the eyes of women who, in the end, left me. And one evening, during intermission at a concert in the Mann Auditorium, when I returned from the restroom, I saw a man who was better-looking than me flirting with her. And she gave him the smile I thought was reserved only for me.

So after the gynecologist told us matter-of-factly that it was no wonder Niva was feeling nauseous, after all, she was six weeks pregnant, my heart was bursting. And Niva said, Maybe it's too soon to celebrate. Maybe we should wait until after the tests. And I said, Now, we celebrate now, and pulled her to me and we waltzed through downtown Ramat Gan. Even though neither of us knew how to waltz.

I felt dizzy after my conversation with Aharona Elbaz. As if I were standing on the brink of an abyss and looking straight down into it.

I leaned against the shelf of records, and a flurry of words began to swirl in my mind. Chances of error. Father or brother. Who to tell. Who. Liat. Now I understand everything. Now I don't understand anything. Momentous decision. Yaela, Assaf. Niva. Do you hear? A daughter. Who's accusing me of harassment. Mom, do you hear? You have another granddaughter. Committee. Momentous decision. What to do. What to do.

With my last ounce of strength, I staggered over to the sofa. That same damned sofa.

The next day, the lawyer-skipper texted me: *Any news?* And when I didn't reply, he texted again: *Remember, committee meeting in three days. We need the information before that.*

I knew he would pounce on the test results as if he'd found a treasure, and that was why I avoided telling him about them for the time being.

I saw patients. I gave diagnoses. I advised on treatment. During the night, serious necrosis had developed in Yona's left foot, and the toes had turned blue. Now, if there was a chance of saving his life, both feet had to be amputated. Did he really want to keep living with severe, chronic pain and no feet? We could no longer ask Yona himself, he had lost consciousness. The physical therapist estimated the chances of rehabilitation, and the social worker advised about sources of support, but I was the one who had to decide. I decided. And decided again. And again. About other dilemmas I faced during my shift. My voice did not shake. My focus did not waver. I went from bed to bed to bed to bed. But throughout the day, I had the sense that everybody already knew about Liat's complaint. I saw, or imagined I saw, a spark of unease in the eyes of the nurses and the residents, and a flash of "thank God it's not me" in the eyes of the senior doctors, my colleagues. The automatic doors opened for me a second more slowly. As if they weren't sure they knew me. The head nurse didn't reply when I asked her about a patient. I spoke to her—and she didn't reply. And I also saw that as a symptom of my lowered status, which had come about because everyone already knew: My time was over.

I remembered when the boy who sat at the same desk with me in high school accused me of stealing fifty shekels from his wallet. The entire class was quick to believe that the boy whose mother cleaned houses in the neighborhood was the thief, and I escaped to the bathroom and stayed there with my copy of *Dune*, while what I really wanted to do, what I should have done, was to stand in front of everyone and shout out the truth: It's not me! It's not! I'm not a thief!

Now too, I wanted to pound the desk and shout so loudly that the whole hospital would hear: I didn't cheat! I didn't harass her! I didn't mean to! Instead, I clenched my fists at the sides of my body, continued to treat my patients, and took solace in the fact that they, at least, still didn't know.

That evening, at home, I took photo albums off the shelf and kept comparing pictures of Yaela and Assaf at various ages with the pictures of Liat on her Facebook page.

In certain shots, her smile was similar to Assaf's. There was no denying it. Something in the map of wrinkles and dimples. And also the eye color—the lightest that brown could be before it became green.

Her nose was similar to Yaela's. Dominant. Almost aquiline. And also the very prominent collarbones.

Her dark complexion resembled mine, as did her high forehead, with an almost receding hairline, her thick eyebrows, and a sort of curve in her lower lip which, on my face, makes me look critical, and on hers, hints at self-irony.

But from whom did she get her slim build? I wondered. Definitely not from me. Perhaps from her mother?

During one of our coffee-cart conversations, Liat had mentioned that her mother was an optometrist. I called information, asked for an optometrist with the name Ben Abu and found three. One in Dimona. One in Ramat Gan. And one in Tel Aviv, who prided herself on being an ophthalmologist as well. I'm not a detective, but thirty-five years in an internal medicine department taught me to eliminate possibilities. I eliminated the possibility of Dimona, because Liat belonged to the generation that would rather live with their parents while at university in order to save money, and if she lived in Dimona, then she would obviously be studying at Ben-Gurion University in Beersheba. I eliminated the possibility of Tel Aviv, because if Liat's mother was a certified doctor, she obviously would have mentioned it in one of our conversations. Therefore, with a pounding heart, I called Eye Contact in Ramat Gan and asked to speak to the manager. When she came on the line, I asked whether she was Liat Ben Abu's mother.

Who's asking? she asked, a bit suspiciously.

I identified myself.

I have nothing to say to you, Doctor, she hissed, and was about to end the conversation.

But before she did, I managed to say, I'm calling about a sperm donation you received from the sperm bank.

I have no idea what you're talking about, she said. But a slight tremor on the edges of her voice hinted that she actually did.

Mrs. Ben Abu, I suggested, let's meet.

There's a café in Ra'anana where Niva used to hold her discreet business meetings. When she wanted to hire a senior employee away from another company or interest an investor in a project based on an idea she wanted to keep top secret, she would set up the meeting at Café Salata.

Café Salata is made up of two dining areas: the visible one that faces the street, and a concealed backyard, which is closed to the public during the day and open only in the evening.

Niva had reached an agreement with the owner that allowed her, and only her, to hold meetings in the backyard during the day, guaranteeing herself walls with no ears. What did she offer him in return? Nothing, I assume. She knew how to ask in such a way that she would not be refused.

Yafit Ben Abu was late for the meeting we scheduled.

By more than a few minutes.

I did not do well with dead minutes on the days that preceded the committee meeting. Bad thoughts invaded every yawning pit of time. Maybe she wouldn't come at all. Or maybe she would, accompanied by a lawyer, but would open the meeting by slapping my face.

To distract myself from doomsday scenarios, I forced myself to stand up from my chair. I walked around the backyard, my hands supporting my lower back, which had begun to hurt since the meeting with Ron Goldberg, and I examined the many photographs hanging on the walls. One of them caught my attention enough to focus on it for a moment: a Tibetan monk, maybe Nepali, old, wearing a red robe, walking through a group of child monks that had split apart like the Red Sea to let him pass.

Hello, I heard a voice behind me.

I turned around.

She did and didn't resemble her. Slim figure. Hair pulled back in a tight bun. Glasses with colored frames. A white button-down shirt with a starched collar.

I reached out for a handshake and she let my hand hang in the air.

Shall we sit down, I said.

Without replying, she sat down and pushed the hair that had escaped from her bun behind her ear. Just like Liat.

Would you like something to drink? To eat? The food here is excellent.

I have no appetite, she said. Just like Liat.

How is Liat? I began.

She's a strong girl, she said.

I'm sor—

Do me a favor and don't give me that "I'm sorry" now, anything but that.

Okay, but still—

Maybe we should get right to the point, Doctor? You said something to me on the phone, right?

I sighed. Then I put the page with the results of the Genetics test on the table. That's Liat's test, I said, and that's mine, and that number shows the matching—

She picked up the page, looked at it above her glasses for a few moments, and then, in the middle of the analysis, stopped and gave me a worried look—

Exactly how did you get a sample from her for the test?

When she . . . visited me in my home, a hair fell.

A hair?

You can extract DNA from a single hair.

Are you saying that you saved her hair?

Yes.

Why would you do that? For what purpose?

I wanted . . . to have something of her.

You wanted to have something of her?

Yes, I know it sounds a little str—

And why is there no logo on this page? No signature? How do I know you didn't forge it?

For official results, you need a blood or saliva sample, Mrs. Ben Abu. But this page was sent to me by professionals who can be trusted, and the chances they have made a mistake are very small.

She read the page for another minute, then threw it in my direction, I mean, she didn't put it on the table between us, but literally threw it toward me, and almost hit me with it.

Let's say this is real, she said, a strong note of doubt in her voice.

Mrs. Ben Abu—

And let's say they found a link between your DNA and hers—

A fifty percent match, to be precise.

You think this will make you her father?

Genetically, we're talking about—

She interrupted me with a murderous look that cut short any further learned explanations from me. Then she took a deep breath, like a girl who was taught to count to ten before answering someone who was making her angry.

Liat had one father, sir. Who died when she was fourteen.

I'm sorry to—

They were very close.

I understand.

No, you don't.

So explain it to me.

What is there to explain? Her voice broke on the word "explain."

A waiter arrived with the tea I had ordered.

Something for you? he asked Liat's mother. Do you want to hear about our specials?

She shook her head emphatically, as if to say: I didn't come here to enjoy myself. When the waiter left, she began to speak surprisingly quickly, the glistening in her eyes prophesying tears. He had a stroke when Liat was at home. It took a long time for the ambulance to arrive, the emergency room was packed because of a terrorist attack, they gave him the wrong treatment. Apparently they could have saved him. Do you understand?

I nodded.

Liat fell apart completely afterward. She stopped eating, stopped running. Did you know she was the national orienteering champion?

Yes, I said (and I didn't say: I follow her obsessively on her Facebook page).

It all came from him, he got her into that. Every Saturday, until her bat mitzvah, he used to take her running, they orienteered all of the Israel National Trail—

It sounds like—

She didn't function after he died, didn't go to school, left the Scouts. There was no label they didn't pin on her. Attention deficit disorder, adjustment disorder. Some idiot psychiatrist even diagnosed her with borderline personality disorder. I knew the entire time that it was just taking time for her to separate from her father. Every person grieves at their own pace—

That's true—

And hers was just slower. I knew that we were in a tunnel and that I had to be in that tunnel with her until we reached the light.

I—

And then, at the age of seventeen, with no advance warning, she got up one morning and said, Mom, I want to be a doctor. So that what happened to Dad won't happen to other people. And to do that, I need good grades. From then on, she was back on track. Do you understand?

Mrs. Ben Abu—

She told me about you, you know? Said you were the only person in the entire department she respected. She wanted to be like you. She said you really cared about the patients. That's why she was so disappointed when you did what you did. Because she thought so much of you.

There was a misunderstanding there, Mrs. Ben Abu.

Misunderstanding? How, exactly?

I waited a moment before speaking. I weighed my words. It was important to be precise. I had the feeling that the next thing I said would be crucial.

Yafit Ben Abu didn't speak either. It seemed as if the stream of words that had erupted from her over the last few moments had exposed more vulnerability than she was used to exposing, and now she was embarrassed.

She signaled for the waiter to come over. And asked for, if possible, a glass of water.

He brought us a pitcher, and when I picked it up to pour, she stopped me and said, I can do it myself.

Look, I began after she took a sip of water, even actions . . . even physical gestures . . . can be . . . misunderstood.

What do you mean?

The movements a person makes, his touch, can be misinterpreted by another person.

Misinterpreted?

I mean, the intention behind the movement is misinterpreted.

Oh come on, she said, putting her glass down so hard on the table that a few drops of water sprayed onto me.

I had no intention of harassing Liat, Mrs. Ben Abu. From the minute we met, the only desire she aroused in me was to look out for her. Protect her.

Is that the story you tell yourself?

It's not a story, it—

Come on, Doctor. I know my daughter and the effect she has on men. Her orienteering coach. Her driving teacher. Her commander in the army—a man my age!— appeared at our door one day with a bouquet of flowers.

I don't think Liat does it on purpose, but something she projects . . . gets men going.

That is not the case with me, Mrs. Ben Abu. The reason I wanted to be close to her is . . . pure. It didn't come from a place of . . . a man interested in a woman.

Just don't tell me it was a paternal thing.

Look, Mrs. Ben Abu—

After all, when she was in your apartment, you had no idea there might be a . . . genetic link . . . between you, and saving a hair from her head like some pervert—

I've already explained to you that—

Her phone rang. Usually, there is a certain compatibility between people and their ringtones. Her ringtone surprised me: Latin pop of the easy-listening kind.

She answered, and after a moment of listening, she instructed her employee about how much of a discount she could give to a specific customer. I had the impression that the break in our conversation had come at a good time for her, enabling her to regain her equilibrium.

My equilibrium, on the other hand, had been shaken by the last things she said. I remembered bringing Liat's hair up to my nose and trying to inhale her scent. Over and over again. What sort of person does something like that?

When she ended her call and spoke to me again, her voice retained a remnant of the professional matter-of-factness with which she had spoken to her employee.

With all due respect, Doctor, you can try to sell that "look out for her" and "protect her" bullshit to the committee. Not to me. Maybe you'll be lucky and all the members of the committee will be men—and then you have a chance they'll buy it. When are they meeting?

This Sunday.

Just a minute, don't tell me that you plan to tell them about the test—

To tell you the truth, Mrs. Ben Abu, that's the reason I wanted to meet with you.

A bitter smile moved across the lips of Liat's mother when I told her that yes, I'm thinking about showing the results of the genetic test to the members of the committee. How predictable you are, that smile said. And how despicable. I continued to explain that, for the time being, she was the only person who knew about the results, and that her daughter's well-being was important to me, otherwise I wouldn't have asked to see her. Then all at once, her bitter smile became a grimace of fury and she stood up, yanked her bag off the back of her chair, bent down to pick up the sunglasses that had fallen out of it onto the floor, shoved them back inside, and stormed out of the backyard. Silently, I cursed the degenerative disc between my L4 and L5 vertebrae, which did not allow me to leap out of my seat and catch up to her. By the time I got out of my chair, straightened up, and took the steps necessary to leave the café and reach the street—Liat Ben Abu's mother had vanished.

I returned to the backyard. I poured water from the pitcher. I said to myself, I'll drink as slowly as I can, maybe in the meantime, she'll calm down and come back.

After two glasses, my phone rang.

First I heard a commotion on the road. Then her voice. Shaking with fury.

I don't understand exactly what you expected, Mr. Caro, for me to give you the green light?

I wasn't expecting—

Sorry to disappoint you. You're getting a red light. You've caused Liat enough damage. So don't add insult to injury. She doesn't know that she was born from a sperm donation. Neither did her father. I had to hide it from him for reasons we won't go into now. And after he died, she was in such bad shape that I couldn't take the chance of destabilizing her more with such a revelation. Do you know she's been at my place for more than a week already? Do you even care how she is? Or are you only interested in saving your own ass?

Of course I—

She hardly gets out of bed, Mr. Caro. She hasn't put a thing in her mouth for days, and yesterday she told me that what happened with you was the "straw," because even so, she had serious doubts about the residency. And now she wants to leave everything and go to Peru. Or Bolivia. I don't know. Can you imagine what it would do to her if it's the committee—the committee!—that informs her there's a chance her father may not even be her father? Do you think that's what she needs now? To suffer that blow?

But—

Listen, she said, then stopped—and it seemed to me that once again she was counting to ten—and continued in a different tone that, surprisingly, contained a hint of shared destiny.

If, with the emphasis on if, that page you showed me is worth something, then . . . thank you. Maybe without you . . . such a marvelous girl might not have been born. But if you care about Liat, if her well-being is really important to you, shred that piece of paper, Doctor. Please.

———

stayed in the backyard for a while after Liat's mother had already hung up. I wasn't capable of looking inward at the chaos raging in my mind, so I stood up to look again at the picture of the child monks, and moved on to the other pictures hanging on the walls of the backyard. A forest clearing. A close-up of petals. A close-up of old-fashioned scales, the kind that were in Albert's grocery store in Talpiot.

The waiter came back with my credit card and said I had points in my account, so he didn't charge me.

Points?

Your name appears in our computer next to your wife's name. You're both members of the club.

What club?

Our customers' club. With every order, our club members receive points for the next order, and your wife accumulated quite a few points with us.

I didn't know that I—

She must have added your name without telling you, sir. You can switch from a single membership to a double membership.

———

t's the small things that break your heart.

Every Sunday, Niva and I had a Skype conversation with the children. First Assaf, then Yaela.

We both saw our children's decision to move away from Israel, with no intention of returning, as our failure. Or, at the very least, a lesion on the heart of our life together. And each of us blamed the other for it.

Couples who have been together for many years no longer need to fight out loud for the fight to be present. In the silence that followed our Sunday Skype conversations you could hear the "people in glass houses" we hurled at each other in our thoughts, almost as if we'd really spoken the words.

"If you hadn't always reminisced about our two fantastic years in Toronto in front of the kids."

"If you hadn't developed such a loathing for the country after you started volunteering for Physicians for Human Rights."

"There's so much wide open space in Canada." "In Canada, people are basically polite to each other." "In Canada, the health system is aimed at the patients' well-being." After that, you're surprised?

"A military country." "An immoral country." "An occupying country." After that, you're surprised?

It's convenient for you to blame politics for everything.

It's convenient for you too.

Has it ever occurred to you, Asher, that maybe it's us? Maybe they had to run away from us in order to flourish? Two opinionated parents. Dominant. Maybe suffocating.

Two parents, Niva? Maybe one? I mean you?

If we had at least given them international names. Yaela? Assaf? What chance do they have to succeed abroad with names like those?

It's not funny.

Assaf's face appears on the screen and I immediately see that he's in distress.

The symptoms haven't changed since he was a child: His gaze wanders; his permanent cowlick, caused by the fact that he has a double crown, is more unkempt than usual; he rubs his neck incessantly; his voice is even more forced than usual. And there's a new symptom from the last few years: It's not enough for him to ask how I am, but he asks again, How's everything. And what's happening. And what else is new. As if he were trying to postpone, as much as possible, the moment the focus of the conversation shifts to him.

But in the end, that moment comes, and he says, Things are a mess. And then chuckles at himself, a chuckle that has no happiness in it.

If we weren't on Skype, I would have rolled my eyes. Because what's new. Instead, I give him a serious look and ask how I can help him. I assume he was fired from his job again because he didn't show up for a shift, and in the few seconds that pass before he speaks, I make up my mind that this time, I'll agree to cover only part of his rent.

Sarah's pregnant, he says.

That's great news!

I'm not sure it's so great.

I don't say anything for a moment, then ask, Why not? You're not sure . . . it's the right time for the two of you to have a child?

I'm not sure it's the right time for *me* to have a child.

I see.

I don't want to hurt Sarah. And I really don't want to kill a living creature.

How many weeks is she pregnant, if I may ask?

Five.

It's hard to call it a living creature after only five weeks, Assafi. By any standard. Almost none of the organs have developed, the respiratory tract doesn't exist, the cortex hasn't yet formed. A cauliflower has more of a mind than a fetus in its fifth week.

It's not a medical issue, Dad.

But—

And I didn't ask you for a diagnosis.

Silences on Skype are more awkward than silences on the phone. He can see me trying to swallow the insult, unsuccessfully. I can see him regretting his sharp tone, but he finds it hard to apologize, so he escapes to his cell phone and checks his messages.

Where's Mom when you need her, eh? I finally decide to say what's going through both our minds, and he smiles in relief and says, Yes. But he doesn't ask the expected question, "What do you think she would say?" After a brief silence, he gives me a screen-piercing look and says, Remember my school trip to Eilat?

I'm surprised he mentions that. But I do remember it. I'd just finished a tough night shift during which I didn't have time to grab even a few minutes' nap. I was on the way home when the phone rang. It was him. Asking me to come and get him. Sweetie, it's a five-hour drive and I just came off a night shift. What happened? I asked. Then he told me. And I thought, bastards. And I thought, man's heart is evil from his youth. So I made a U-turn at the light and drove to Eilat. Express. No stops. Except one, to fill the tank with gas and myself with coffee. And I arrived in less than four hours at the large parking area where there were many empty buses and one with a child and a teacher in it. I signed a form for the teacher and drove away with him. On the way, Assaf said, Thank you for coming, and I said, Of course I came, Assafi. And he said, I called you because I knew Mom would tell me to deal with it. And I said, Even grown-ups find it hard to deal with viciousness. And he said, It's about time you told me the truth. Which one? I said, trying to joke. But he said seriously, That I'm adopted. What are you talking about, I shouted, you're our son. Believe me. I was there at the delivery. So how come, he said, you and Mom and Yaela—his voice broke—are good at everything you do and I just screw up all the time?

Of course I remember, I say now and wonder, is he trying to say that he wants me to go and bring him back from Montreal? But instead, he says, Being a parent is a heavy load. Sometimes a shitload.

But—

Imagine if I have a kid like me.

You weren't—

I'm not sure I'm ready for that kind of sacrifice, you know?

I—

And I might never be ready. Maybe it's just not for me.

Time will tell.

"Time will tell." Wow, Dad, that's an expression I haven't heard for ages.

What can you do, kid, your dad's an antique.

Then he played me some new pieces by his group, the Immigrants. I didn't like jazz before Assaf began to play it. Everything always sounded too random to me, too irresponsible. But through him, I learned to respect the freedom the style allows both the musician and the listener, and during a department evening that took place in our home a few years ago, I even played a disc of his group in the background and was so pleased when people asked me: Whose wonderful music is that?

Now I complimented him on his playing, which had lost some of its affectations over time, and he thanked me and said he had to hang up because Sarah would be there soon.

I said, Good luck, and hung up, thinking, why "good luck"? What a ludicrous thing to say. And I thought, we spoke for half an hour and I didn't tell him anything—not about Liat, or the complaint, or the DNA test, or my agonizing indecisiveness about whether to reveal the results to the committee—and I thought, exactly how do you say a thing like that to your son?

———

On the night between Sunday and Monday, I couldn't fall asleep. In general, since Niva is no longer with me, I find it difficult to fall asleep. I have at least two sleepless nights a week, and then I read articles. Or watch reruns of the Storytellers' Festival and try to identify familiar faces in the audience of the Givatayim Theater. And make myself a glass of hot milk. And go over to the drawer where the medications are to take a sleeping pill. But I don't take any out of the fear that I'll become addicted. And I look in the mirror, and see in it Shlomo, my twin brother, the way he might have looked if he weren't dead. Then I go back to bed and try to sleep on Niva's side. Then return to my side. And fall asleep. And my recurring nightmare flashes through my mind: I'm being bombarded by bullets on the main street of Suez City and I search for cover but don't find any, search for cover but don't find any. And I wake up, waiting in vain for Niva to tell me that everything will be fine. And I think: If only she had an identical twin sister. A living memento. Then I get up for another glass of milk and see the previous glass, dirty, on the living-room cabinet. And I think: With Niva, that would never happen. And I think: It's chronic, this longing of mine for her. Chronic. And I turn on my phone and go through our old texts.

Most of them are practical. Pick me up. Don't forget to buy. I left something for you in the fridge. But occasionally, like gold, a "Chicken Little" glitters between us. Or even a "My love."

Until I switched my subscription to Haaretz newspaper to a subscription to their Internet site, the rumble of a motorcycle and the thud of the rolled-up newspaper hitting the door signaled the end of the night. But on Monday morning, it was a knock at the door.

The walk from my bedroom to the front door gave me enough time to picture Liat standing there, with a stethoscope in her hand. And to be horrified by a more likely possibility, that it wasn't Liat standing there but her mother, her hand in the air ready to slap my face as soon as I opened the door.

But on the other side of the door stood a man.

He was holding a huge tray of sweets.

I couldn't remember where I knew him from, but I nevertheless bowed my head modestly and said, Thank you, thank you from the bottom of my heart. I planned to add, This wasn't necessary, really, it wasn't, I was just doing my job.

But then he said, in a strong Arabic accent, I'm sorry for your loss.

Seeing my puzzled expression, he added, Your wife helped my son. Because of your wife, my son is alive.

I looked at him with new interest. He was dressed in an unusual combination of elegance and sloppiness: A university lecturer's jacket covered a T-shirt, and below the hems of his fancy cloth pants were dirty white sneakers.

Come in, why are you standing outside like that, I said.

It's okay, the man said, glancing around quickly, and handed me the tray.

I said, There's no need, really, it's too much.

Looking resentful, he said, Respect me, please.

From the way he shifted his weight from foot to foot, I could make a fairly accurate guess that he also suffered from chronic lower back pain. And that for him, like for me, the hardest thing was standing straight right after he got out of his car.

I took the tray.

He almost started to leave, then changed his mind, took his phone out of his pocket, and held it out to me. A small boy with big eyes shaded by uncut bangs, wearing a Barcelona soccer uniform, stared out of the screen, smiling innocently.

That's Omar, he said. When he was eight, he looked like he was three. Nothing grew. Even his heart was small. And his lungs. On Saturdays, a mobile clinic comes to our neighborhood. I mean, a Jewish one. The doctor there said it was very dangerous, we have to treat him. There are hormones but they're very expensive. Not subsidized. And then your wife got the pills for us. She brought them to our house by herself. Free. I... When she didn't come to the clinic, I asked where she was. Then I wanted to come to her shiva. With my boy. But the border was closed, you understand?

I nodded.

Your wife was—he said, then stopped, searching for the right word—a very good woman.

Yes.

Islam rasak. May... your mind be peaceful. That's what we say in Arabic.

Thank you.

Yalla, I have to go back to work, the man said, turned around, and left me with the huge tray in my hands.

I put the tray on the dining-room table. I tasted tiny bits of the baklava, the knafeh, and the other sweets on it, and as I did, I wondered about the way two people who have been together for many years allow themselves to hand over entire areas of life to the exclusive responsibility of the other.

I was responsible for dealing with the bank. For the weekend shopping in the supermarket. For filling out forms. For paying fines. For writing birthday wishes. For preparing the cars for winter. And for getting the air conditioners ready for summer.

Niva was responsible for, among other things, our political conscience.

For the first few years, she still used to suggest that I join Saturday activities. I look out for the human rights of the patients in my department, I would tell her, that's hard enough. And I knew my response conveyed a tinge of superiority over someone who chose to work for a profit-making pharmaceutical company, and perhaps that's why she felt the need—which I felt exempt from—to make up for that by doing something for the general good.

For the first few years, she still told me about the experiences she had as a volunteer. She tried to infect me with her enthusiasm. Showed me pictures of sick people, read me letters of thanks. Urged me. Come on, Chicken Little, how long will you sit on the fence.

Later on, she gave up on me. And when I would ask, How was it?, she would brush me off with general answers. Or say that she was too tired to talk. Or shift the conversation toward ideology, deliver fiery speeches, and then be disappointed in me again when I wasn't prepared to say amen to her ever more radical views, implying that I had no moral backbone.

I moved the remaining sweets to a smaller tray, which I covered in plastic wrap so I could take it to the department. I looked at the clock. I still had half an hour before I had to go to work. A bit pressured, but that's all there was. I went to the shelf of records and looked for an appropriate soundtrack. I couldn't decide between several options, but finally chose Cat Stevens. Something in his voice, Niva always used to say, is clean. And she also said, The way he plays the guitar. It sounds as if he's sitting around a campfire with us. I put the needle on the grooves before the first song and sat down on the couch. Cat Stevens began to strum. And then the song, "Where Do the Children Play?" And then, almost in a whisper, I began to tell the Niva in my mind about my agonizing indecision. First she chuckled that séances were really not her thing. And why Cat Stevens? He converted to Islam. Then she grew serious. And listened.

While I was on the way to the hospital, the lawyer called.

I got the results from Genetics, I replied before he asked.

So? he urged me, his voice particularly tense.

Liat and I are not related by blood, I said.

Oka-a-ay, he lengthened the last syllable as if he were trying to decide what to do now, and I could imagine him running his hand along his tie.

Silence on the line. A juggler wearing a pointed hat was juggling balls in the air at the traffic light. One of them fell and he picked it up and kept juggling. I had the thought that maybe this would be the last time I took this route to the hospital. After all, the committee had the authority to order my immediate suspension from work. And then: Walking down the main corridor to the department, a barrage of looks fired at me from every direction. And then: Collecting my personal items into a box. Riding down to the parking area in the elevator. And then: The item in the newspaper. The phone call from Yaela in the middle of the night. The surprise in her voice. Still more surprised than shocked. Is it true, what they wrote in the newspaper, Dad? Did you really do what they say you did?

Did you do what I asked? Did you write down what happened, step by step? The lawyer interrupted the stream of my horrific scenarios.

Yes, of course, I replied.

So I suggest that tonight we go over what you wrote and rehearse it. I don't want them to trip you up with a question you can't answer.

Fine.

In the meantime, I'll prepare the legal side. I found a few interesting precedents. Even if they suspend you, there's no reason you should lose your benefits. We'll meet at the entrance to the hospital director's office at eight forty-five in the morning.

As I read everything I'd written up to this point, it became clear to me that actually, those pages contained mainly what I couldn't say to the committee. That without realizing it, and quite thoroughly, I had mapped out all the things that had to remain outside its discussions—if I didn't want to add to Liat's pain.

So what about me? Chills ran down my spine. What will I say in my defense when I'm in the hot seat tomorrow? How will I find shelter from the who-would-have-believed-it look of the people there, some of whom certainly know me, went to school with me, perhaps worked with Niva for a period of time. I'm no longer a child, I can no longer escape to the bathroom and hide out there with a copy of *Dune* until the storm passes. And what, damnit, if I can't be a doctor anymore? I never took a skipper course or a tour guide course, professionally, it's who I am—

To anesthetize my anxieties, I watched the fifth, deciding round of the French Open. Thirty-seven-year-old Roger Federer against thirty-one-year-old Novak Djokovic. Actually, it was a rerun of the match. But there are advantages to being alone: There's no danger that someone might accidently reveal the results.

Federer was leading. As always, he played more elegantly and even scored a few points in the set. But in the end, he lost, as expected, to the younger, more flexible Serb.

Before going to sleep, I took one last look at the image of Liat in the orienteering race on Google and enlarged it a bit. Her yellow tank top with the thin straps emphasized her dark skin, her neck glistened with sweat, and the gold metal rested two fingers above her cleavage— the exact spot my hand had fallen on.

Only after a long minute of staring at the cleavage did I realize: My pulse had quickened. My throat had grown dry. And involuntarily, desire arose in me.

I slammed the computer closed in horror.

Where have you been? Why don't you answer your phone? My lawyer asked cheerfully at eight forty-five in the morning in the hospital director's office. I turned it off, I explained. I didn't want any distractions before the meeting.

The meeting's been called off, Doctor.

Called off?

Ben Abu withdrew her complaint!

Goldberg's secretaries pretended they weren't listening to our conversation, but the taut tendons in their necks made it clear that they weren't missing a single syllable.

I pulled the lawyer out of the director's office.

What do you mean, withdrew the complaint? Why would she do something like that? I asked in a hushed voice, almost a whisper, and a reason suddenly occurred to me: Maybe Yafit had told her as a preventative step.

I don't know, Doctor, the lawyer continued happily and too loudly, and I don't care.

So that's it? I go on with my life?

No complaint—no committee, the lawyer said. Goldberg asked to speak to you face-to-face, but I assume he just wants to feel like he's had the last word.

Look at that, Asher, Goldberg said. He was standing at the aquarium and gesturing for me to come closer.

I moved closer.

He pointed to a small fish, silver-gray with black diagonal stripes that was swimming relatively quickly around the small corner rocks.

I saw that it was alone, so I brought it a mate. And what did the fish do? Ate it. And there's no one to complain to. No one who will explain why it did such a stupid thing. It's as silent as a fish, you might say.

I nodded.

Come, sit down, he said, pointing to a chair.

I sat down.

He lit his pipe and smiled broadly at me. Did you hear my sigh of relief at seven this morning? Did it reach all the way to your apartment in Hadar Yosef?

I smiled back, automatically.

Asher, Asher, he went on, you have no idea how upset I was about that whole story and how happy I am that it's behind us.

I'm happy it's behind us as well, Ronnie.

But Asher—he leaned so far over to me that his entire body was almost lying on the huge, empty desk—we need to be sure it won't happen again.

Of course.

Things are not like they used to be, Asher, there are apps.

Apps?

You can meet women easily. All kinds and colors. All you have to do is open a profile for yourself, and the rest will take care of itself. You can find love with the help of those apps. And you can also find comfort. If you know what I mean. Too much loneliness is dangerous, Asher. An excess of loneliness is the number-one reason people do stupid things. A person who is alone for too long begins to lose touch with reality. Starts to think, for example, that a girl his daughter's age can really be attracted to him. Do you understand what I'm saying?

Yes, I do.

In general, residents and nurses are not a good idea, Asher. You had a miraculous escape this time. I have no idea why Ben Abu withdrew the complaint. Sometimes they do it only because they don't have the emotional strength to relive the experience during an investigation. That's why many sexual harassment cases are closed. Not for lack of evidence but for lack of strength. But if there's another complaint against you, Asher, one more complaint, that will mean a pattern. And a pattern is what counts in such things. So, with all due respect, and with all the friendship between us, you'll be out of here so fast you won't know what hit you. Do you understand me?

Yes, I do.

The phone rang. He picked up the receiver, put a hand on the mouthpiece, and said, It's the deputy minister's office. I have to take it. Only good news from now on, eh?

I walk to the department. The automatic doors open without any delay. I put on my white coat and start my rounds, a cluster of residents trailing behind me. Liat, of course, is not among them. No one mentions her. No one wonders out loud: Where has Liat Ben Abu disappeared to? We walk from bed to bed to bed to bed. A remark Liat made during one of our coffee-cart conversations echoes in my mind: We hurry out of the patients' rooms as if we're running away from something. The beeping of monitors is everywhere. It's always everywhere. But today, for some reason, I'm more aware of it. I hesitate slightly with the first patients. Or more precisely, I'm slightly absent. But gradually, my voice steadies and I return to my body.

Lying in the last bed is a woman of about fifty who is in terrible pain. She moans even more loudly as we gather around her bed. Patients sometimes do that when the doctor is there, the way children do when they want to call out to their parents. I ask her questions. I'm compassionate. Finally, I ask one of the residents to summarize her case. He gives details on all the tests and X-rays that had been done to locate the source of the pain, explaining that there were no findings, and ends with a suggested diagnosis: Fibro. Not fibro so fast, I say. And ask for two final tests.

The woman says, Can I ask what fibro is? I explain to her that it's short for fibromyalgia, pains that have no immediate medical explanation. What do you mean, no explanation? The woman said with a groan. Is that why I've been in the hospital for a week already? To hear that you have no idea what's wrong with me?

There is a group of illnesses—I maintain a patient tone, not allowing even the minutest trace of impatience to come through in my voice—called cryptogenic illnesses because their cause is unknown. That doesn't mean that they can't be treated or we can't ease your pain.

But it really hurts, Doctor, she says. And I say, I know, and I don't minimize the importance of that. Would you like us to increase the dosage of the painkillers we're giving you? I ask, and she nods. I take out the syringe of morphine that I always keep in my pocket, pass it to the resident, and say to my patient, I'll come back at three to check on you. But don't kill me if I'm a few minutes late. She smiles a sick person's smile, which always has a bit of sadness in it. But nonetheless—a smile. That remark always works for me. And I don't care that the residents have heard it hundreds of times already.

I continue on to two surgical consultations. And to an X-ray meeting. Then I return to her bed at five after three. She's asleep. I write a note—*I hope your pain is better. See you again at rounds nine o'clock tomorrow morning. Best, Dr. Caro*—and ask the nurse to give it to her when she wakes up. I've learned over the years that uncertainty is worse than pain.

I go over to the head nurse to order a few tests. She answers my questions without any hesitation, and tells me, among other things, that Yona the amputee is recovering from surgery, his condition is stable, and he'll be back in the department to stabilize his diabetes. Death had come to visit him, then turned around and left.

I take off my lab coat and drive home. I open the car window to let a bit of the outside in. There's a yellow blooming outside, but it's not really spring. Every year, Niva used to get hoarse this time of year, at the change of seasons, and when we were in Toronto, she actually lost her voice. I should be relieved. But instead, I feel heartburn, as if I'm having emotional reflux, because the acids rising in my esophagus come from sour feelings.

At home, I turn on Niva's phone and stare at her screen saver for a long time: the four of us at the entrance to a Bob Dylan show at the Royal Albert Hall in London, happy that we'd managed to get tickets from a scalper at the last minute. We still didn't know that the performance would be terrible and that it would include an especially lackluster version of "Blowin' in the Wind," after which a woman in the audience fainted, apparently in protest. And so I found myself—after cries of "Is there a doctor in the house?"— trying to revive her in a side room while the audience in the hall continued to applaud in the vain hope that Dylan would be decent enough to do an encore. I focus on Niva's expression in the picture. All of her says contentment. She had the extraordinary ability to feel contented. Really and truly contented.

For me, there was always something missing.

I tap Messages, hesitate for the last time, trying to decide how to phrase it, and in the end, I send Liat two words: *Thank you.*

She didn't answer me. The two gray checks that turned blue indicated that she saw the message. And chose not to respond.

Her Facebook page remained silent in the weeks that followed.

I checked it constantly. Even during Skype conversations with Assaf and Sarah, which had become more frequent because of the desire they both had to consult with me about the developing pregnancy—

I would surf, under the table, to Liat's page.

And over and over again, I'd find that no new pictures had been uploaded. And no tirade against senior doctors who exploit their position of power to harass young female residents.

With half an ear, while typing discharge forms, I heard the Head Gossip tell one of the nurses that Dr. Ben Abu had decided to take a year off from her residency and travel to Bolivia as part of a Doctors Without Borders delegation. Then—as I pretended to be totally focused on a patient's file—the Head Gossip began telling the nurse about the results of the genetic test her husband had taken a while ago.

You won't believe it, she said.

So tell me, what?

Nine percent of his genes come from the Australian continent.

No kidding.

It seems that some aboriginal did it with his grandmother's grandmother. I think we'll have to take a trip there this year to find his roots.

They both laughed briefly. A workplace laugh. The laugh of two women who have enormous responsibilities and can take a break from them for only a moment, no longer.

A sharp pain shot through my lower back as I continued to "read" the files.

To keep from standing crookedly and exposing my distress to everyone, I remained sitting, turning the office chair into a sort of improvised wheelchair and dragging myself in it from bed to bed to bed while doing my rounds.

Later, when the pain had diminished somewhat, I went down to the coffee cart and stood in the short line, but when it was my turn, I couldn't buy anything. The coffee-cart girl gave me an inquiring look and asked loudly, Yes, sir? I looked at her and asked, Is it okay if I stand here, next to the counter, for just a minute? And she nodded and said, But move aside a little, sir, so you won't be in other people's way.

I moved aside a little and stood in front of the sugar stand. I supported my lower back with one hand so I wouldn't collapse onto the floor, so I wouldn't end up flat on my back in front of patients and passersby. What do doctors do on the days they can't be doctors? I heard Liat's voice ask in my mind. What do doctors do when their lives are just too big for them?

A few months later, I heard the sound of a new message on Niva's phone. I went over to it, expecting I'd find, as always, a request from someone who wanted to interest her in a new start-up, and I'd have to give them the bad news.

There was an image on the message.

It took me a few seconds to see that it was Liat. Her long hair was cropped now, in the style of that Irish singer, I think her name is O'Connor, and her eyes looked larger and seemed to glow in her suntanned face.

She was wearing a doctor's white coat over a black T-shirt and pants with pockets on the sides, and her smile was so broad and so relaxed and confident that the stethoscope lying on her chest seemed to be responding with a smile of its own.

She was holding an Indigenous child, about four or five years old, in her arms. A flat nose, thick lips, black hair divided by crooked parts and gathered into two braids. She was wearing a kind of cloth, or sack, and two strings were tied around her wrist, one green, the other yellow.

The girl wasn't looking at the camera. Her eyes were fixed on Liat, as if to say: I trust you. I have faith in you. What would I do without you.

Under the picture Liat had added two sentences from the book we both love:

Proper teaching is recognized with ease. You can know it without fail because it awakens within you that sensation which tells you this is something you have always known.

In a Skype conversation with Assaf a few days later, he told me that the tests they had been so afraid of were fine. And also that Sarah felt better.

Maybe it would still be a good idea to give birth in Israel? I asked, and he said, I don't think so, Dad, our whole life is here. And after a brief silence, he added, but you're invited to come. I mean, I spoke to Sarah about it and both of us would be really happy if Niva . . . Did I tell you that Sarah agreed to the name?

You wrote to me about it, I said (and didn't say that instead of happiness, I had felt such profound sorrow that big Niva would not get to meet little Niva that I couldn't reply).

In short, Assaf went on, it would be great if little Niva knew her grandfather from day one. Besides, what could be better than our own live-in doctor? Do you think you can ask for a month or two off without pay? Let's say starting around the beginning of October?

I booked a plane ticket to Montreal.

One way.

Then I put the Schubert record on the phonograph: Sonata no. 664 in A Major.

Ta-ta-tam, tam-ta-ta-ta-tam—

The piece opens with the melody I love so much, and then it's woven into it over and over again, sounding different each time:

Like a children's game.

Like an invitation to dance.

Like a heart pounding after a near accident.

Like a severe scolding.

Like relief after pain.

Like growing old.

Like something you were able to grasp for a moment, and then lost once again.

Evening turned into night outside my window. The house is empty. There are no sounds of children coming from the living room.

Water is not running along Niva's body in the shower. The Schubert sonatas continue to play in the background, the volume low.

If I have to confess everything, this is the time.

A MAN
WALKS INTO
AN ORCHARD

Author's Note

In the title and throughout the story there are references to the Talmudic treatise about four Jewish sages who go into an orchard (*pardes* in Hebrew, which also refers to the "orchard" of esoteric biblical knowledge and critical interpretation), and only one emerges unscathed. A translation of the tractate appears at the end of the story.

February 2017

Ofer and I walk in the orchards every Saturday. Once we used to walk with the kids, but now that they're older, they like to get up later on Saturday. We get up early. I drink coffee. Ofer drinks fake coffee made from dates. We change into sports clothes, drive a few minutes, and leave the car at the barrier, even though it's usually open and some people drive straight through. Inside, we walk on the bicycle path that was paved a few years ago, and if someone on a bike comes along, we step off it. The orchards bear fruit three months a year, from December to February. Oranges, grapefruits, clementines. There was one year when the owners tried to grow red grapefruit. It apparently didn't work, because later on, we didn't see them anymore.

On the way, I pick an orange for myself, if there are any, and Ofer always protests. Says it's not right. That it's like those Israelis who steal faucets in hotels. Nature belongs to all of us, I say. And hand him a segment. And he always gives in and takes it. When I think about it, he didn't take the orange slice I offered him that Saturday. I held out a juicy orange segment and he didn't take it. But how could I have known it was a sign? As always, we walked down toward the garbage dump where garbage hasn't been dumped for years, which is why the city was trying to rebrand it as the Hill of Love, and then we turned right in the direction of the sewage treatment plant. We usually walk a little ways past it to where we can see the houses of the adjoining moshav, but the smell coming from the plant was stronger than usual that day, so when I told Ofer I was nauseous and wanted to go back, he put a hand on my shoulder and said, Sure, no problem.

On the way back, two men ran past us, and one of them said good morning. Actually, it was Ofer who said good morning to them first, and they replied. It's a habit left over from the years he lived in America with his first wife. When he was there, he thought that good-morning, good-morning ritual was the essence of everything he couldn't stand about Americans. Now he himself did it. After they passed us, he was silent, and I knew that was because he was slightly jealous of them. Until his illness, he used to run and he even completed the Tel Aviv Half Marathon. In any case, I was sure those two men could have been located, and they would have confirmed that, at that point, Ofer and I were still walking side by side and not fighting or anything.

Not that we didn't fight sometimes on our Saturday walks. I get much angrier than he does, and a couple of times I even said, I don't want to talk anymore! Leave me alone! I'll go the rest of the way on my own! And he would wait for me, doing stretching exercises on the rocks. Because I cool down as quickly as I get worked up. When I'd come back, I'd already be missing him a little, and he looked so sexy in his running shorts and white T-shirt. Always white. And I would think to myself: That hunk is yours. Don't be like your mother, who wasted her life being annoyed with your father over every little thing, until one day he had a stroke and died. Then she turned him into a saint and went to his grave every Friday to summarize for him everything that had happened that week in Israel and the world.

I don't think Ofer is dead. Even though I know that, with every day that passes and he's not found, that possibility makes the most sense. And even though, at night, I dream the same dream over and over again in which his side of the bed turns into an abyss.

What did we fight about? The kids. Of course. Mainly when they were little. I didn't understand how he could be so calm about them. He didn't understand why I was so stressed. I couldn't stand the fact that he turned me into the bad guy in front of them. He couldn't stand the fact that I criticized them. I don't have much faith in psychologists and went grudgingly for therapy with Ofer, but something Ami, the psychologist, said during one of our sessions is etched in my mind: "There are parents who love their children from the bottom up, and others who love theirs from the top down." Meaning that there are parents who, first of all, need to calm their worries, and only then can they appreciate their children. And there are parents who, first of all, have to appreciate their children, and only then are they willing to see what still worries them.

That remark clarified things for me. Maybe it did for Ofer too. Or maybe the kids just grew up and buried themselves in their phones (Matan) or in their social lives (Ori), and now, we're mostly grateful for every minute they're kind enough to spend in our presence.

What else did Ofer and I fight about? Real estate. And sex. Real estate because I wanted us to take out a loan and buy an apartment as an investment and he said that buying an apartment as an investment is for rich people and he wasn't prepared to put himself under that kind of pressure. And sex because as soon as he changed his eating habits, his desire to sleep with me dwindled. Or maybe the change in his eating habits was an excuse and after eighteen years together, he was tired of me. In any case, it hurt. It hurts that you always have to be the one to initiate and it hurts that he doesn't get a hard-on when he's in bed with you and you have to go down on him for hours to turn him on. But what hurts the most is that while you're having sex, you realize that he's actually doing you a favor. Maybe you should take Viagra? I would say every once in a while. Not only to hurt him back but also because I thought it might really help. But that would only push him further away. Viagra? You must be kidding, he'd say. What am I, a hundred years old? Besides, you know very well that I'm against pills, he'd say. Or he wouldn't say anything, he'd just turn his back to me and go to the balcony and invite Ori to have one of their heart-to-hearts, or drive with Matan to a Hapoel Jerusalem basketball game, or call a meeting of the NGO for that night—anything to go to bed after I'd fallen asleep.

Until lately, I would tell Ofer about guys who came on to me in the hope it would excite him. Some of the stories were true and some I made up. For example, I created a thirty-year-old guy named Nitai who'd begun working in our office recently and was constantly flirting with me. With every description, I laid it on thicker. First Nitai only made eyes at me. Then he said something flattering about the skirt I was wearing. Then he began saying things like, "You smell fantastic. Is that perfume or body cream?" Or "That neckline can't be legal." Or "Would you like to go out for a drink after work?"

Have a drink with him if you want to so much, Ofer said during one of our walks in the orchard. He was trying to sound indifferent, or maybe he really was indifferent, I couldn't tell. Which alarmed me so much that I said, You're kidding, right? He's just a kid. I'm not into him at all. I'm into you.

I'm trying to re-create the final moments now. We were walking hand in hand. Yes, hand in hand. Feeling good about each other that morning. A van carrying three, possibly four Thai workers passed us. Their faces were covered with a kind of cowl, and one of them waved hello at us. At the time, I used to hear that the Thai workers from in the orchards ate dog meat, and that all the dogs that had gone missing in the neighborhood had actually been taken by them to their rickety old shed behind the garbage dump and cooked in a large pot every evening. But I don't believe they did anything to Ofer. And even before that, I thought the rumor about the dogs was out-and-out racism. In fact, I'm quoting Ofer. That's what he called it, "Out-and-out racism."

After the Thai workers had passed, we heard music in the distance. Trance party music.

A nature party, Ofer said.

We haven't been to a nature party for so long, I said.

Not since the Dead Sea.

Could be, I said.

I wonder where it is.

It's coming from the direction of the garbage dump, isn't it?

The Hill of Love, please call it that, Ofer said.

There's that flat area between the hill and the Thai workers' shed, I said, perfect for a party.

Maybe it's where the horse farm is.

Never thought of that, I said.

We didn't speak for a few moments because we'd reached the steep climb before the vehicle barrier, and it's not easy to talk while you're climbing it. When we reached the barrier, Ofer said, I'm dying to pee. Hold my phone for a minute? Sure, I said. And he walked onto a path between a row of trees while I waited for him on the road. A minute. Another minute. Another minute.

He didn't come out.

I called him, and his phone vibrated in my pocket. Then I remembered and walked into the same row of trees he'd walked into and called him: Ofer! Ofer! He didn't answer. My heart began pounding. I pushed away branches and searched through the green of the trees and the gold of the oranges for the white of his T-shirt, but didn't see it. So I went back to the road. Because I thought I might have picked the wrong row, and maybe he'd come out of the orchard while I was in it. But he wasn't there. Right then, an old man wearing a helmet came walking by, and I stopped him and asked if he'd seen a man in black athletic shorts and a white shirt. He said no, and asked what had happened. I told him, and he asked, Do you want me to help you look for him?

I said, I don't know, I don't want to bother you, maybe I'm making a mountain out of a molehill.

He took off his helmet and, sounding like the old-timers who had been soldiers in the Palmach, he said, Miss, this is Israel, we always have to be on our guard.

Again, we entered the row of trees. Again I called out his name. Again he didn't reply. The old soldier also shouted his name in his hoarse voice. Then we returned to the road and I was so stressed that I began to cry. I hadn't cried for so many years. Bike riders and hikers stopped and asked what had happened. Suddenly I couldn't speak. I couldn't get a single word out of my mouth. So the old man explained to them. Someone said, Call home. Maybe he's already there. So I called Ori, who answered in a sleepy-annoyed voice: Mom, I'm sleeping. I wanted to ask whether Dad was home, but I couldn't get a word out. So I handed the phone to the old man, who said, Hello dear, I'm here with your mother and she wants to know if your father is home. I heard

Ori's voice say, Just a minute, I'll check. A few minutes later, I heard her say, No.

Later, everyone who went out walking or riding in the orchards that Saturday joined in the search. Ori came as well. Matan stayed home. At the time, we still didn't know why. People walked in the rows between the trees, trampled on leaves and rotten fruit searching for a man who resembled the man in the picture I found on my cell phone, which had been taken a few years earlier at one of the events held by his NGO. He was standing next to the donors, wearing a slightly-too-large suit, his Adam's apple prominent, as always, his hair a bit mussed, and his eyes—the reason I fell in love with him—shone at the camera. I wanted to tell them that when he's excited, they flash yellow sparks. And when he smiles, they slant almost the way the Thai workers' eyes do. But my throat had completely dehydrated. As if a barrier of dryness had developed near my uvula, preventing words from passing. So I just showed the picture to anyone who asked and remained standing on the road, paralyzed with fear. I couldn't move my legs. I couldn't move my arms. When the sun stood high in the sky, someone came up to me and asked, Did you call the police? And someone else said, They won't come. The rule is that they have to wait at least twenty-four hours before they declare a person missing. And the first someone answered him, Not if they suspect terrorism. She has to tell them that she saw someone in a kaffiyeh running away through the bushes or something like that.

But I couldn't say anything. Not a thing. So I handed my phone to the Palmachnik, who called the police and said authoritatively to whoever answered that they couldn't wait because there was no way of knowing who had ambushed Ofer in the orchard, and maybe we were in the middle of a terrorist kidnapping, and anyone who knows anything about terrorist kidnappings knows that the first few hours are critical. His silences between one sentence and the next grew longer, making me think that whoever was on the other end of the line was taking him seriously. A few minutes later—it might have been more, because at that point, I'd lost my sense of time—the police arrived and closed off the area, because if a gang of terrorists was involved, there was a chance that its members were still in the vicinity, and as much as they appreciated the efforts to mobilize the general population to help in the search, they couldn't allow ordinary citizens to wander around the orchard without weapons or supervision.

They asked me whether I had any idea of who might want to hurt Ofer. I shook my head. Nevertheless, during the drive to the police station, I texted Dan: *Are you there?*

We agreed not on Saturdays, he texted back.

Despite that, I wrote, *Ofer has disappeared.*

What do you mean, disappeared?

I texted a question, *Did you tell anyone about us?*

Of course not. Then he added, *I have to go. We're in the middle of a family dinner.*

I waited a little longer to see if he would write something nice like "Hugs" or "Everything will be fine," but he didn't even text his usual command: "Delete." So I decided that no matter how this business with Ofer ended, I was through with Dan and his grandmother's apartment in Holon. And I also knew that my decision was worthless.

At the station, they put me into a windowless room and left me there for an hour. Maybe three. Time moved differently, like in a dream you want to wake up from and no matter how much you bang on its walls, you can't. Then they took me out of the windowless room and led me to a room that had windows where a woman detective sat. She introduced herself as Tirza, and with her bob and starched collar, she reminded me of Hana Futterman, the Talmud teacher who once said to me, in front of the entire class, Chelli Dagan, why are you sitting there like some floozy, close your legs.

The detective asked me a lot of questions before she realized that I wasn't capable of answering: How is your relationship with your husband? Did he have an emotional crisis recently? Did he show signs of suicidal tendencies? Was he involved in political activity? Did he have a weapon at home?

She also said, We're pursuing several lines of inquiry at the moment. Look at me, please. You need to know that your silence is not doing you any good, Chelli. That was when the penny dropped, and I realized that I might be one of the lines of inquiry they were pursuing. I pressed my knees together before I was rebuked for that too. I took a pen and piece of paper from the table and wrote: *I'm not talking because I've lost my voice, not because I have something to hide. I feel like I'm in a dream.* Then I saw her right eye grow round with empathy while her left one continued to suspect me, because a detective like her had probably heard everything.

Then she said, Write. If you can't speak, write down your version of what happened. I didn't understand what "your version of what happened" meant. What other version could there be? Ofer went into the orchard and didn't come out. No one else was around when it happened. Who else besides me could tell them what happened there? But the detective handed me a pad of yellow paper and said, Let's go. When she saw my eyes widen, she explained, I believe that you're upset, but unless proven otherwise, we can't eliminate the possibility that you were involved in your husband's disappearance, and however unpleasant that may be, we need to do our jobs. At this very moment, we're scanning your cell phone, including texts you think you've deleted. And we've sent a policewoman to your home to pick up your laptop. In the end, we'll know everything we need to know about you, Chelli. Even now, we know quite a bit: You came to Israel from Argentina when you were seven. Your father, who was an opponent of the ruling military junta, was kidnapped and held by them for a few months, then unexpectedly released on the condition that he leave the country immediately—am I right so far? In the army, you were a combat fitness instructor and spent a month in a military jail for insubordination. You have a deep-sea diving license and a license to drive trucks. For the past five years, you've been teaching new immigrants at an immigrant absorption center, as a volunteer—good for you—and the Mamanet volleyball league chose you as their player of the season. The logistics company you've been working for as financial director for the last five years chose you as an outstanding employee, but you continue to conceal from your colleagues the fact that you still have to complete a paper to actually receive your master's degree and not just claim you have it. Do you understand, Chelli? There's no point trying to hide things from us. The more you share real information with us, the better our chances of finding your husband.

I wanted to tell her that they were absolutely on the wrong track.

I wanted to tell her that if something happened to him, if something really happened to him, I'd lose my mind.

But I was incapable of speaking.

So I picked up the pen and wrote down everything that had happened from the moment we went out for a walk in the orchard, minute after minute.

Then I left a line empty, as if I'd pressed Enter on the computer keyboard, and added a question: *What about the terrorism angle? Are you really checking it or has the Israeli police decided to focus all its efforts on me?* She picked up the page, read what I'd written and nodded slowly, as if I had disappointed her.

Then she said, Your husband's disappearance, Mrs. Raz, has none of the characteristics of terrorism. There were no warnings about the possibility of a terrorist kidnapping in that area. No organization has taken responsibility for a kidnapping. But even so, we and other security forces are taking actions to eliminate that possibility. I understand, she went on, that you're worried, but I need you to help me help you. What you wrote here— she pointed to the page—is not enough. You gave me basic information. Thank you. But I need us to go deeper into the things that are not so nice to talk about, okay?

As I nodded, I thought about Dan, but she said, As a beginning, I'd like you to write five things that people don't know about Ofer. And please, don't write only the things you think are relevant to the investigation. You don't know what is or isn't relevant for us. And sometimes, it's the seemingly minor things that give us the lead we're looking for. Hobbies, deviations, secrets from the past, anything goes.

She kept that page, but I remember clearly what I wrote.

1. His illness. Autoimmune. Very rare. Strikes only one in one hundred thousand people. Ofer decided to treat it with yoga and extreme changes in his nutrition. He amazed his doctors by pretty much succeeding. The attacks disappeared almost completely. But still, there are things he can't do anymore. Like running a half marathon or rowing a kayak. Or carrying me to bed.

2. His first wife was much more beautiful than me, but a total nutcase. Among other things, she threw a kitchen knife at him and tried to run him over with their SUV. He ran away from her and from the States in the middle of the night, without leaving so much

as a farewell note. And came back to Israel penniless.

3. During the years after he left his American wife, he threw himself completely into nature parties. Including drugs. Including dancing himself into unconsciousness. Including trying to hitchhike after a party, stark naked, on the road to the Dead Sea, and being stopped by the police (I don't think he has a criminal record).

4. He stopped all that after we had the kids. Ofer was born to be a father. Really. For me, being a parent is all trial and error, but for him, being a father came naturally from the first minute. Actually, people might know that about him. He opened an interactive forum for fathers when the kids were still small, where he shares experiences and sometimes gives advice, "Not as an expert but just as someone who's been there."

5. He posts short stories under a pseudonym. He has a blog called "One Hundred Times One Hundred." His dream is to complete one hundred stories of one hundred words each, and then publish a book. Just last week he posted his ninety-ninth story.

I choked down a powerful wave of panic that rose in me as I wrote, and handed the page with the five items to Tirza. I hadn't written with a pen for years, only the computer keyboard, so my hand was already hurting.

Tirza read it and asked, What's the pseudonym he used on his blog? I was surprised that, of all things, that was what interested her, but nonetheless I answered, Zalman International, and rolled my eyes so it would be clear that no matter how much I loved my husband, I thought it was an idiotic name. Let's see what the last thing Zalman posted was, she said and typed the name into the search engine. Maybe we'll find something there.

I knew what she'd find there. I could have recited that story by heart. And, in fact, all the stories that Ofer posted.

A Fraction of a Person
A question in my daughter's arithmetic notebook:
There are x number of pupils in a class, divided into
groups. How many are there in each group? It's
my day with her, so I'm helping her. Even though
math is her mother's field. Her solution is three and
three-quarters per group. There's a mistake, I say,
you can't have a fraction of a person. We find the mis-
take. The next day, I drive her to school slowly, trying

to extend the moment to infinity, because I know that when she gets out of the car, my meter will reset.

It's interesting, the detective said, that he writes as if he's a divorced man.

It's only a story, I wrote on the pad and showed it to her.

You can't really know, she said, maybe Ofer had been feeling like "a fraction of a person" recently?

We all feel like that sometimes, don't we? I wrote. And saw how her right eye grew round with empathy and her left eye continued to be suspicious.

Can I text my kids? I wrote and showed her the pad again, focusing on her right eye.

She nodded and handed me her phone.

I wrote to Ori: *Hi Oriki, I'm in the police station. Without a phone. I'm trying to give them as much information as possible about Dad so they can find him. I hope you're okay. A policewoman will come to take my laptop. You can give it to her. And don't get stressed. It's part of their procedure. I'm texting you now on the detective's phone. You can text me anything you think is important to this phone.*

I changed the word "detective" to "policewoman," and sent the text.

The detective took her phone from me and read what I had sent.

Tirza said, She's really something, your daughter.

I looked at her, puzzled. How do you know?

She got all the Girl Scouts in her troop to go out searching, she said. After we made sure there were no terrorists in the orchard, we gave them the green light, and for the last few hours, they've been combing the area in groups.

Is Matan with them? I wrote.

As of now, your son is at home. I'd say that...he has a slightly different approach to the whole thing.

Different approach?

A policeman came into the room, gave her a document, and left. She read it and looked up at me questioningly.

Who is Dan Medini and what is your relationship to him?

That's none of your business! I wrote. With an assertive exclamation point. But inside, I felt as defeated as a little girl who's been found in a game of hide-and-seek.

Your son gave us his phone number. That's how we found your correspondence, Mrs. Raz. Documented on these pages are all the texts you exchanged over the past year.

This new information—Matan knows about Dan— struck me like a blow. Once, when I was playing Mamanet, a ball hit me in the face, and I had the same feeling now. Dizziness. The sense that I was about to fall down.

The pain that began after a delay. Why didn't he say anything to me? My poor baby. Walking around with a secret like that. It's no wonder he's been so down recently.

Mrs. Raz, she continued in the tone of a teacher explaining something to a child, if you had an extramarital affair your son knows about, it's possible your husband might have known too, and that might have something to do with his disappearance. And if your lover, or someone related to him, has a motive to hurt your husband, that could also have something to do with his disappearance.

I took a page and wrote at the top of it: Dan Medini. Lover. Then I wrote: I'm ready to tell you everything so you can understand why there's no way Dan is connected to Ofer's disappearance and not waste energy following that up while Ofer might be in danger. But you have to promise me that if you get in touch with Dan, you'll do it discreetly. We're talking about peoples' lives here.

Tirza read it, nodded in agreement, and gave me back the page.

Before I continued writing, I erased the word "lover." It suddenly looked inappropriate. After all, there isn't and never has been any love between me and Dan.

He came to a meeting in our office on a Sunday. Maybe if he'd come on a Monday, nothing would have happened. But I'd just been through a Saturday without a single tender touch from Ofer. And then that Dan came into the conference room with all those shoulders of his. The owner of a security company. Speaking softly. Barely audible. Hewing out every word with effort. Staring at me while the other people said words like "estimate" and "bonus," and on his way out of the room, found an excuse to get my email address. A price quote. Yes, he asked for my email address so he could consult with me, the financial director, about a price quote. Since when do you consult about a price quote? You give a price quote. And that's it.

Two hours later an email from him popped into my box. *I like you. I want to see you.* Just like that. Straight to it. No games, no question mark.

I don't think so. I'm happily married, I replied.

Me too, he wrote. *What time do you finish work today?*

He didn't pick me up from work that day. But he definitely picked me up two weeks after that. In the interim, we barely communicated. He didn't send me links to songs he loved, and I didn't write that I'd dreamt about him at night. It wasn't the way I'd imagined such things happen. We met in the backyard of a café in Ra'anana. It wasn't even dark yet. Next to us, on the wall, hung a photograph of old-fashioned scales like the ones that were in the grocery store in Buenos Aires where we bought a few things when we didn't want to go to the supermarket.

Dan didn't waste time on preambles.

His second sentence (the first was "Are you comfortable sitting next to the air conditioner or would you like to change places?") was "I want to put my cards on the table."

Then he told me about his son. The boy had been in a depression which, at first, they thought was just a mood and, later, just some adolescent thing that would pass. But then he took a whole packet of Nurofen, and Dan and his wife realized it was serious, and that their only mission in life for the next few years was to keep him alive until he stabilized. It had been going on for three years now, and it was wiping them out. Draining all their strength. And lately, he'd realized that he had to do something to counterbalance that stress. Something that would reenergize him. And then he saw me at the meeting, laughing, enthusiastic, constantly moving my hands when I spoke.

He put his hand on mine when he finished speaking. And I didn't move it.

Because as he spoke, I received an answer to my burning question: No, there was no chance I would fall in love with him. He was inarticulate. Not stupid but inarticulate. He had no sense of humor. And no layers. What he was is what he was: broad shoulders, deep voice, and hungry eyes.

How about we go to a less public place? he suggested, and I nodded.

I have the keys to my dead grandmother's apartment in Holon, he said.

Together in your dead grandmother's bed. I smiled. Sexy.

He didn't smile back.

Are the sheets are clean there? I asked.

Ah, yes, sure, he said.

And that's how it began.

In American TV series, when there's adultery, it almost always destroys the marital relationship. But the truth is that sometimes the opposite happens. From the moment I started sleeping with Dan once every two weeks, then once a month, my relationship with Ofer only got better. I stopped feeling hurt. I stopped complaining. I was filled with gratitude for the freedom Ofer granted me, even though he didn't grant me anything officially. I wanted very much to repay him, even though he didn't know anything about it. Every time I saw Dan in his late grandmother's apartment on Kugel Street in Holon, which still smelled strongly of chicken soup and medicine, only made it clearer to me how much more Ofer was than Dan. More intelligent. More interesting. More fun. More everything. I was flooded with renewed love for my handsome man, and on the morning he walked into the orchard, we really had strolled hand in hand. Like high-school sweethearts.

I tore the page off the pad and handed it to the detective. While she was reading, I thought, this is the first time I've told anyone about Dan. How strange it is that even if that someone is a police detective with a starched collar and not a girlfriend, I felt relieved, the way you do after a confession. And I also thought: Where is Ofer now? Maybe the Thai workers are eating his spleen at this very moment. And I wondered: How did Matan know? And I thought: There's no way that detective won't judge me harshly. Very few women are willing to see an extra-marital affair as something that can help the marriage. That's exactly why I didn't tell my girlfriends anything.

The detective looked up from the page and said in a voice that seemed to hold some personal, not professional, anger: You seem very pleased with yourself, Mrs. Raz. I don't see even a drop of guilt feelings here.

I said nothing, and she went back to her professional tone: We'll have to talk to that Dan of yours. And at the same time, find out what his wife does or doesn't know. Revenge is a motive that shouldn't be taken lightly.

I gestured with my hand for her to give me back the page, and I wrote furiously, the speed distorting my hand-writing: You promised me you'd be discreet with this!

Besides, I'm telling you that you're wasting time with anything related to Dan and his family. Maybe instead of that, you should be questioning the Thai workers. Don't you think that's a more realistic direction to take?

We spoke to them, she said, and for the moment, we find no connection between them and your husband's disappearance.

For the moment? I wrote.

She ignored my question mark and continued with her own question marks. Who else could have wanted to harm your husband, Mrs. Raz?

No one, I wrote. And tears of frustration and despair began to fall from the corners of my eyes, because truly, no one would have wanted to harm my wonderful man. I didn't want the tears to flow. I didn't want to be that woman who cries during questioning. But I couldn't stop them either.

Do you want a glass of water? the detective asked. I wanted to say: I want a glass of water and a sleeping pill so I can go to sleep and wake up in two days, after you've found Ofer alive and well. Instead, I wrote: Yes, thank you. She went out and returned with a glass of water and let me sip and breathe before she said in her good-cop tone, Although you may have received a different impression, I'm on your side, Mrs. Raz, and I also want your husband to be found as quickly as possible. And alive.

But for that to happen, I need your help. I'd like you to make a list of all the circles he belonged to. And I'm asking you to make the effort to come up with the names of anyone in those circles who could have held a grudge against him. And why.

I took the yellow pad. Reluctantly.

First circle: Cool Dad—the fathers' forum. All its activities take place on the Net, except for the three or four times a year they meet for a barbecue. Why should anyone there hold a grudge against him? He was a volunteer and didn't make a penny. Maybe someone who . . . maybe advice he gave to someone on the forum led to disaster? That's hard for me to believe, even though I always told him he should avoid advising people because he really wasn't an expert.

Second circle: A Good Question—the NGO he established that helped young religious people, mainly from the ultra-Orthodox sector, during the first steps of their entry into the secular world. He himself had gone through that. Entirely alone. And it had been very hard for him. Yes, the ultra-Orthodox sector isn't crazy about that NGO, and they post notices on the walls in their neighborhood calling him a heretic and accusing him of encouraging young people to abandon their religion. But the truth is that he's very careful not to actively persuade people to cross the lines, only to help the ones who had already decided on their own. Maybe he hadn't been careful enough?

Third circle: His family in Modi'in Illit. They haven't spoken to him and he hasn't spoken to them for thirty years, except for his sister, who calls from a pay phone to wish him happy birthday once a year. Obviously they hold a grudge against him. But the act of cutting off all communication with their son is violent enough. I don't think they would go beyond that.

Fourth circle: The support group of people who suffer from the same disease he has. They were at our house several times. Gentle people, all of them. As if that illness struck gentle people in particular. The thought that one of them would harm Ofer seems very far-fetched.

I waited a little while longer, maybe I'd think of a fifth circle, and then handed her the page.

Without reading it, she said, Tell me, how open do you think your husband was with you? Before I could reply, she went on, While you were writing, I read another few stories on his blog. For instance, look at this, she said and handed me her phone.

Spots
Her husband said she should have them checked. So she went to see Dr. Bar, who was bending so close over her now that she smelled her every breath.

Sunspots, the doctor finally said, and she nodded in agreement, although she knew the truth: They were spots of impossible loves. During her married life, three loves had been removed from her heart, and each time, a heart-shaped spot appeared on her cheek. But we can't treat sunspots in summer, Dr. Bar said, because of the sun in this country. Come in at the beginning of winter and we'll discuss treatment.

And the one after it—even more disturbing, Tirza said.

The Robot Was the Only One

The robot, programmed to vacuum the floors, found her body. It bumped into different parts of it, retreated, and worked around them. The note lay near her ear. It sucked it in and shredded it.

During the shiva, it heard explanations of her actions. It noticed that human beings couldn't handle mysteries. It knew—its inner eye had scanned the letter before shredding it—that none of the explanations were exact, but didn't think it should correct the explainers, which included her husband. The truth, it had learned, tends to hurt human beings unnecessarily.

I didn't react after reading the stories. I knew them, of course. But maybe because the protagonists were women, I never thought they should worry me.

The detective continued, interpreting my lack of a response as an admission: Maybe when you were hiding a lover from him, Mrs. Raz, your husband was hiding a mental breakdown from you?

I averted my eyes.

Mrs. Raz, I want to repeat a question I've already asked you. Is there a chance that Ofer was suicidal?

I wrote: No. But the two letters were small, cramped, the n-o of a woman who was no longer sure she was right.

The detective's phone rang. After listening briefly, she said, She's here with me, and then asked, Can you send us a picture?

A moment later, we heard a text message sound. She turned the phone so I could see the screen and said, A member of the search team your daughter organized found this shirt. Near the railroad tracks. Do you recognize it?

November 2017

It happened at night, so at first I thought I was dreaming it. Dreaming that he was on my bed. Dreaming that he was stroking my head. So I asked him, Papi, is that really you? And he said, Pull my beard really hard and if it hurts, that's a sign it's me. So I pulled his beard. Not too hard. And he said, Aiee. Only then did I allow myself to cry.

Maybe because my dad once returned from hell, I was sure that at some point, Ofer would just show up too.

Because I am reading what I wrote nine months ago, I don't understand: How could I have been so complacent?

After they found Ofer's shirt, they also found his pants nearby, along with his underwear, sneakers, and socks.

They didn't find his body. For a few more months, the police continued to investigate, raided the houses of suspects in Modi'in Illit and Mea She'arim, questioned

Dan under caution, and even summoned me to a return interrogation when I got my voice back.

But in the end, they admitted they didn't have the faintest idea what had happened. Or in professional language, they didn't have any leads.

Their assumption was that Ofer had most likely cut through the orchards to the sea, a twenty-minute walk, tied a rock or something else to his leg, and drowned himself. But bottom line, they had no proof of that either.

I thought, and still think, that Ofer was too attached to the kids to abandon them like that. Without even a letter. But apart from Ori and me, everyone gave up. On the one hand, the case of Ofer's disappearance remained open because they couldn't close it without a body. The search, on the other hand, stopped and Tirza told me that we would have to wait until new information was uncovered. It happens in a lot of unsolved cases, she explained. Suddenly someone blurts out something during the investigation of another crime, or one of our undercover guys in prison breaks the case.

How much time can it take? I asked her. Years, she said. Then she put her hand on mine, for the first and last time, and said, Sometimes decades. I said, I love him, Tirza. Everything that happened with that Dan—

She interrupted me and said, I know.

Matan switched to boarding school. No matter how much I explained and apologized, he couldn't forgive me. If I hadn't been such a whore, it wouldn't have happened, he said one evening. His voice was changing, so he said the word "whore" in a high voice, a girl's voice, and that made me smile for a second. A fraction of a second. Which drove him crazy. You're smiling? What is there to smile about here, he said. If I put a knife to your throat, will you smile too? Or will you finally tell us where Dad is? He took a box cutter out of his pocket and waved it at me, then all at once he broke like a vase, collapsed in pieces at my feet, put his head in his hands as if he had a terrible migraine, and said, I can't anymore, I can't anymore, I can't anymore. And I thought, Neither can I, kid, neither can I, but I didn't say anything, I just stroked the air above his head.

The principal of the boarding school knew Ofer from the NGO, so he agreed to admit Matan in the middle of the year.

I sat in his office. Behind him was a picture of Golda Meir, the school's namesake. He said, It's just unbelievable what happened to Ofer. Unbelievable. And he also said, Matan looks very much like him, you must be aware of that. They're both so amiable on the surface, but hidden beneath that is a kind of... tenacity. Then he looked me in the eye and added, You know that, as parents, we're supposed to feel a sense of . . . failure if . . . our little chick wants to leave the nest, when really . . . really we should be proud of him for being able to spread his wings.

I nodded as if I agreed, but I still felt the sense of failure spread through me as we spoke, combining with the what-will-happen-to-my-child feeling and the Ofer-how-could-you-leave-me-to-deal-with-all-this-shit-alone feeling, and the what-is-it-about-me-that-pushes-everyone-away feeling—

I explained to the principal that it was a temporary arrangement. Until his anger passed. And he moved his head like someone who had seen too many times how temporary arrangements became permanent. Then he had me sign all sorts of forms, and no matter what form I signed, I felt as if I were signing away my son.

Several days later, Ori drove Matan to the boarding school. He wouldn't let me take him. And when I looked out the window at the car moving away, I thought, Once upon a time there was a family that is no more.

Dan cut off contact. After the police called him in for questioning, he sent me a short email: *We can't meet anymore. Sorry.*

And that was that. To my reply, *It's a shame, but I understand*, he didn't respond.

Judging from his Facebook page, his family was more of a family than ever, and every once in a while he would post a picture of them hiking in various places in the country, so either what happened in Holon had remained in Holon, or his wife knew and decided to forgive him for the sake of their sad son.

No one has touched me for nine months. No one has even hugged me.

Except Ori.

When she comes home on leave from the army, she immediately drops her duffel bag on the floor to free both arms and then we hug tightly for a long time because missing someone plus missing the same someone equals solace.

She arranges to meet her girlfriends very late at night so we can have dinner together and then look at a few pictures. She takes the albums off the shelf and sits on the living-room couch, extends her never-ending legs forward, and also opens her laptop. I sit down next to her, and together we look at the pictures of Ofer from different periods, looking for signs.

Mom, doesn't he look stoned in that picture?

Tell me, was he a little sad on his last birthday or is it just the lousy lighting?

She sleeps late on Saturday so I have time to drop off plastic boxes of quiches for Matan at the gates to the boarding school, and when she wakes up, the shakshuka

Ofer used to make is waiting for her, with onion and red pepper cut into strips and Feta cheese and a pinch of hot pilpelchuma. I know that the cover version isn't as good as the original, and I know that if Matan were at the table with us, she would give him a quick glance that said exactly that, but only she and I are here, so she eats everything and sops the sauce off the plate with a piece of challah and says every time, Mom, you outdid yourself this time.

After the shakshuka, we read stories from the blog. Ori believes that there are signs concealed in those stories and that if we read them carefully enough, we'll break the hidden code and then we'll discover what happened to Ofer.

I don't think so. They're only stories, not the book of Zohar. But I try to go along with Ori and her "discoveries."

She read story number thirty-two aloud to me.

The Inner Panther
After he recovered, Zion tried to be the panther he once was: He tried to run, climb, ride his bike, not ride his bike, play tennis, stop playing tennis, tried everything until he finally accepted the next affront as a fact: At a certain age, our bodies lose flexibility.

But our minds—no.

Our minds, the last year of his life taught Zion, are flexible forever, prepared to leap toward the unknown, if only we accept the risk.

Our minds can always say yes. To new love, new music, the possibility that the story isn't over yet.

After she read it to me again—she dragged me with her to the Biblical Zoo in Jerusalem. Why would Dad choose the name Zion, of all names? She explained it to me. He's directing us to Jerusalem! And where in Jerusalem are there panthers? Only in the Biblical Zoo!

I thought Ofer had chosen the name Zion as a homage to Zion, a character in Galila Ron-Feder's young adult book series, which I knew he'd read secretly in the yeshiva when he was a teenager. I thought it was his way of saying that Zion had grown up, had maybe even split from Batya and had begun a new life. But I didn't say anything. We wandered around the Biblical Zoo for hours, and when I saw a teenage guide whose walk reminded me of Matan's, I took my phone out of my pocket and called him. He didn't answer, again, and Ori said, Give him his space, Mom. Then she asked to go back to the cages of the lions, tigers, and leopards—all of which, it turned out, are considered panthers. I didn't understand what she expected, that if she stood in front of them long enough, one of them would open its mouth and tell us where Ofer was? But I didn't say anything, I bit my lips, and finally she said, Did you know Dad took me here once for a fun day instead of taking me to school?

No, I said, I didn't know.

He didn't want you to get upset that I was missing school.

Now I was offended, and said, I wouldn't have been upset. A few seconds later, I said, To tell the truth, I would have been.

She laughed and said, I really miss talking to him, I really miss standing on the balcony with him asking his advice about all kinds of little things.

So do I, I said.

And she said, I miss the texts he used to send me.

And I said, Like, *It's been a while since I told you how much I love you.*

And she said, Or, *I'm so proud of who you are.*

And I said, I miss dancing with him in the living room.

And she said, "Super Trouper."

And I said, "Cotton Eye Joe."

And she said, I miss the profane things he said at Friday-night dinner.

And I said, I miss Friday-night dinners.

And she said, I miss going out for a walk with him after Friday-night dinner and looking at the stars.

And I thought, but didn't say, I miss something that's hard to put into words, maybe...connection? The feeling that everything I do, even if I sleep with another man, is connected to Ofer—

And I thought, I also miss certainty, I want to know something for certain—

And I thought, If I say *that*, I'll fall apart. And falling apart in front of your daughter is not like falling apart alone, at night, because when you're zapping channels, of all the movies in the world, you come across Ofer's favorite, *Mulholland Drive*, at the exact moment when the singer with the tear on her cheek begins to sing "Llorando."

And Ori—how smart that kid is—put her arm around my waist and said, I know it seems unreal to you that Dad's not here, Mom, but if every one of his short stories is a small piece of the puzzle, maybe in the end we'll manage to put it all together and understand where he is.

And I said, Amen, sweetheart.

And she said, It's a lucky thing Dad can't hear you say amen.

And we continued to stand there in front of the panthers' cage until they announced over the loudspeaker that the zoo was about to close.

Story number forty-nine also sent us on a journey.

The Recurring Nightmare About Noa Elkayam
I dreamt about you again. We were in a taxi in
Haifa. We were twenty. And also forty-eight, wearing
white navy uniforms, but you had wrinkles and I had
gray hair. We got out of the taxi, and right before we
said goodbye, you asked me: How are you? I thought
you really wanted to know, so I replied: Lonely,
and tried to pull you closer. You recoiled. Of course
you did. I should have known you would. Even in a
dream.

Nonetheless, now that I'm awake, I want to ask:
How are you?

Ori found the Facebook page of the love of Ofer's youth (her real name was Puah Ohayon—Ofer hardly ever spoke about her, and when he did, there wasn't the slightest trace of mythology in his voice) and arranged to meet her on Friday.

On the way to Haifa, she said, You probably don't have any desire to meet Dad's first girlfriend. But we agreed to do everything, right?

I nodded and thought to myself, Who cares. The main thing is that you and I have time together. When we passed the palm trees of Atlit, I remembered how once, when Ofer and I were on our way to see friends in Haifa, it started to pour, and right at that spot, he pulled over to the right and said, Kelach Stream. And we began to climb the winding road toward Beit Oren until we reached a little bridge. Then he stopped the car and said, Come on. I said, It's a deluge out there. And he said, That's the point, a deluge! Take my coat. We got out of the car and stood on the bridge and looked at the enormous amount of water rushing below it, and Ofer said, Wow, Kelach Stream only flows like this once or twice a year. And there are years when it doesn't flow at all! I pretended to be as excited as he was, even though all I wanted was to go back to the heat of the car, and even though I couldn't shake the feeling that I was a reluctant participant in a reenactment, that some other girl had already stood on this bridge with him once, looking at that narrow wadi, which only in our dry country could be called a stream.

You think Dad was really lonely? Ori interrupted the memory.

I sighed. Since Ofer disappeared, I've been sighing like that, like an old person. Like my mother.

Dad was surrounded by people who loved him, I said. The people from the forum. The people from the NGO. And the people he helped. Do you remember how they talked about him when they came to see us after—

Yes.

He had the ability to walk into a room and capture everyone's heart.

That's true. He charmed even my bitchiest teachers.

And he worked at it, your dad. At being loved. He knew how to be there for anyone who needed him. He went to events. He called to wish people happy birthday.

And besides, he had us.

Right.

So—

I don't know, honey. Maybe loneliness is a personality trait, not a situation. And maybe someone who runs away from home at the age of seventeen and is cut off by his family will always have a vacuum…to fill.

You think that space became so large that…there's a chance that…and maybe our iRobot really did shred Dad's letter…

I've already told you: No. He loved you both too much to do something like that.

And you.

And me, yes.

We'd arranged to meet Puah Ohayon at Seasons, a café on the beach. She said she'd be sitting outside. And the first thing I thought when I saw her was: What does it mean that all the women Ofer loved before me are better-looking than I am?

A cascade of light brown curls. (What woman our age has a cascade of hair?)

A generous smile.

A face too flexible to have ever undergone "aesthetic treatments."

Great taste in clothes. (Aren't women from Haifa supposed to dress like old spinsters?)

A bit curvy. Just the way men like women to be.

(I've never been attracted to a woman the way I'm attracted to you, Ofer told me when we were first together. Something about your mind turns me on.)

Puah Ohayon gave me a long handshake, which enabled her to examine me exactly the way I had examined her. And be disappointed. I could actually see the thought written in a subtitle like in that R.E.M. clip: Of all women, *she's* the one Ofer chose?

Then she hugged (why hug?) Ori and said in a social worker's voice (maybe she really was a social worker?), I've thought about you a lot since Ofer . . . (People don't know what the next word should be: Disappeared? Faded away? Went off to bizarre places?) It must be a nightmare for you.

Totally, Ori said.

The truth is that I wanted to give you a call, Puah said, looking at me. But somehow . . .

It's okay, I said.

A waitress arrived. Took our order.

A lifeguard warned the swimmers about strong currents.

A golden retriever that reminded me a little of Boy, the one Ofer and I had before the kids, walked past us without its owner or a leash. When Ori was born, Boy (named after Boy George) went into postpartum depression because of the drastic lowering of his status, and he would lie on his cushion in the living room for hours without moving. When we came home from the hospital with Matan, he took a preventative step and ran away to a new life through the tear in the fence of our shared garden. If I remember correctly, we didn't even hang notices with pictures of him on trees in the neighborhood.

Thank you for agreeing to see us, Ori said.

Of course, Puah Ohayon said.

Like I said to you on the phone, Ori went on, the police have stopped looking for my dad, but we still haven't given up.

That's very good.

And we're trying to check out all kinds of leads ourselves.

I'll be happy to help you. Even though, like I said on the phone—

My dad posted stories on his blog, using a pseudonym, Ori said.

I didn't know, Puah Ohayon said. But I didn't think she looked completely surprised.

One of them was this story, Ori said, passing her story number forty-nine.

Puah took the page, and the more she read, the redder her neck became.

She touched her nose with her finger once. Once, in a dramatic gesture, she moved her cascade of curls from right to left.

When she finished, she wiped an invisible tear from the corner of her eye and said, Forty-nine. That was the number of our bus. We used to take it from the base to my parents' house. And she said, He always loved writing. I still have the letters he wrote me from his officers course.

When did you see each other last? Ori asked.

See each other? Puah Ohayon was flustered. Ofer and I didn't... didn't see each other. He would call once a year to wish me happy birthday. And once a year, I would call to wish him happy birthday. That was it. When I heard that he... I was shocked. I'm still shocked. Who would have wanted to hurt that kind of person?

When is your birthday? Ori asked.

January twentieth.

So you spoke three weeks before he went into the orchard.

Yes.

Was there anything unusual about the conversation?

Unusual? No. I don't...think so. We spoke mostly about me. Ofer asked what I wished for on my birthday. He always asked that.

And what did you say?

That I wished to keep being brave.

Brave?

I left my husband two years ago. And I live with a woman.

No kidding.

I wished to keep being brave in other aspects of my life too. And Ofer—well, I don't have to tell you how wonderful he was—said, After what you've been through, everything else is a piece of cake.

And he didn't say anything about himself?

Right now, I don't remember anything special. I think he mentioned that you, Ori, were going into the army. And we laughed about how time flies. After all, we met in the army.

How did you really meet?

The waitress arrived with our orders. The lifeguard ordered the swimmers to get out of the water. A teenage boy with Matan's shoulders came out of the water with a surfboard. Tonight, I thought, like every Friday night, I'll send him a WhatsApp. And like every Friday night, he won't reply. But I'll see the two blue checks that shows he is alive.

Puah Ohayon put a straw in her mouth and took a long draw of her fruit shake, and only then did she ask Ori, Are you sure you can deal with hearing about your father's love life?

We think the stories are tracks my dad left behind for us to follow, Ori replied in a too grown-up voice. And the tracks lead to you.

Puah hesitated for a second. As if she couldn't decide which results of her memory search engine she wanted to double-click on.

He came into my office on the base during lunch break, she finally said. An officer and a gentleman. He really did look a little like Richard Gere, with those almond-shaped eyes of his. He asked for some form or other, but that was clearly just an excuse. I don't remember what we talked about, I only remember that I had a really strong feeling during the whole conversation that he'd ask for my number at the end. But it didn't happen. So I waited a few days, got hold of his phone number, called him, and asked if he wanted to go to see *Ghostbusters* together.

Wait a minute, Mom, you were actually the one to make the first move with Dad too, right? Ori asked me.

Yes, I confirmed. Dad was a bit shy. Maybe it had something to do with—

The environment he grew up in, Puah and I said together.

We smiled at each other. And for a moment, an imaginary line connected us: Two women who knew the same man.

Pretty quickly, we moved in together in a small unit attached to my parents' house, Puah went on. Remember, he'd left religion only two years before that. And he didn't just leave it, he cut himself off totally from his family and his community, so I think that...he was looking for a family just as much as he was looking for a girlfriend, and really, he did become a member of our family. My mom really fell in love with him. When we broke up, she took it harder than I did.

Why did you break up? Ori asked. And I was almost tempted into answering in unison with Puah, after all I could guess the answer: We became good friends. I was twenty-one, Puah went on. I was curious about how it would be with other men.

I expected Ori to ask, And how was it?

Instead, she leaned forward a bit and said, The police raised the possibility, among others, that Dad committed suicide. Maybe by drowning. Does that fit your picture of him?

I need a cigarette, Puah Ohayon said.

I reached into my bag and took out my pack—I'd gone back to smoking after Ofer disappeared because there was no longer anyone to warn me that it wasn't healthy—but then she said, No thank you. I'm dying for a cigarette now, but I stopped. A month ago. My partner can't stand the smell.

Good luck with that, I said as I put the pack back in my bag.

Puah Ohayon put the straw in her mouth again and drew on it for a while. Then she said, No. The truth is that suicide doesn't seem like Ofer to me. When I read in the paper that the police think it was suicide, I thought to myself that they must want to close the case. The Ofer I knew wasn't capable of doing such an egotistical thing.

Ori nodded with the enthusiasm of someone who was on the same wavelength.

On the other hand, Puah added, people change.

Tell me, Ori asked, in the conversations you had, did he ever share anything about things that . . . worried him?

Puah turned to look at the waves and seemed to speak to them: I'm trying to remember if he said anything else in our last conversation.

Not just in your last conversation, Ori explained. In general.

I think that—she looked back at us—there were two things...he kept going back to in our conversations over the last few years. One of them was the change he made when he left his job in marketing and established his NGO, Soft Landing. He had a lot of concerns before setting it up. To tell the truth, I laughed at him. I said, You left your family when you were eighteen and didn't look back. You left your American wife when you were twenty-five without blinking an eye. Since when are *you* afraid of changes? You don't understand, he told me, there were no children then. When you're a dad, you're willing to make concessions that...you never believed you would ever make. And you're not, you're *really* not in a hurry to take risks.

But what exactly...was he afraid of? Ori asked.

He wasn't sure it would last financially. It was very important to him—she turned to me—that you supported the change. He always said how much he didn't take that for granted.

Really?

I understood that you also helped him with the numbers, with the whole financial side.

Yes.

And what was the second thing? Ori interrupted. You said there were two things he was preoccupied with.

The kids, Puah said. I mean you and your brother. Matan, right? I think he was worried mainly about him. About how he'd manage in real life. Now I remember that, also in our last conversation, when we talked about you going into the army, he said that he was completely unconcerned about you but was pretty worried about the day Matan would go into the army. And that, recently, Matan had crawled back into his shell, those were his words. And that it was impossible to reach him.

Yes, I said.

Really, how is he? Puah asked. How is he dealing with everything that's ... happening?

I exchanged a quick glance with Ori. Very quick. Not longer than a tenth of a second. But long enough for her to understand that I didn't want to get into that. Didn't want another pair of judging eyes to fix on me. I torment myself enough as it is.

Overall, he's doing fine, given the circumstances, Ori said and changed the subject quickly: Tell me, is there anything else Dad shared with you that might be relevant to the puzzle we're trying to piece together?

Puah thought for a while as she twisted a curl with annoying slowness, then finally said, That's it, sorry. I think you know better than I do what was going on with Ofer over these past few years.

We can only try to guess, I clarified, but not really know.

Puah nodded sympathetically, but a bit impatiently, the way a therapist looks at the clock on the wall behind you and sees that the time is up.

Ori signaled the waitress to bring us the check.

I got up to go to the restroom, more out of a desire to get away from the conversation than a real need to use the restroom. On the way there, next to the cash register, was a huge aquarium filled with colorful fish. Suddenly, the whole idea of an aquarium seemed cruel to me. To take a living creature used to the open sea and cage it that way? Why? I felt like smashing the glass. So that all the water would come pouring out of it.

When I came back, Puah Ohayon was immersed in rereading the story.

Is it okay if I keep this? she asked when she finished.

Yes, Ori said, you can also read the rest of Dad's stories. Just Google "Zalman International" and you'll reach his blog.

Zalman International? Puah Ohayon tried not to laugh. Because of the circumstances. And then she laughed. A beautiful, hearty laugh that also infected us.

None of us said, "Ofer and his silliness," but the thought flickered in the air.

Right before we said goodbye, I mustered the courage to ask what I'd wanted to ask during the entire conversation: Tell me, do *you* dream about him sometimes too?

Puah looked into my eyes as if checking to see if I would believe her, and said, Honestly, no.

Before I backed out of our parking spot, I asked Ori to turn around to see if anyone was behind us. She already knew: Since Dad went into the orchard, Mom hasn't been able to look at herself in the mirror. Not even the car mirror. Every time I did it in the last few months, I was devastated by what I saw: Who is that woman with the messy hair and starkly prominent cheekbones, and worry bags under her eyes, and a divorcée's bitter wrinkle over her upper lip? Who is that woman and what does she have to do with me?

I can't believe that the police didn't even bother to get in touch with that Puah, Ori said after we set off.

I didn't say anything.

Isn't it a basic thing to do? Ori persisted.

I don't know anymore what's basic and what isn't, I thought. But I said, Yes, it's basic.

Which means that it's up to us, Ori said. We're the only ones who can find Dad.

I'm not sure anymore that there's a chance of finding him, I thought. And said, Right.

Ori browsed through the binder of stories and said, I have to remember to print out number forty-nine at home. I want all of them to always be within reach.

She became engrossed in reading for a few blessed minutes, and then said, Listen to this, Mom:

Leaving the Hospital
If to change, then the world. If to sin, then without
guilt. If to travel, then far. If a man, then a woman, if
a woman, then fine. If to make something, then peace.
If peace, then now. If we're left, we'll love. If we're left,
we'll love. If there's time, it's running out. If to dance,
then wildly. If it's past, then forget it. If a prisoner,
then escape. If to think, then to do. If to do, then to
err. If to err, then now. If we're left, we'll love. If we're
left, we'll love.

Do you think a person who wrote something like that would commit suicide, Mom?

I answered immediately, No. And remembered the first time I'd come across those lines. Later on, Ofer expanded the story a bit to reach one hundred words, but it was originally written for me. A few years ago, my appendix burst and somehow, it got complicated, and to this day, it's not clear why. They didn't treat the infection in time. Or maybe they did, but not the right way. Bottom line, I was hospitalized for two weeks with an acute infection. Most of the time I was completely out of it because of the painkillers, but one night, I woke up and saw him sleeping beside my bed. He'd put two chairs together and had folded his body into them. Wearing jeans and a white T-shirt. Covered with a thin hospital blanket. And on the blanket was a piece of paper with a love poem written on it.

By the way, Mom—Ori tore me out of my memory, out of the sweetness of the memory—have you noticed that Dad wrote like a woman a lot?

Like a woman? I replied, swallowing a smile as I remembered him coming out of our bedroom before a for-women-only performance by Etti Ankri, the ultra-Orthodox singer, wearing a long dress. And high heels. And a wig that was once part of Ori's Purim costume. He looked at me and I tried not to laugh, but I laughed and asked if I could take a picture of him, and he said absolutely not. Then he took off the high heels because there's a limit, and put on a pair of flat shoes he'd bought in Berlin instead. When we got to the car, I opened the door to the passenger seat for him the way a gentlemen does for a lady, and he said, No way, and got into the driver's seat. On the way to the concert, we passed a bottle of red wine back and forth for confidence, and right before we pulled into the parking lot, I said, We can still change our minds, sweetie, and he shook his head. At the concert, we thought a woman from his office was sitting two rows in front of us and was about to turn around and see him and point and shout, "A man!" But it didn't happen. As part of her encore, Etti Ankri sang the song we'd chosen for our wedding ceremony, and I put my hand on his dress, and he put his hand on mine. When we got home, he carried me from the car to our bed because he still could, and we made love at full volume because we still felt desire for each other.

I meant—Ori pulled me out of the memories again—that even though Dad is a man, he liked to write from...a woman's mind. Listen to this, for example, she said, pointing to one of the stories in the binder and reading it aloud:

Frida Kahlo from the Suburbs
The first time she dressed up as Frida Kahlo was for
Bezalel's Purim party. A guy there was worth the
money she spent for a flowered scarf, black braids, a

yellow silk shirt over a long matching dress, and high-heeled boots decorated with red beads.

The guy was a loser. But she kept the costume for years. Tonight she wore it to her husband's office Purim party.

Afterward, he asks her how it was.

Fine, she says, thinking: No one knew who I was dressed as.

They're great people, he says.

The greatest, I say.

Maybe Dad is walking around in a costume, Mom? With a new face some plastic surgeon gave him?

Oriki?

Yes, Mom?

Is it okay if we're quiet for a while?

Are you giving up?

No, of course not, honey. I just feel like hearing some music.

I turned on the radio. David Broza was singing—

Back home after twenty years
At first it all seems the same
Two horses tied to the fig tree
A cardboard sign with an arrow pointing
"To the Wedding."

I knew that, in a few seconds, he'd sing the chorus, which was dangerous for me to hear now—because, as Ofer once quoted to me from a book by a poet whose name I've forgotten, "Music is the bait at the end of the fishing rod that is cast into the depths of our soul, and it dredges up all that has been submerged"—so I turned off the radio before the dangerous-for-me chorus began and did what Ami the psychologist advised me to do at moments when the pain threatened to become unbearable: I pictured us coming home and discovering that Ofer has been waiting for us the entire time, wearing his white T-shirt, and we go inside and he doesn't say a word but keeps me wrapped in his large arms for an entire week.

The next morning, I drove Ori to the central bus station in Modi'in, where she takes a bus to her base. On the way, she received a call. She knew I couldn't stand her chattering with her girlfriends when I'm driving, so she already had her finger on the red button to decline the call, but then—

Hi, Puah, she said, I'm putting you on speaker. Mom's in the car too.

Hi, Puah, I said.

Hello to both of you. I'm calling because . . . Yesterday, you asked me whether I dream about Ofer, and I said no. Because I really don't. But all of a sudden, I dreamt about him last night. And the dream was so . . .

bizarre that I had to tell someone about it. Is it okay that I called?

Of course, I said. We're in a traffic jam anyway.

So in the dream, Ofer and I are standing and looking down at the Kelach Stream. It's something we actually did once. And then he bends over the railing to see better. And falls. But that doesn't upset him at all in the dream. And even though the flow is strong and he's wearing clothes in the rushing water, he calls to me happily: Puah, come on, don't pass this up! I hesitate. Because the rocks sticking out of the water look dangerous. Meanwhile, the current is dragging him downstream, and I think: It doesn't matter, all streams flow to the sea. So I drive the car we had then, my mother's red Fiat Uno, toward the sea, and park in the lot of the Camel restaurant, except that the sign on the building says Paradiso, not Camel, and then the scene cuts to an image of me sitting on the bank of a stream which doesn't actually exist near the Camel restaurant, waiting for Ofer to come. But he doesn't come. And with every second that passes, I'm more and more worried that he's been carried off to somewhere else, that maybe I'm not waiting in the right place.

And then?

That's it. I don't remember anything after that. Sorry.

You have nothing to be sorry about.

I haven't really helped you.

Who knows? You've given us another piece of the puzzle.

You'll let me know if there's anything new?

Of course. And you let us know if you have…any more dreams.

We reached our destination.

We hugged tightly in the car. Ori took me in her arms as if I were a little girl.

Don't go, I wanted to tell her.

Take a day off, I wanted to tell her, I'll write you a note like the ones Dad used to write for you when you didn't want to go to school: "Ori Raz won't be coming to the unit today due to reasons beyond her control."

Instead, I told her what I knew she wanted to hear: I think Dad is calling to us through other people's dreams. I think he's asking us to not give up.

There's no way we're giving up, she said resolutely. But also a bit impatiently. Like someone who wants to leave. To be with girls her age.

Don't forget you have sandwiches in the pocket of your duffel bag, I said.

I won't.

And talk to your brother.

Of course, she said.

She got out of the car. Opened the trunk. Took out her duffel bag. Slung the strap on her shoulder and walked to the station, tall and beautiful, like her dad, and didn't turn her head even once.

February 2018

It's embarrassing to admit, but in the end, I just gave up. How long can you look at the same albums and read stories you already know by heart and follow trails that aren't really trails to the Grand Canyon Mall in Haifa, to a vineyard in Kfar Vitkin, to the Kibbutz Ga'ash beach, to the Ben Shemen Forest, to Masada, to the Dolphin Reef in Eilat? Yes, we even went all the way to Eilat.

Until, one Saturday, Ori said to me, Mom, I had a really tough week on the base. Some moron from munitions stole an APC and tried to drive it home. Is it okay if, this Saturday, we . . . don't look for Dad? Maybe do something else together?

Like what? I asked, trying to hide my relief.

I don't know. Maybe . . . my friend was in a kind of workshop. It's called HeartBeat.

New Age workshops are your dad's thing, not mine.

Come on, Mom, it's a kind of drum circle. And the idea, if I understood correctly, is that drumming helps you go back to your inner rhythm if you've lost it for some reason.

Okay.

Okay what?

It sounds like a load of crap, Ori, but *yalla*.

The next day, we went to the workshop. And drummed on large drums the instructor handed out. And I didn't feel for even a second that it "helped me go back to my inner rhythm." I felt there was no chance I could get back my inner rhythm until I knew what happened to Ofer and until Matan started talking to me again. But I liked the instructor, a kind of Viking, with long hair in a ponytail and a shirt cut off at the shoulders and slightly sad eyes. I thought he needed the workshop as much as we did, and I enjoyed the simple pleasure of the touch of my palm on the tight skin of the drum and the mathematicalness of the rhythm, and the moments when the circle succeeded in creating a joint rhythm, which made me feel, for the first time in a long while, that I was part of something, and I enjoyed the rare moments when I was totally into the drumming and could put aside my thoughts for a second—

And most of all, I enjoyed seeing my Ori so animated. She stood up to dance with the drum. Waved her hand high in the hair and slapped the tight skin as if she were, at the very least, Shlomo Bar, the famous drummer.

After the workshop, I felt unable to go home with my entire body filled with a desire that had no object, so we went out for a drink. I mean, I drank and Ori was the designated driver.

Later on, a kind of tradition formed. Every Saturday night, we went to drum with Omri the melancholy Viking on the roof in downtown Tel Aviv, and then we went out for a drink in a nearby bar. And every time, guys would come on to Ori, and she would brush them off, explaining to me afterward that she "wasn't there yet." Once, an older man with a gangster's scar on his cheek actually came on to me. And I used her simple sentence. "I'm still not there," I told him. All the way home, Ori and I laughed about the mysteriousness of that remark. Because where the hell is there? And even though we laughed, we knew very well where it was. In any case, without deciding officially, we stopped looking for Ofer.

And then—one Saturday when Ori was still sleeping—I received a phone call from the boarding school. And the instructor on duty said in a voice that tried to be soothing but sounded stressed: Your son. On the way to the hospital. Jumped out of the window. Second floor.

I woke up Ori and we raced there. At first, I drove, but after I almost ran a red light at an intersection and braked at the last second, Ori offered to drive and I agreed, because I felt that in another minute, I really would cause an accident. And all the way to the boarding school I cursed the principal, silently and not silently, in Hebrew and in Spanish, that *hijo de puta*, who had convinced me to give Matan space and be proud that my chick had spread his wings. Spread his wings, *la puta mierda*. Spread his wings and jumped out of a window—

In the emergency room, they told us that Matan had been moved to the internal medicine department. Third floor. We rushed to the elevator, but then Ori realized that they hadn't told us which internal medicine department, so we hurried back to the emergency room and asked. We were greeted by Dr. Caro in Internal Medicine "C." I was glad it wasn't some young doctor. How can you trust a doctor who's younger than you are? The good news, Mrs. Raz, said Dr. Caro, is that your son's condition is not critical. Right now, we're only talking about serious injuries, and at the same time, we're checking to see if there is any damage to his internal organs, even though the chances are quite slim—

Thank God, I said. What a relief.

And Dr. Caro, who from the first moment reminded me more and more of my father, said seriously, What we have found in his blood tests are extremely high levels of glutamate and aspartate, which is characteristic of ketamine users.

Ketamine?

It's a party drug, Mom—

Are you sure, Dr. Caro? Because Matan—

You'll have a lot to talk about when he wakes up.

What do you mean, "When he wakes up?" He's in a coma?

He's not in a coma, he's under the influence of a very strong drug.

But how long will it take for the influence to pass?

Hopefully, a few hours.

We sat at his bedside and hoped.

His hair had grown long. And he had a new, small beard, kind of like a goatee. And his face had filled out a bit.

And the intense longing for him that I had held in my body for all the months he didn't want to see me erupted like a geyser.

Fuck "give him space." There is no more space.

I leaned over and kissed his forehead. The smell of his scalp was still like his father's, the best in the world.

My little boy, I said voicelessly. My little boy.

Ori must have felt the intensity of my emotions because she put her hand on mine, and with her other hand, she found information about ketamine on her

phone and placed it between us so I could read it too:
Originally an anesthetic for horses. The user enters a dis-
sociative state. Detached from reality. Lack of awareness.
Exaggerated sense of abilities. That is, the user thinks
he can do everything. Some users don't remember what
they experienced. Like with dreams. Slow and gradual
awakening. Damage to cognition can be irreversible.

The more I read, the deeper I sank into my chair. One
of the sites even said that users may wake up and not
remember who they are. And that sent chills of catastro-
phe from my scalp to the bottom of my spine.

I went outside to smoke.

Ori followed me and asked for a cigarette.

Since when do you smoke? I asked in surprise.

Since now, she said. And coughed immediately after
her first drag. Which reminded me suddenly that she
was a young girl. Just a young girl.

Don't take the smoke into your lungs, I told her. Take
a puff and exhale it right away.

Okay, she said, and took a drag. And inhaled. And
coughed. Then she looked at me. I didn't know Matan
did drugs, Mom. If I had known, I would have told you.

Of course, I said. I never thought otherwise.

I won't survive it, she said—and coughed again, tears
filling her eyes—if we lose him too.

We won't lose him, I said firmly. And crushed the butt of my cigarette. Because I didn't want to leave Matan alone for too long. Ori crushed hers too. And we went back to sit at his bedside.

Ori rested her head on me. Exhausted from so many unknowns.

I stroked her hair and blamed myself. For letting Matan go to the boarding school. For not insisting he come home on Saturdays. For letting Ori deliver messages between us. For holding conversations with him in my mind—and not in reality. For making do with leaving quiches in plastic boxes with the guard twice a week and not breaking through the barrier at the entrance and going straight to his room. For telling myself that we each cope with Ofer's disappearance in our own way, and that Matan's way was to disappear himself. For telling myself that he was in good hands. After all, the principal was Ofer's good friend, and if there was cause for worry, he would definitely let me know.

I prepared myself for a situation in which Matan woke up with his memory completely erased and I would have to remind him who he is: How when he was pacifier-two, he used to do acrobatics on the slides and swings in the playground, and the other mothers were alarmed at first, and in the end, applauded him. And how when he was front-toothless-six, we were driving to a capoeira class and Eviatar Banai's song "Till Tomorrow" was playing on the radio, and when I stopped at a light and looked at him in the rearview mirror, I saw that he was crying, and when I asked, What happened, Matanchuk, he said, Mommy, that song gave me a heart-tack. And how when he was slightly-pimply-eleven, he boycotted me for a week, didn't say a word to me, because he caught me reading his diary. And how when he was very-pimply-thirteen, he ran away from home, saying he would never come back to this prison. And how when he was broad-shoulders-fourteen, he started volunteering for Ofer's NGO and took it upon himself, through meetings and phone conversations, to support boys his age who wanted to leave the ultra-Orthodox world they'd grown up in. And how when he was voice-changing-fifteen, he announced on Thursday that he was doing Friday-night dinner, and put together a wonderful Mexican meal that included tacos and black beans and chili con carne and nonalcoholic cocktails. And how when he was brokenhearted-sixteen (Hili Galili, that slut, cheated on him with his best friend), he decided, inspired by *Forrest Gump* (we saw the movie so many times together as a family that, during it, we'd already begun acting like we did at *The Rocky Horror Picture Show*), to run and not stop. And yes, after a few kilometers, he slowed down to a walk, but to our surprise, he really didn't stop walking. And he even grew a beard. Like Forrest. And slept in the homes of all sorts of newly secular kids he met through the NGO. And within two weeks, he reached Ein Yahav, in the far south of the country, and then called us and said that's it, he'd reached his goal, his legs already hurt more than his heart. And could we come and pick him up.

If Matan wakes up, I won't let him forget who he is, I promised myself, like a little girl making a deal with God. But when Matan opened his eyes, he tightened his grip on my hand and said in a perfectly lucid voice, I want to go home, Mom.

We didn't actually sit down to talk until four days after he came home. At first, he stayed in his room (how smart Ori had been to warn me not to touch his things so that if he wanted to come back, he would feel wanted). Then he began to come into the kitchen, cut himself some vegetables for a salad. Nosh a bit of the curly halvah I'd bought for him (along with the mini ice-cream bars, artichokes, and pineapple) as a kind of peace offering. And on the fourth day, we went out to the balcony to smoke, and a few minutes later, he came out as well and sat down on the other side of the table that Ofer had built. May I? he said, pointing to the pack. I handed it to him and restrained myself from asking, "Since when do you smoke?" He took out a cigarette. And lit it. And

together, we looked at the view for a long moment: build-
ings that looked remarkably like ours. And then he said,
It looks good on you, the short hair.

I had no choice, I said, my hair lost its shape.

And then he said, Listen. And didn't say anything for
a long time. Such a long time that I was afraid that, here it
is, with a slight delay, the irreversible cognitive damage—

Until finally, he said, I had a kind of moment, Mom.
In the middle of the trip.

I kept myself from saying, "You mean the moment
you thought you were a dolphin and jumped from the
second floor to the sidewalk?"

I exhaled smoke. And turned half my body to him to
show that I was listening.

Suddenly I could speak to God, he said.

Oh no, I thought.

Not the God of religious people, he was quick to reassure me. Not the kind you have to pray to, not the one
whose commandments you have to follow.

There's another God?

Sure. The inner God. That place inside you that
knows.

And what did he tell you, your inner God? I asked. I
was careful not to sound cynical.

Don't be cynical, Mom.

I'm not.

Matan crushed the cigarette in the ashtray, and only then did he turn his whole body to me. I messed up with you, Mom, he said.

Are you talking about the box cutter? I said. It's understandable. We were all terribly upset, we're all still terribly upset.

That's not it, Mom. It's something else, he said, and his voice broke.

Only then did I realize that he was about to reveal a secret that had stood between us all this time.

I made a mistake, he said.

And my heart had already begun to guess.

Remember that Dad and I always did the shopping on Fridays?

Yes.

So on the Friday before he ... went into the orchard, I asked him to stay in the car a little longer. And told him. About that Dan.

I see.

Don't ask me how I knew about him.

I'm not asking.

And the weird thing was that it didn't seem to bother him at all.

Really?

He said, Thanks for the information, Matanyahu. And I said, Come on, Dad, don't tell me you don't care.

And he said, in the same calm tone, How long have you known about it? And I said, Two weeks. And he said, That's a lot of time to walk around alone with such a thing, kid. It's good that you told me. It's good that you got it off your chest. And I asked him, But what are you going to do about it? Talk to Mom? And he said, Come on, let's take the bags out of the trunk. And he got out of the car. And like always, he took most of the bags into the house himself. Later, at dinner, I watched him, looking for signs. But he acted normally, right?

Right.

He even said his "profane" things.

Right.

So I said to myself that maybe I was wrong. Or maybe you even told him before then. I don't know. I heard that these days, there are all kinds of . . . arrangements . . . that couples have—

Yes.

Anyway, I went to sleep feeling fairly calm. And then, when he disappeared—

You connected the two things.

He nodded and took a drag of his cigarette. And blew smoke rings that looked more like question marks than rings.

I wanted to reach out and stroke his head, but I wasn't sure how he would react. So I restrained myself.

And then he said, Even now, I still hope that maybe he was just doing a Forrest Gump, Mom.

If only, I said with a sigh.

And because he grew a beard, no one recognizes him. And one day, he'll just call from some nowhere town in Australia and say, That's it—

I've reached my goal, my legs hurt more than my heart.

Exactly.

I'm not sure that's going to happen, Matanchuk.

I know, but I can dream, can't I, Mom?

Dreaming is a must.

Matan asked for another cigarette. I handed it to him. At some point, I'll have to tell him not to overdo it, I told myself. At some point, I'll have to talk to him about the ketamine too. At some point, I'll have to tell him he could have died from it. But not now. Now I have to bite my lip. Because everything is very delicate. Because he's sending out antennae in my direction. One wrong word, one unnecessary chuckle—and he'll go right back into his shell.

To make a long story short—he crushed another butt—when I spoke to God . . .

The inner one.

The inner one, yes, I realized that I was angry at you because I was really angry at myself. I blamed you because I really blamed myself.

Images flashed through my mind: Ofer refusing to take the orange section I offered him. Ofer putting his hand on my shoulder when I said the smell from the sewage treatment plant was making me nauseous, his touch more pressing, slightly heavier than usual. Then suddenly giving me his hand. Why did he walk hand in hand with me after Matan told him about Dan? Maybe he already knew it would be the last time we'd walk hand in hand in the orchards and wanted to end it well. Even when he fired employees, he first found them other jobs.

Don't blame yourself, Matani, I said.

Easy to say.

Until we know what happened, there's no point in laying blame. What if it was a terrorist attack? What if someone was really settling a score with him?

You think that's what happened?

I don't know what happened. But I can tell you that what the police say doesn't jibe with what I know about Dad. Maybe he was going through a bad period. Maybe he really was upset about...what you told him. But I don't believe that he...did anything to himself. And if he did. Why haven't they found his body?

Hey, Ori appeared behind us. Good morning to you both.

What's happening, Giraffe, Matan said.

What's happening, Dolphin, she came back at him.

They make you look fat, those pajamas, he said.

It's making you smell, that cigarette, she came back at him.

And I thought: Why is it that something I couldn't stand—those little barbs of theirs—has become something that makes me happy.

When I woke up late on Saturday, the house was already filled with the smell of cooking.

A man in black sweatpants and a sparkling white T-shirt was standing at the stove with his back to me.

The back of his neck was the back of Ofer's neck. His beautiful arm muscles protruded from the sleeves of his shirt exactly the way Ofer's did. His sharp shoulder blades were exactly like Ofer's when he was young.

Need help? I asked Matan.

Not at all, he said, giving me a half smile. The first half smile in a year.

I sat down to read the weekend supplements. Ofer liked to get the real, printed paper in the morning, at home, and read it with his date coffee. I couldn't cancel the subscription—canceling the subscription was admitting something I wasn't prepared to admit—but I hadn't really read the paper this last year, and now, too, my eyes passed over the letters without making sense of them, and my thoughts focused on the fact that, at some point, I would have to talk to Matan about the future. To find out whether he was going back to boarding school or not.

Meanwhile, Ori woke up. Sniffed. Came into the kitchen.

Need help? she asked Matan.

Not at all, he told her.

The shakshuka had exactly the same taste as Ofer's. Not almost. Not nearly. Not more or less. Exactly. You have to know how much hot red pepper to add, Matan replied to the question Ori didn't dare ask so as not to make me feel bad.

After the meal, Ori took out the albums. And opened her laptop. And said, Mom, the Dolphin and I thought we should go over the pictures and stories again. Maybe we'll get a brilliant idea that you and I didn't have. Want to join us?

Start without me, I'll join you in a little while, I said.

And really, I planned to join them.

Since Ofer disappeared, I'd been going for walks only in our neighborhood. Around the block. And sometimes, twice around the same block. I didn't dare to go farther. And I didn't plan to go farther this time either, but at the first traffic circle, instead of going straight, I turned right, and at the second traffic circle, instead of turning back, I kept going straight, and then I turned off onto the lane of gardens that connects the playgrounds for almost a kilometer before it reaches the main road, on the other side of which is the park, on the other side of which is the cemetery where my dad is buried, and whenever I walk past it, I say to myself, Hey, Papi, I'm sorry, Papi, that I didn't tell you more often how much I love you—

I think that only after I passed the cemetery did I realize that I was going in the direction of the orchards, and there was still a voice inside me that said, that warned, what will happened to Ori and Matan if you also . . . but I silenced it and kept walking, passing the stable and the barking dogs that guarded the stable. Ori rode here for a few years and was really good at it, sat tall and straight in the saddle, so beautiful with her curls spilling out of her helmet, until at some point, it began to be competitive, with championships and points, and she told us that she didn't like competitiveness, and I thought to myself that she was like Ofer in that way because I actually love competitiveness, and I especially love winning, and Ofer said to her, No problem, Oriki, if you want to stop the horseback riding.

And now, here I am at the barrier where Ofer and I used to stop the car, and there really are quite a few cars here, even though I was told that after Ofer disappeared, people were afraid to come here, but in the end, the runners went back to their route and the bike riders went back to their route and now here I am, who would have believed it, once again that smell of the citrus fruit remaining on the trees, and now there's no one to tell me not to pick any, but even so, I don't pick any and keep walking, don't give my hand to anyone, thinking that Ofer will appear in front of me any minute in sweatpants and a white T-shirt and say, So, have you calmed down? And explain that he hasn't disappeared at all, I was the one who disappeared for a year because we fought and I was angry and now I've come back mollified, and here's the hill of garbage which, at this time of year, can almost seem like it really is a Hill of Love because everything is green and blooming—

People with dogs come toward me. Ofer always wanted us to get a dog again, but I didn't want a dog and I didn't want another child, what's wrong with two, two is one more than the one that I was, why is it my fault that he grew up in a house with eight kids and that's his standard. So at least a dog, he said, and I said, Since the kids were born, I'm off dogs, they don't make me feel anything, sorry, you married the wrong girl, Ofer. I told him that so many times: You married the wrong girl, Ofer. As a joke. As a way of ending the argument with a ridiculous conclusion, and maybe that's what happened in the end, he became convinced that he really did marry the wrong girl. And now that smell from the sewage treatment plant, you have to get past those hundred meters, take a deep breath, long deep breaths, and then it subsides to a bearable level. I once tried going with Ofer to a yoga retreat up north that had a breathtaking view of the Sea of Galilee, but I couldn't connect to all that meditation, I couldn't stop my nagging thoughts, just the opposite, it made me have even more nagging thoughts, and the yoga gave me lower-back pain, and the worst thing was the food, all those sprouts and leaves that made Ofer well and made me hungry, and finally, at lunchtime on Saturday, when he went in for another session, I took the car and drove to a gas station and ordered four chicken shish kebabs. But here I am now, already past the strongest stench, and soon I'll come to the place where we used to look out over the houses of the moshav, and I used to think but not say, If we had bought an apartment as an investment ten years ago, we could already have bought a house in this moshav, and he used to think but not say—actually, I have no idea what, I don't know anything about his thoughts, his inner world had become blocked to me as the years passed. Let's go back, I hear him say, and almost feel his hand on my shoulder, on my right there are still grapefruits on the trees, but back then there hadn't been, and this is the exact spot where he gave me his hand—

Good morning, said a woman who appeared in front of me walking faster than me. Good morning, I replied as if I were Ofer, as if I were Ofer's American wife who threw a kitchen knife at him and then tried to run him over with their SUV, and only at the last minute did he jump aside—

Maybe he'd stopped sleeping with her too? Maybe she came to Israel and waited for him among the fruit trees, determined to succeed this time. What would make a woman throw a kitchen knife at her husband? He always claimed she was a complete lunatic, and really, in the only picture of her I saw, she had a wild gleam in her eye, but who knows if that's true. I never heard her side of the story. After Ofer disappeared in the orchard, I wrote to her on Facebook and she replied in American that she was really sorry to hear it, but Ofer always had a tendency to disappear suddenly, that's who he was, she wrote, totally devoted until something bursts inside him and he runs away from you without leaving so much as a goodbye note, and I replied that the police didn't think that was it, and that Israel wasn't a country where you could disappear so easily, and she wrote again that she was sorry to hear about it and asked me to please write to her if there was anything new, but she never bothered to ask again. How can people who were once so close become such total strangers, how can people who thought they were so close discover they were actually strangers—

How about that, the music. Without my noticing, it has been playing in the background as I walk, and now that I've turned back toward the city, it's louder—party trance. We haven't been to a nature party for a long time, Ofer said, since the Dead Sea, Ofer said—

And then he gave me his phone and car keys and went into the orchard—

I walk into exactly the same row he walked into then, the music gets a bit louder, the sound of the bass guitar tickles my body as if I've moved closer to the party, and I decide to walk in that direction—decide isn't the right word, my legs carry me in that direction. A year ago, I remember, the music had stopped even before the police arrived, and in the following weeks, I asked them over and over again to find out where it was coming from, but they said they'd checked the territory and checked their sources and there was no evidence of a nature party in the area; sound waves are misleading, Detective Tirza said, maybe you thought you heard a party nearby but it was actually as far away as the next town—

I step on rotten fruit and stray branches scratch me. It had rained a few days ago and the ground is still a little muddy, so my white sneakers are turning brown, but I don't care, I continue walking toward the bass guitars that keep getting louder and pound inside my body like another heart, and even though there is no trace of Ofer on the ground, I have a strong feeling that I'm following the path he took, that he went into the orchard to pee, but then said to himself, *Yalla*, I'll go a little farther, I wonder what that party is, and then was drawn to the music because music is the bait at the end of the fishing line—

And forgot that I was standing and waiting for him on the road, or maybe he didn't forget, maybe he remembered and nonetheless, as I'm doing now, chose to go on—

We met at an Independence Day party in the garden of some woman from the office—toward morning, the deejay played part of the soundtrack of *Trainspotting*, and Ofer threw himself into the dance, stomped wildly on the grass. His shirt became drenched in sweat and it was clear that he was completely transported by the music, and I watched him dancing with closed eyes and thought about what it would be like to sleep with him, and later I went over to him and wished him a happy Independence Day and said, I've never seen a man dance that way, and he was embarrassed and stammered in a way that opened all my buckles—

I turn right at one of the paths through the trees because I think that I may have moved farther away from the party now instead of getting closer to it—Detective Tirza was right, sound waves really are misleading—but now I'm moving closer again. The path bypasses the garbage dump on the right and passes the Thai workers' shed—I heard that after Ofer disappeared, the police raided it, found that they were illegal, and sent them back to Thailand, but the runners have returned to their routes and the bike riders have returned to their routes and those Thai workers or new ones have returned to work, the shirts hanging outside to dry are signs that there's life here—why can't their employers get them a dryer, Ofer would probably say—

The more I walk, the clearer it becomes that he went this way before me, the basses are coming closer and now I hear drums, or at least cymbals. I pass the beehives, maybe a swarm of bees attacked Ofer on the way to the party? That happened to my dad. When we first came to Israel he didn't have a job and he sometimes took over for his friend who was a beekeeper—today they're called apiarists—and when he made one wrong movement, the bees attacked him and, despite his protective clothes, stung him all over his body and he was in intensive care for a few days, and my mom never stopped saying loudly to anyone who visited what a failure her husband was—

But even if bees stung Ofer to death, the question remains, Where is his body? Maybe the Thai workers cut him up, out-and-out racism, out-and-out racism, even my thoughts are already in the rhythm of the music that is getting closer and closer, I mean, whenever I think, okay, I'm there, but then no, not yet, and suddenly there's a clearing in the orchard. And on the branch of a tree is a cardboard sign with an arrow pointing to one of the paths through the trees, but it doesn't say "To the Party" or "To the Wedding." There's just an arrow for those who possess hidden wisdom of the Kabbalah. Or maybe it's one of those parties where you're sent a code on your phone and only that will get you in—

And I walk among the trees that bear fruit I've never seen in reality, I pick one and make a hole in it with my pinkie and suck and suck, and the liquid begins to flow through my body instead of blood and blurs my consciousness, and an invisible speaker who sounds like my Talmud teacher Hana Futterman dictates the four ways of interpreting the Talmud: *pshat, remez, drash, sod*—

The party is already very close, reach out and touch it, the bass guitars set the rotten fruit on the ground dancing, and I quicken my steps but move forward more slowly, my pants stretch on me as if I'm running but everything is in slow motion—

And then the scene cuts to a panther, or someone dressed as a panther, standing at the end of the path who asks me for the code, but I have no idea what it is, and he asks for the code once again, and I try "Frida Kahlo," and he shakes his head, and I try "Puah Ohayon," and he shakes his head and tells me I have one more chance, and I try "pursue a lead," and he shakes his head, and I have no leads, so I say, I'll come from the other direction, what can you do to me, and he says, There's someone like me at every entrance, and I ask, Are they all dressed as panthers or is each one different animal? But he doesn't smile, and says, I'm sorry, and he says, Lady, this is a private party—

I consider looking for a rock to crush his head with, but then think of consequences, I consider seducing him with the delights of my body, but I'm not at all sure anyone would be interested in the bodily delights of a forty-two-year-old woman, and I'm not sure that my seductive powers are still potent, so I decide to go with the naked truth and say, Listen, I'm looking for my husband, something bad happened and I need him with me, and I know he's at the party because he told me he was coming, and I wouldn't bother him if the first hours weren't critical, if it weren't really urgent—

How do I know you're not undercover? he asks me. I am undercover, I almost say. I'm invisible. I've been disguised as a functioning woman for a year already, but inside, I'm falling apart—

And then I realize that he's asking if I'm an undercover cop—

And I say, The police and I are done, and I say, Those idiots say there's a good chance he committed suicide, but my Ofer would never do something like that—

And I see in his eyes that he's alarmed, and I see in his eyes that he's still a child, and if he's still a child, I can—

Imagine your mom looking for your dad urgently, I say. It's a matter of life and death, I say and touch his huge arm, not a flirtatious touch, a maternal touch—

And he moves aside and says, Okay. And puts a party bracelet that has PARADISO written on it on my wrist and says, But I'm warning you, lady, find him and get out of here quick!

I go inside, and for the first few seconds, I don't see anything, just trees and a heavy red curtain spread between two of them, like the curtains they have in theaters, the kind that close from both sides when the show ends and the actors have already taken their bows. I approach the curtain, my heart pounding in the rhythm of the trance music, and my steps rapid, like the trance music, and I grab the edge of the fabric and pull it aside, and it takes me a few seconds to take in what I see in the wings—

Everyone is naked. Men and women. Not half naked, not three-quarters naked, completely naked and not ashamed, and everyone's body is gyrating to the rhythm of the music, and it looks like the end of the world and it looks like a battlefield in the world war—

And someone with heart-shaped sun spots on his cheeks comes up to me and says, Welcome, and tells me to close my eyes and stick out my tongue, and I do what he says, otherwise he'll see that I don't belong and I'll lose my last chance to know what happened to Ofer, and he puts a pill on the tip of my tongue and hands me a glass of water and I take a sip and swallow it without knowing what it is, and he says, It needs a few minutes to take effect, you can give me your clothes, I'll take them to the dressing room, and I realize that I have no choice but to get completely undressed, mortified that I haven't waxed, but I don't let that stop me and I take off my shirt and sports bra and my pants and my plain underpants, since Ofer disappeared, I have no secrets, and he hands me a recycled paper bag, and I put my clothes in it, and he takes the bag and asks what my alias is, and I say, Zalman International, and that doesn't faze him and he says, Enjoy, Zalman—

And it's clear as death to me that I can't stand on the sidelines the way I used to at parties because I was the new girl in class, the new immigrant from Argentina who only knew how to dance unsuitable dances like *gato* or *carnavalito*, so I move closer and try to fit in, and at first, I'm too aware of my own and everybody else's nakedness, like I was at that spa in Berlin I went to with Ofer a few years ago when I bolted after half an hour because I felt like my dark skin was terribly conspicuous and all the Nazis were staring and in another minute, they'd say *Juden raus*, but gradually the music engulfs me and the energy of so many people dancing sweeps me into gyrating with them, unconcerned about how I look, undisturbed when my body occasionally touches other bodies, heat touching heat, maybe we're all one gyrating body, not separate ones, one body with many legs and many hips and many arms, but if we're one body, the question pulses in me, then what kind of body are we, male or female?

And then the pill starts to take effect. I mean, at first I don't realize that it's the pill, but I feel like something inside my head is changing the way computer settings change, and at first I don't understand what the essence of the change is and keep dancing in the trance rhythm, which has become a bit slower and more hypnotic, more seductive, I look for the deejay's stand but don't find it, apparently God is a deejay, apparently I've come to the Garden of Eden and the pill they put on my tongue is the apple and we're all a second away from being cast out and I'm Adam and I'm Eve I'm Adeve—

And I notice that, when I'm beside the men dancing closer and closer to me, I'm a woman, and when I'm beside the women dancing closer and closer to me, I'm a man, no genders, no boundaries, shifting freely, the body doesn't change its form but the internal feeling is flexible, if a man, then a man, if a woman, then fine, there's a switch I can flip easily to shift from side to side, shift from feeling totally a woman to feeling totally a man, and I notice that when I'm a man, I'm less tense about whatever danger is approaching, about the possibility I'll be hurt, and on the other hand, a possibility of bursting out opens inside me—

And just as my curiosity is aroused about how it would be to have sex this way—

I feel a hand in mine, and a man, perhaps a woman—it's not entirely clear to me and I don't really care, I don't look down to see—a man or a woman pulls me after him/her and we move away from the multi-bodied organism and the music until it grows fainter, until we reach two nearby trees that have a purple curtain stretched between them, and he/she pushes the curtain aside and I see a square-shaped clearing surrounded by bushes, and there's a mat on the ground, the kind you buy at a gas station, the kind I used to spread on the ground in the park for Ori and Matan when they were little, and he/she lies down on it and gestures for me to lie down too, and I hesitate for a second because I still have a wedding ring on my finger and I'm still married to Ofer and I still don't know where he's hidden, but I say to myself, Go with the flow, it's the only way you'll find out what happened to him, and when I lie down, he/she asks if I want to be a man or a woman this time, and for a moment, I hesitate—

And then I reply, a man. Because if there's already an opportunity, then why not? Then we make love, that's the phrase, we don't have intercourse, we make love, moving slowly at first, and then quickly, and then very quickly, and I feel like I'm a man, I mean, my body is still a woman's, but I feel like a man in this sex act, I'm horny like a man I go straight for it like a man I penetrate like a man I come like a man, I mean, I don't ejaculate, but my orgasm is nothing like the orgasm I know, it's shorter and more explosive, and afterward, I'm totally emptied, I don't have the strength for another round, and it's only for him/her that I move my hips another few times until—

And when it's over, I feel a powerful urge, totally sexual, to get an explanation and to understand what the hell is going on here, and he/she shrugs and says they have no idea, but that shrug is too forced, so I persist and ask, Who here does have an idea, who? And he/she replies, Maybe God, and I ask them to take me to him now because my need for an explanation is so strong now that it hurts my balls—

And he/she agrees and gives me a hand to help me stand up, and even though I'm still feeling languid from that draining male orgasm, my soul is burning to know, so I let myself be pulled along, and we again approach the trance dancers, and again we're among the multi-bodied organism, and the smells of sweat enter my nostrils, so many kinds of sweat smells enter my nostrils, and standing in the middle of the multi-bodied organism is, of all the people in the world, Omri, the melancholy Viking, his hair loose, as long and as beautiful as a woman's hair, and he's pounding a large drum that's hanging from his neck, improvising around the trance dancers, and I think to him, Hey, how are you, and he thinks to me, It's not easy to wait, and I think to him, It's not easy not to wait either, and neither one of us speaks a word, we speak only in thoughts, and I begin to dance in front of him the way I once used to dance at parties at the Dead Sea, not giving a damn, my eyes closed, and when I open them a little while later, Dr. Caro is standing in front of me, and he gives a small bow and asks, May I? I nod and he takes my hand gently and we begin to dance a waltz, slow, formal, the way a father dances with his daughter at her wedding, the way my father danced with me at my wedding, and I say in surprise, What, you're here too? And he says, of course, Chelli, everyone's here, this is the graduation party, and he pulls me closer, a bit too close, and we spin through the gyrating bodies, through all the arms and necks, and come out at the other side of them onto a path of marble fragments, layer upon layer of pure marble fragments that are crushed under our feet, and at the end of the path is an elevated shed that looks a bit like a lifeguard shed, but much higher, and there's a ladder leaning against it, and Dr. Caro releases me from his too-tight embrace and says, From here, you're on your own, Mrs. Raz, and I put one foot on the first rung to make sure it's stable and begin to climb, but as soon as I go up a rung, a new one is added, so I begin to climb faster to beat it, but that doesn't help because the new rungs are also added faster, until I finally give up and stop trying, and that's when the ladder abruptly turns into an escalator that carries me upward—

And in the lifeguard's shed there's a deejay who is God, and God who is a deejay, and how logical that is, because whoever controls the soundtrack controls the world, and she's wearing a white sharwal and a black shirt and there's a deejay stand with two phonographs and a laptop and all the appropriate equipment, and she has large black headphones on her ears and a perfect view of the multi-bodied organism that enables her to see exactly what the music is doing to them/it, and she doesn't even notice that I've come inside, she's busy switching between two tracks, doing that thing that deejays do, playing two tracks at the same time as a way of signaling the change that is about to come, so I wait for the changing of the tracks to be over—

And only then do I touch her shoulder, and she turns around and doesn't look surprised, just the opposite, she looks as if she's been waiting for me to arrive, but she hasn't been waiting the way you wait for good news but the way you wait for Judgment Day, and she takes off her headphones and says Hello, Chelli, and I say Hello, and I say, I want to know what happened to my Ofer, and she smiles a rotten smile and says, If I tell you I'll have to kill you, and I think, I'll take that chance, and she hears my thought even though I didn't say it, and she says, I'm serious, and I say, So am I—

And then there's a cut and she starts to cry, God is crying and teardrops fall on the world and on the party, and the multi-bodied organism under us wallows in mud like at Woodstock but doesn't stop dancing to the rhythm of Omri's drum, and she says, I'm terribly sorry, you have no idea how sorry I am—

And I say, Stop being sorry and tell me—

And she says, He came to the party we had here exactly a year ago, he didn't have an invitation, but one of the guards who had once been ultra-Orthodox knew him, so he let him in, and at first he was a little shocked, like everyone, but soon enough he loosened up and danced his heart out for hours, he danced wildly, threw himself completely into it as if he'd been waiting years for the chance to let it all hang out, and then I saw him go to the mat with another guy and then with another guy and then he collapsed in the middle of the dance floor, he must have had a bad reaction to the pill. Later I read that he had a rare disease, so maybe that had something to do with it, we don't know everything about the side effects of the pill and that's why we're so selective—

Not selective enough. It seems—

We always have a paramedic on duty and he tried to revive him, but it became clear fairly quickly that he was gone and we couldn't report it to anyone, do you understand?

No, I really don't understand.

We couldn't report it because that party never existed and that pill never existed and we couldn't let the police start asking questions—

But why?

Because the pill isn't legal, and the lab that makes it isn't legal, and the fact that anyone who takes it can feel like both a man and a woman without giving up either possibility is something that doesn't exactly please any government in the world, not to mention the religious establishment—

Why? What exactly are they afraid of?

Don't you see how revolutionary it is, Chelli? How that freedom of movement between the sexes challenges the laws of nature?

But where is Ofer? I say angrily. With all due respect to the laws of nature, what did you do with my husband's body?

It's in a good place, Chelli.

What do you mean, a good place?

That's all I can tell you.

But why didn't you find a way to let me know? Do you have any idea what I've been through this last year?

God bends her head in shame and says, I'm sorry, I'm really sorry, but now I'll have to kill you—

And she pulls a box cutter out of her sharwal—

But before she can release the blade and cut the bulging artery in my neck, I jump out of the very high shed and land softy on the ground, like a cat, and a huge flash of lightning splits the sky, and I get up and keep running for my life in the pouring rain, I don't look back, but I know that a pack of panthers is chasing me, I feel them closing the gap, and I run and run and run among the trees, getting scratched, stumbling, getting up, getting scratched, and the citrus juice spills down my thighs to my ankles. Until I can't anymore, until my strength is gone, until my legs fail me, until enough—

hen I opened my eyes, Ori and Matan were standing over me.

I touched my body with the palms of my hands the way you do when you're looking for your wallet.

I was dressed.

I heard birds chirping in the distance.

I didn't hear sounds of a party.

What happened? Ori asked.

I don't know, I said.

Can you get up? Matan asked.

I can try, I said.

They each grabbed one of my hands and gently pulled me up.

My loves, I said.

Is everything okay, Mom? Matan asked.

Dad is dead, I said.

But Mom, Ori began to object, we really can't know until they find a body—

Dad is dead, I repeated. I know.

_____

And they didn't argue with me or say that I was crazy or ask how I knew. They just remained silent for a long while. And then the three of us hugged in the middle of the orchard. A clumsy hug, because how can a threesome hug. And I thought, Once upon a time there was a family that is no longer what it was but is something else now.

And on the way back, Ori turned on the radio, and of all the songs, it was playing again—

Back home after twenty years
At first it all seems the same . . .

And I knew that after the first verse, the chorus it was dangerous for me to hear would come—but I didn't turn off the radio. I let the pain come. I let the unbearable pain pass through me.

And later, we went into the house and Ori became engrossed in a video chat with her friend, and Matan became engrossed in a phone conversation with an ultra-Orthodox kid who needed support, and his empathetic tone was exactly the same as his father's.

So I turned on my computer. And wrote the missing

story. The final story of the one hundred times one hundred project.

The words had been in my mind for a long time and I just needed to copy-paste from my mind to the page—

Hole

There was a hole in his wife's white T-shirt the police gave him when they closed the case of her disappearance due to lack of evidence. Near her heart. A tree branch probably tore the fabric, because his wife wasn't the type to wear a shirt with a hole in it. And whenever he took it out to think about her, he couldn't stop looking at the hole or thinking about the absence of what was supposed to be where the hole was. It took him years to understand that a hole is also something you can see through.

When I finished writing, I counted the words to make sure there were exactly one hundred. Including the title. Because I knew it was important to Ofer, that detail.

Then I uploaded the story to the Zalman International blog.

And even though I knew I would never write again, I briefly understood the comfort Ofer found in writing. The way it had enabled him, the entire time, to endure the loss of all he had relinquished.

Below is a paraphrase of the Talmudic treatise mentioned at the beginning of the novella:

Four men entered the Orchard—Ben Azzai, Ben Zoma, Acher (Rabbi Elisha ben Abuyah), and Rabbi Akiva. Ben Azzai looked and died; Ben Zoma looked and went mad; Acher destroyed the plants; Akiva entered in peace and departed in peace.

ESHKOL NEVO, born in Jerusalem in 1971, is one of Israel's most successful living writers. His novels have all been bestsellers in Israel and published widely in translation. His novel *Homesick* was long-listed for the 2009 Independent Foreign Fiction Prize; *World Cup Wishes* was a finalist for the 2011 Kritikerpreis der Jury der Jungen Kritiker (Austria); *Neuland* was included in the *Independent*'s 2014 Books of the Year in Translation; *Three Floors Up* (Other Press, 2017) was adapted for film by the acclaimed Italian director Nanni Moretti; and *The Last Interview* (Other Press, 2020) was a finalist for the National Jewish Book Award. Nevo owns and co-manages the largest private creative writing school in Israel and is a mentor to many up-and-coming young Israeli writers.

SONDRA SILVERSTON has translated the work of Israeli fiction writers such as Etgar Keret, Ayelet Gundar-Goshen, Zeruya Shalev, and Savyon Liebrecht. Her translation of Amos Oz's *Between Friends* won the National Jewish Book Award for fiction in 2013. Born in the United States, she has lived in Israel since 1970.